SUPERNATURAL SLEUTHS

With the same editor:

Tune in for Fear
Hallowe'en Hauntings
Ghost Tour
Christmas Spirits
Nightcaps and Nightmares
Greasepaint and Ghosts
Dead of Night

SUPERNATURAL SLEUTHS

Stories of Occult Investigators

Edited by
PETER HAINING

WILLIAM KIMBER · LONDON

This collection first published in 1986 by
WILLIAM KIMBER & CO. LIMITED
100 Jermyn Street, London SW1Y 6EE

ISBN 0 7183 0597 3

Photoset in North Wales by
Derek Doyle & Associates Mold, Clwyd
and printed and bound in Great Britain by
Biddles Limited, Guildford and King's Lynn

Contents

In memory of
ELLIOTT O'DONNELL
Ghost Hunter *Extraordinaire!*

Acknowledgements

The editor and publishers are grateful to the following for permission to include copyright material in this collection: A.P. Watt & Co Ltd for 'A Victim of Higher Space' by Algernon Blackwood; Hutchinson Publishing Group for 'Case of the Haunting of Grange' by Sax Rohmer and 'The Case of the Red-Headed Women' by Dennis Wheatley; The Estate of Seabury Quinn for 'The Poltergeist'; Clayton Magazines Inc for 'The Sinister Shape' by Gordon MacCreagh; League Publications Inc for 'Panic in Wild Harbor' by Gordon Hillman; Robert Hale Ltd for 'The Case of the Bronze Door' by Margery Lawrence; and Donald M. Grant Publisher for 'Apparition in the Sun' by Joseph Payne Brennan.

Introduction

The world-wide success of the film *Ghostbusters* has undoubtedly created a great public interest in ghost hunting. As the *Sunday Mirror* put it in a typically colourful report last December, 'An army of spook sleuths has grown up following the success of this film. They are feverishly following any lead that might help them hunt down a haunting. For this new breed of ghost busters are deadly serious about their ghoulish hobby!'

However, while the screen activities of the three young men to rid New York of a fearsome collection of ghostly phenomena of all shapes and sizes are unashamedly fictitious, it is true that hardly a week goes by on either side of the Atlantic without a new haunting being reported to such genuine ghost hunters as the Society for Psychical Research in Cambridge or the American Paranormal Society in New York, whose investigators are anything but like those of the film's trio of madcap heroes! In fact, they bring a quiet dedication and painstaking method of enquiry to every case they tackle. And having known some of these men and women over a number of years, I can vouch for their integrity and the fact that they, perhaps more than anyone else, can say with certainty that stories of ghosts are not just ... *stories*.

It is, though, true that the ghost hunter has been an important figure in supernatural fiction for a good many years. Indeed, some of the best known of these occult investigators have been bracketed with such illustrious sleuths as the great Sherlock Holmes. Fans of macabre fiction will no doubt already be familiar with men like John Silence, Carnacki and Dr Taverner. What, though, of James Loxley, Moris Klaw and Dr Muncing, to name just another three? You may not have heard of them before, but you certainly will in the pages of this book in which I have endeavoured to assemble all the masters of the craft of spook hunting.

Among some of the other surprises in store are the fact that the man who started that great humorous magazine, *Punch*, Mark Lemon, actually wrote the first short story of a ghost hunter, and although Sir Arthur Conan Doyle never sent the intrepid Holmes on the track of any supernatural phenomena (though he was fascinated by the subject) he *did* write a rather unusual story about an occult sleuth which is not to be found among his collected works and has been out of print for many years. Rescued from oblivion, too, are a story of Mr Psyche who was such a favourite with readers of the *Windsor* magazine; Gordon Hillman's splendid American investigator from the pages of *Ghost Stories* magazine, Cranshawe; and the redoubtable Miles Pennoyer whose door at number 7, Queer Street, has – like the book of stories in which he appeared – not been opened for many years.

As someone who has been ghost-hunting myself (a night in a haunted house which produced a sudden and incredible sensation of bitter cold, but no actual sight of anything), I know the demands which are placed on a person's powers of objectivity as well as on his or her nerves when such investigations are undertaken. These elements are splendidly highlighted in the stories which follow, and the reader will doubtless be fascinated to read just how many of the fictional supernatural sleuths were actually based upon real people. In some cases what you read actually *happened* – only the names have been changed.

So, are your nerves ready for a ghost hunt?

PETER HAINING
October, 1985

I

The Ghost Detective

Mark Lemon

'The Ghost Detective', written in 1866, is the earliest short story which has been traced featuring spirit detection, and in it will be found several of the elements which undoubtedly helped inspire the whole school of occult detectives. Mark Lemon *(1809-1870) is, though, an unlikely writer to have created such a story, because his fame rests primarily on having been the founder of the satirical magazine* Punch, *and its editor from 1843 until his death. His early work was as a journalist on magazines such as the* Family Herald *and* Once A Week, *after which he turned to writing farces and operettas for the stage as well as novels and children's stories. He was quite obviously gifted with a lively imagination, and records indicate that he wrote his first short stories for the* London Journal *(of which he was later the editor for a time), and made a particular point of contributing to the special Christmas numbers. It was for one such issue that he wrote 'The Ghost Detective' in which a phantom intervenes in the affairs of a sorely-pressed family. The expert on Victorian supernatural fiction Montague Summers, has suggested that the story 'might well be a relation of actual fact'. Whether this is so or not, its influence on stories of supernatural sleuths is undeniable ...*

'You take an interest in Christmas legends, I believe?' said my friend Carraway, passing the claret.

'Yes, I think they are as good as any other,' I replied.

'And have faith in ghosts?'

'Well, I must answer that question with an equivocation. Yes – no.'

'Then if you care to listen, I can, I fancy, remove your scepticism,' said Carraway.

I professed my willingness to be converted, provided I might smoke whilst my friend talked, and the conditions being agreed to, Carraway commenced:

'When I first came into the City – now some thirty years ago – I formed an intimacy with a young man in the wine trade, and we passed most of our leisure time together. He was much liked by his employers, whose principal business was with publicans and tavern-keepers, and after a time my friend became their town traveller – a position of trust and fair emolument. This advancement enabled my friend, James Loxley, to carry out a long-cherished desire, and that was to marry a fair cousin to whom he had been attached from his boyhood. The girl was one of those pretty *blondes* that are so attractive to young fellows with a turn for the sentimental, and a tendency to sing about violet eyes and golden hair and all that. I was never given that way myself, and I confess Loxley's cousin would not have been the woman I should have chosen for a wife had I ever thought of taking to myself an incumbrance. I had had a step-mother, and she cured me of any matrimonial inclinations which I might have had at one time. Well, Loxley thought differently to me, and his marriage with his cousin, Martha Lovett, was settled, and I was appointed best man upon the occasion.

'The bride certainly looked very pretty in her plain white dress – very pretty, though somewhat paler than usual, and that perhaps made me think more than ever that Martha was not the wife my friend James should have selected, knowing as I did that they would only have his salary to live upon, and that much would depend upon her to make his means sufficient for decent comfort. However, they were sincerely attached to each other, and that, I was told, was worth one or two hundred a year, which I did not believe. Martha was greatly agitated at the altar, and at one time I thought she would have fainted before the ceremony, as they call it, had finished. As it was, she had a slight attack of hysteria in the vestry, but the pew-opener told me that was nothing unusual with brides, especially with those who had been widows.

'The wedding-breakfast was a quiet affair – nothing like the sacrificial feasts of the present day – and we were all merry enough until the happy pair were to leave for their own home, and then poor little Martha hung about her mother's neck and sobbed – much more than I thought was complimentary to her new husband – but then I was not a fair judge of the sex, having been worried all my life by a step-mother.

'When Loxley and his wife were fairly settled in their new home I used frequently to pop in for a game at cribbage or a chat with my old friend, and a more loving couple I never saw in my life. Not being by any means rich, they had babies, of course, and in less than three years there were two most charming creatures – when they didn't cry or poke out their eyes with tea-spoons, or perform any other of those antics which are the delight of parents, but can only be designated as inflictions to unattached spectators.

'I have thought it only fair to mention these little matters; you will see wherefore by and by.

'Loxley had invited me to take my Christmas dinner with him, and a pleasant day we had! He was partial to keeping Christmas with all the honours, and his little dining-room – it was his drawing-room also – was sprigged about with holly, even to the picture frames. He had only two oil paintings – portraits of his father and mother, both long deceased, but the likenesses, he said, were so good, that he could always fancy his parents were present.

'Well, as I have mentioned, we passed a happy day and night; Loxley had arranged to go with me for a couple of days into the country, on a visit to a good old uncle of mine, as an atonement for keeping me away from the family dinner.

'The visit was paid; but I was rather annoyed at the effort which Loxley evidently made to appear entertained, and I thought he was home-sick, or vexed that I had not invited his wife to join us, as there were lady visitors at my uncle's. Whatever was the cause of his frequent abstractions, I could only regret it, as I had given him such a good character for cheerfulness and pleasant companionship, that one of my cousins twitted me, with rural delicacy, for having brought a thorough wet blanket from London.

'During our journey back to town Loxley was silent and thoughtful, and I longed to ask if anything troubled him. But we had passed such a jovial Christmas Day together that I could not suppose he had any other anxiety than what the restoration to the arms of his Martha would remove. We parted, however, without any explanation being asked or volunteered.

'On the second day after our return, I was astounded at receiving a message from Loxley to come to him at the Mansion House. The officer who brought the note told me that Loxley was in custody, charged, he believed, by his employer with no less an offence than embezzlement.

'Such an accusation seemed at first to me, who had known Loxley so long, so intimately, preposterous – impossible. As I walked to the Mansion House a cold sweat seized me, and for a moment I thought I should have fallen, as the strange conduct of my friend during the past two days came to my recollection. Had he found his means too small for his home requirements? Had he been tempted, and yielded as good men had done before him? No, no! – a thousand times, no! – if I knew James Loxley rightly.

'He was standing at the prisoners' bar when I reached the Mansion House, and I was not permitted to speak to him. He saw me, however, and knew his friend was with him.

'The junior principal, who had recently joined the firm of X and Co – by the bye, he had for some reason never taken kindly to Loxley – was giving his evidence. He said: "That John Rogers, a customer of the house, had caused a great deal of trouble with his overdue account, and that it was thought he would prove a defaulter. Mr X (the prosecutor) had heard accidentally that Rogers had received a large sum of money, and as Mr Loxley was away from business Mr X had called upon the debtor to demand payment of his debt. Mr X was received with much insolence by Rogers; and his conduct was accounted for subsequently by the production of Loxley's receipt for the money, dated the 24th of December. The man had paid £40 by a cheque to Loxley, and no such amount was credited in the books of X and Co. Rogers produced his banker's book, and the cheque with Loxley's signature on the back. It was found, also, that a person answering by description to Loxley had received two notes of £20 each, one of which had been paid at the Bank of England in gold early on the morning after Christmas Day."

'This evidence was confirmed by John Rogers, who had given the cheque; by the banker's cashier, who had paid it; and by the Bank of England clerk, who had given gold for the note.

'Loxley was asked – having received the usual caution – if he wished to say anything.

'He answered:

' "Yes;" and he thought he had been hardly used by his employers, that an explanation of the matter had not been required from him by them before he had been taken into custody as a thief. He had also heard of Roger's accession to money; and having the interests of his employers in view, went at once to the man and with great difficulty succeeded in obtaining payment of the debt. He received the cheque, but, fearing that Rogers might stop the payment of it at his banker's, he, Loxley, cashed it immediately, placing the notes he received, as he believed, in his pocket-book. As it was Christmas Eve, he did not return to X and Co's, the house being closed, but walked home with a friend he had met in the banking house when he received the money for Roger's cheque. On the morning of the 26th he had intended calling at X and Co's on his way to his appointment with me; but, finding he was late, he attached no consequence to the omission, having a holiday. When he was at his journey's end and in his bedroom, he was looking in his pocket-book for some matter or the other, and for the first time missed the banknotes he had received for the cheque. He was completely perplexed, being certain that he had placed the notes in the case, and that he had never lost possession of them. He had employed the morning of his return to town in searching – vainly, he knew – all conceivable places at home for the missing notes, and of course without success. Before he could go to X and Co's offices he was taken into custody."

' "One of the notes was cashed at the Bank of England early on the morning of the 26th, was it not?" asked the Lord Mayor.

'The bank clerk who cashed the note said "Yes, it appeared so, but he could not remember exactly whether it was presented by a man or a woman. He thought it was not paid to the prisoner."

' "But it was paid, and in gold," said the Lord Mayor. "The embezzlement of employers' money is one of the gravest offences against the law, and must be severely punished and put a stop to. The statement of the prisoner is very plausible –

very feasible, perhaps I should say – but I cannot feel it my duty to decide upon its truth or falsehood. He must be committed for trial."

'Loxley bowed his head and remained immovable, until a shriek in the passage of the court reached him, and he started as from a dream. He instantly looked to where I had been standing, and I understood his meaning. He was right. He had recognized the voice of his wife, who, having heard where they had taken her husband, had followed after. I found her as I had seen her on her wedding day – hysterical, but the attack was very violent; it was with great difficulty I conveyed her to her mother's, and thence to her own home.

'I said all I could to comfort her. I told her my own conviction of Loxley's innocence, my full belief in the explanation which he had given, and the certainty of his speedy liberation. But I spoke to a stricken woman, to a distracted wife, a half mad mother. She sat for some time with her children in her lap, rocking to and fro, and sobbing as though her heart would burst. She cried to me to succour her husband, to bring him home, if not for her sake, for that of her innocent children. She would not let her mother speak, but continued to appeal to me until – yes, I own it – until I fairly broke down and could not answer her. And all this while the green holly garnishing the room, and the faces of the father and mother looking on placidly from the walls.'

The recollection of the painful scene he had been describing made Carraway silent for a time, and I remarked that he had the satisfaction of knowing he had done his duty to his friend, whether he proved guilty or innocent.

'Yes,' continued Carraway. 'I had that satisfaction, though I did not desire to blow my own trumpet in what I have said. Well, when the elder X, who had been away from town, heard of the matter he was inclined to believe Loxley's statement, and blamed his son for his precipitancy. The matter, however, was beyond his control now, and the law had to vindicate its supremacy.

'The trial came on, and the gentleman whose professional business it was to prove Loxley guilty necessarily did all that was possible to show the weakness of the defence. He asked why Loxley had not instantly returned to town when he had discovered the loss of the notes? Why had he not written to his employers? Why had he not mentioned his loss to me – the friend whom he had called to speak of his character? No satisfactory answer could be given for such omissions. What had become of the other note? If a dishonest person had found the notes – supposing them to have been lost – would they not have changed both of them for gold? The most favourable construction which could be placed upon the case was the supposition that the prisoner had need of twenty pounds and had taken his employer's money, intending, very likely, to replace it. That was no uncommon case. The pressure of what seemed to be only a temporary difficulty had often led well-meaning men into such unpardonable breaches of trust. And now, having placed the case as fairly as he could before the jury, his duty was done, and it rested with the twelve intelligent men in the box to pronounce their verdict.

' "Embezzlement," the judge said, very properly, "was a serious crime, and must be repressed by the punishment of offenders. The jury had heard the prosecutor's statement – proved by highly respectable witnesses; and the prisoner's defence – unsupported by any corroborative evidence. The jury had to judge between them."

'Without leaving their box the jury, after a brief consultation, pronounced a verdict of "Guilty," and my friend – my dear friend, James Loxley – was sentenced to transportation.

'This terrible sentence was almost fatal to Mrs Loxley. Her delicate constitution would have given way under her excess of grief had not – well, had not I set before her the duty she owed to her children, who had a right to a share in her affection. Poor thing! she struggled bravely to overcome her great sorrow, but I doubt much if she would have succeeded but for what I am now about to relate to you. Stay – I must mention one or two matters before I tell you that portion of my story.

'The Loxleys occupied only part of the house in which they lived. They had their own furniture, but the landlady of the house provided servants, excepting a little girl who acted as nurse.

'The general servant who waited upon the Loxleys was one of those patient drudges often found in lodging-houses. Her name was Susan, but Loxley had given her the sobriquet of "Dormouse," as she was a drowsy, stupid – perhaps sullen is the better word – girl, who moved about more like a piece of machinery than a living being. She never showed any feeling, either of displeasure or gratification, excepting in her strong attachment to Loxley's children. That arose, perhaps, from her womanly instinct. But when Mrs Loxley's great trouble came, when the girl had come to understand what had befallen Mr Loxley, and that misery and ruin had overtaken them and their children, Susan's whole nature appeared to undergo a change. She seemed to watch every want, every movement of Mrs Loxley. More than once she was found sitting on the stairs near Mrs Loxley's door, when the poor lady was in her paroxysms of grief, as though desirous to lend what aid she could in subduing them. I was so struck by the devotion and sympathy of this poor, stupid creature that I could not help noticing her, and on one occasion offered her money. She refused to take it.

' "No, thank'ee, sir," she said; "that's not what I want; but I should like to be of use to poor missus, if I could, sir."

'I told her she had been of great use, great comfort, to Mrs Loxley, who had seen, as I had, how much she felt for her misfortunes.

' "Yes, sir, that's true enough. And what will they do to Mr Loxley, sir?" she asked.

' "He will have to suffer a great deal, Susan – great misery; but neither you nor I can help him."

'The girl burst into tears, and cried so bitterly that Mrs Loxley overheard her, and I have no doubt questioned her when I was gone.

'Mrs Loxley's mother was staying with her, the elder Mr X having insisted upon making a temporary provision for the unhappy wife of the man he still believed to be innocent – I say Mrs Loxley's mother was staying with her daughter. She had gone to bed in an adjoining room, as Mrs Loxley frequently begged to be allowed to sit alone, as she found it difficult to sleep. I have reason to believe that after her mother had gone to rest, Mrs Loxley had an interview with Susan; but, for reasons which will appear, I never questioned her on that point. It was past midnight, according to Mrs Loxley's statement, when, sitting with her head resting on her hands, she saw the door of her room open, and her husband enter; saw him as plainly and like himself as she had ever seen him. She rose up; but the figure motioned her to remain where she was. She complied; now conscious that it was not her husband in the flesh upon which she looked. The figure sat down in his accustomed place, and then appeared to gaze steadfastly on the portrait of his father, still ornamented with the faded holly twigs which had been placed there at Christmas-time. This continued for some minutes. The figure then rose up and, looking towards Mrs Loxley with a most loving expression on its face, walked from the room, opening and closing the door after it.

'Mrs Loxley tried to follow, but could not. She was not asleep, she had not been even dozing – she was sure of that, but had seen with her waking senses the apparition of her husband, then lying in Newgate prison.

'What followed seemed equally inexplicable to me, who had more than once witnessed her tendency to hysteria and fainting. She said she had felt no alarm at what she had seen. She was stupefied for a few moments, but not alarmed. She went to her mother; but finding her quietly sleeping Mrs Loxley lay down beside her without disturbing her. In the morning she narrated to her mother what she had witnessed during the past night, and subsequently repeated her story – word for word, her mother said – to me, in the presence of her landlady and the maid Susan.

'The effect upon the poor, dull-witted servant was very remarkable. She fixed her eyes on the portrait which had attracted the notice of the apparition as though she were fascinated by it. She then asked Mrs Loxley, with a voice and look of terror, "Did you speak to the ghost, missus?" And when Mrs Loxley replied "No," Susan inquired, "And didn't the ghost speak to you?"

'Mrs Loxley answered that she had told all that had occurred, adding nothing, keeping back nothing; and this assurance seemed to have a consolatory effect upon the girl, who then busied herself with her work. I had made inquiries at the prison, as Mrs Loxley foreboded illness or death to her husband, and learned that my unfortunate friend was in health, and had become more resigned to the cruel future which awaited him. Mrs Loxley appeared to be satisfied with this account of her husband.

'The night which succeeded Mrs Loxley proposed to pass in the same manner; but her mother insisted upon remaining with her, and that night no apparition came.

'Mrs Loxley was disappointed, and attributed the absence of the spirit to the presence of her mother, and it was now her turn to insist. Mrs Lovett went to her room, having promised to go to bed and not seek to watch or return to her daughter. It was impossible, however, for the old lady to sleep, and she listened to every noise in the street, and to those unaccountable sounds which we have all heard in our lonely rooms.

'It was again past midnight, and Mrs Loxley had, she admitted, worked herself into a high state of expectancy, when, without the opening of the door, the figure of her husband stood in the room. Again it regarded her most tenderly for a few seconds, and then fixed its gaze on the portrait of Loxley's father. It had not seated itself, as on the former visitation, but stood, with its hands folded, as though in supplication. It then turned its face to Mrs Loxley and opened its arms, as if inviting her to its embrace. Without a moment's hesitation she rose, and almost rushed to the bosom of the shadow. But the impalpable figure offering no resistance, she dashed herself against the panelling of the room, and the withered holly sprigs in the frame of the picture above her fell rustling to the ground. The shade was gone!

'Mrs Lovett, hearing the noise against the panel and the scratching of the falling holly, immediately went to her daughter. Mrs Loxley had not borne the second visitation so bravely as she had done the former one, and it was necessary to call for assistance, as a violent attack of hysteria succeeded the vision.

'The "Dormouse", usually most difficult to arouse, was the first to hear the calling of Mrs Lovett and to go to her assistance.

' "Has she seen it again?" asked Susan, almost directly she had entered.

' "Yes."

' "And did he speak to her this time, missus?" asked Susan. Mrs Lovett could not satisfy the girl's curiosity, but when Mrs

Loxley revived sufficiently to tell what she had seen, Susan repeated her inquiries and appeared to be relieved when she heard that the ghost had been silent.

'I was sent for early in the morning, and, having dispatched what pressing business matters I had, I went to Mrs Loxley. She was, as before, perfectly circumstantial in her account of what she had seen, not varying in the least from her first statement; and she and her mother believed that she had seen with her corporeal eyes the spirit of her living husband. I could not bring myself quite to this conclusion. I therefore suggested that it was possibly the association of the portrait with her husband, acting upon her over-taxed brain, that had conjured up these shadows. Mrs Loxley admitted the possibility of such a solution and readily acceded to my proposal to take down the portrait which had attracted, as it seemed, the attention of the figure, and then to abide the result of another night, if Mrs Loxley felt equal to courting the return of the vision.

'I rang the bell for the maid, and requested her to bring the steps.

' "What for?" she asked quickly.

' "To take down one of the pictures," I replied.

' "There ain't no steps," she said firmly.

'I could have sworn I had seen a pair in the passage as I entered, but I might have been mistaken, and I did not press the request. The picture was easily removed by my standing on a chair.

'As I turned to place the picture on the floor I was perfectly thunderstruck to see the change which had come over Susan. She stood transfixed as it were, her mouth and eyes distended to the full, her hands stretched out, as though she were looking upon the ghost which had disturbed us all.

' "What is the matter with the girl?" I exclaimed, and all eyes were directed to her.

'Susan fell upon her knees and hid her face almost on the ground and screamed out, "I'm guilty, missus! I'm found out! I knowed why the ghost come! I'm guilty!"

'We were all astounded! After a few moments, as I stood on the chair with the face of the portrait towards me, Mrs Loxley uttered a shrill cry and rushed to the picture. From the inside of the frame to which the canvas was attached she took out a note for £20 – the note which had formed part of the forty which Loxley had received and had lost so mysteriously!

'There was no doubt who had been the thief. Susan had already confessed herself guilty, and I did not hesitate to obtain what other confession I could from her. It seemed that Loxley had been mistaken in supposing he had placed the notes in his pocket-book. Owing to his surprise at meeting the friend he had spoken to at the banker's he had placed the notes in his trousers-pocket, and the force of habit had induced him to think he had otherwise disposed of them. These notes, so carelessly placed, he had drawn forth with his hand whilst ascending his own stairs, and Susan had found them. The half-witted creature showed her prize to an old man employed to clean shoes and knives, and he counselled the changing of one of the notes, with what success we know. Susan received none of the money, as the old scoundrel declared himself a partner in the waif, and told Susan she might keep the other note. But what Susan saw and heard subsequently had so terrified her and filled her with remorse, that she dared not dispose of her ill-gotten money, but, strangely enough, concealed it behind the portrait of Loxley's father.

'My friend, by the exertions of X, sen, was soon liberated, and by the honourable conduct of the same gentleman, who did all he could to repair the wrong unwittingly done to Loxley, an excellent appointment was found in Australia. There James and Martha and their progeny are now, and thriving, I am glad to say.

'I'll trouble you for the claret,' added Carraway. 'And now do you believe in ghosts?'

'I must make the answer I did before,' I replied. 'Yes –no. I think the apparition was provoked by the cause you at first suggested – namely, the association of Loxley's with his father's portrait and Mrs Loxley's over-taxed brain. You have heard, no doubt, of the well-known case of M Nicolai, the Berlin banker, who, according to his own account, having experienced several unpleasant circumstances, saw phantasms of the living and the dead by dozens, and was yet convinced they were not ghosts. Mrs Loxley might have also been dreaming, without being aware of it, as others have done; and it is rather against the ghost, if he appeared only to discover the lost note, that he came not when Mrs Lovett was present.'

'But the note was found behind the portrait at which the ghost looked so earnestly. How can you account for that?' asked Carraway.

'Well, I am so much a doubter of spiritual manifestation that I can satisfy myself, though not you, perhaps, on that particular. Suppose this stupid Dormouse had taken it into her silly head that Mr Loxley's ghost had come for Mr Loxley's money, and under that impression had placed the note behind the picture after she had heard Mrs Loxley's account of the first visitation, in order to get rid of the money which the ghost wanted?'

'I don't believe that!' said Carraway. 'I believe it was a real, actual ghost!'

'I don't,' I replied, 'and so we end as we began. I'll thank you for the cigars.'

II

Selecting a Ghost

Sir Arthur Conan Doyle

It has long been a source of surprise to admirers of the cases of that great detective, Sherlock Holmes, that he was never called upon to deal with the supernatural. All the more so when it is recalled what an avid interest in the subject his creator had, for Sir Arthur Conan Doyle *(1859-1930) not only investigated several reports of hauntings but also attended seances at which attempts were made to contact people 'on the other side'. Yet the explanation for Holmes' aversion to psychic investigations was explained in his own words addressed to the good Dr Watson. 'This agency,' he told his friend, 'stands flat-footed upon the ground. The world is big enough for us. Ghosts need not apply.'*

It would, though, be quite wrong to think that Conan Doyle did not write stories about the supernatural, for among his books are titles such as Dreamland and Ghostland *(1886) as well as haunting tales like 'The Captain of the Polestar' and 'The Great Keinplatz Experiment'. Curiously, though, the story here which Doyle wrote in 1883 and was published in* London Society, *has never been included in his collected works. It is notable, I think, not only because it reveals Conan Doyle as another very early writer on the theme of ghost hunting, but is actually the first story in which the ghost hunter is employed to* find *a spirit for a house rather than get rid of one! 'Selecting A Ghost' has a nice twist in the tale, and I am especially pleased to be giving the story its first anthology appearance here.*

I am sure that Nature never intended me to be a self-made man. There are times when I can hardly bring myself to realise that twenty years of my life were spent behind the counter of a grocer's shop in the East End of London, and that it was through such an avenue that I reached a wealthy independence and the possession of Goresthorpe Grange. My habits are conservative, and my tastes refined and aristocratic. I have a soul which spurns the vulgar herd. Our family, the D'Odds, date back to a prehistoric era, as is to be inferred from the fact that their advent into British history is not commented on by any trustworthy historian. Some instinct tells me that the blood of a Crusader runs in my veins. Even now, after the lapse of so many years, such exclamations as 'By'r Lady!' rise naturally to my lips, and I feel that, should circumstances require it, I am capable of rising in my stirrups and dealing an infidel a blow – say with a mace – which would considerably astonish him.

Goresthorpe Grange is a feudal mansion – or so it was termed in the advertisement which originally brought it under my notice. Its right to this adjective had a most remarkable effect upon its price, and the advantages gained may possibly be more sentimental than real. Still, it is soothing to me to know that I have slits in my staircase through which I can discharge arrows; and there is a sense of power in the fact of possessing a complicated apparatus by means of which I am enabled to pour molten lead upon the head of the casual visitor. These things chime in with my peculiar humour, and I do not grudge to pay for them. I am proud of my battlements and of the circular uncovered sewer which girds me round. I am proud of my portcullis and donjon and keep. There is but one thing wanting to round off the mediaevalism of my abode, and to render it symmetrically and completely antique. Goresthorpe Grange is not provided with a ghost.

Any man with old-fashioned tastes and ideas as to how such establishments should be conducted, would have been disappointed at the omission. In my case it was particularly unfortunate. From my childhood I had been an earnest student of the supernatural, and a firm believer in it. I have revelled in ghostly literature until there is hardly a tale bearing upon the subject which I have not perused. I learned the German language for the sole purpose of mastering a book upon demonology. When an infant I had secreted myself in dark rooms in the hope of seeing some of those bogies with which my nurse used to threaten me; and the same feeling is as strong in me now as then. It was a proud moment when I felt that a ghost was one of the luxuries which money might command.

It is true that there was no mention of an apparition in the advertisement. On reviewing the mildewed walls, however, and the shadowy corridors, I had taken it for granted that there was such a thing on the premises. As the presence of a kennel pre-supposes that of a dog, so I imagined that it was impossible that such desirable quarters should be untenanted by one or more restless shades. Good heavens, what can the noble family from whom I purchased it have been doing during these hundreds of years! Was there no member of it spirited enough to make away with his sweetheart, or take some other steps calculated to establish a hereditary spectre? Even now I can hardly write with patience upon the subject.

For a long time I hoped against hope. Never did rat squeak behind the wainscot, or rain drip upon the attic floor, without a wild thrill shooting through me as I thought that at last I had come upon traces of some unquiet soul. I felt no touch of fear upon these occasions. If it occurred in the night-time, I would send Mrs D'Odd – who is a strong-minded woman – to investigate the matter, while I covered up my head with the bedclothes and indulged in an ecstasy of expectation. Alas, the result was always the same! The suspicious sound would be traced to some cause so absurdly natural and commonplace that the most fervid imagination could not clothe it with any of the glamour of romance.

I might have reconciled myself to this state of things, had it not been for Jorrocks of Havistock Farm. Jorrocks is a coarse, burly, matter-of-fact fellow, whom I only happened to know through the accidental circumstance of his fields adjoining my demesne. Yet this man, though utterly devoid of all appreciation of archaeological unities, is in possession of a well-authenticated and undeniable spectre. Its existence only dates back, I believe, to the reign of the Second George, when a young lady cut her throat upon hearing of the death of her lover at the battle of Dettingen. Still, even that gives the house an air of respectability, especially when coupled with blood stains upon the floor. Jorrocks is densely unconscious of his good fortune; and his language when he reverts to the apparition is painful to listen to. He little dreams how I covet every one of those moans and nocturnal wails which he describes with unnecessary objurgation. Things are indeed coming to a pretty pass when democratic spectres are allowed to desert the landed proprietors and annul every social distinction by taking refuge in the houses of the great unrecognised.

I have a large amount of perseverance. Nothing else could have raised me into my rightful sphere, considering the uncongenial atmosphere in which I spent the earlier part of my life. I felt now that a ghost must be secured, but how to set about securing one was more than either Mrs D'Odd or myself was able to determine. My reading taught me that such phenomena are usually the outcome of crime. What crime was to be done, then, and who was to do it? A wild idea entered my mind that Watkins, the house-steward, might be prevailed upon – for a consideration – to immolate himself or someone else in the interests of the establishment. I put the matter to him in a half-jesting manner; but it did not seem to strike him in a favourable light. The other servants sympathised with him in his opinion – at least, I cannot account in any other way for their having left the house in a body the same afternoon.

'My dear,' Mrs D'Odd remarked to me one day after dinner, as I sat moodily sipping a cup of sack – I love the good old names – 'my dear, that odious ghost of Jorrocks' has been gibbering again.'

'Let it gibber,' I answered, recklessly.

Mrs D'Odd struck a few chords on her virginal and looked thoughtfully into the fire.

'I'll tell you what it is, Argentine,' she said at last, using the pet name which we usually substituted for Silas, 'we must have a ghost sent down from London.'

'How can you be so idiotic, Matilda?' I remarked, severely. 'Who could get us such a thing?'

'My cousin, Jack Brocket, could,' she answered, confidently.

Now, this cousin of Matilda's was rather a sore subject between us. He was a rakish, clever young fellow, who had tried his hand at many things, but wanted perserverance to succeed at any. He was, at that time, in chambers in London, professing to be a general agent, and really living, to a great extent, upon his wits. Matilda managed so that most of our business should pass through his hands, which certainly saved me a great deal of trouble; but I found that Jack's commission was generally considerably larger than all the other items of the bill put together. It was this fact which made me feel inclined to rebel against any further negotiations with the young gentleman.

'O yes, he could,' insisted Mrs D, seeing the look of disapprobation upon my face. 'You remember how well he managed that business about the crest?'

'It was only a resuscitation of the old family coat-of-arms, my dear,' I protested.

Matilda smiled in an irritating manner. 'There was a resuscitation of the family portraits, too, dear,' she remarked. 'You must allow that Jack selected them very judiciously.'

I thought of the long line of faces which adorned the walls of my banqueting-hall, from the burly Norman robber, through every gradation of casque, plume, and ruff, to the sombre Chesterfieldian individual who appears to have staggered against a pillar in his agony at the return of a maiden MS which he grips convulsively in his right hand. I was fain to confess that in that instance he had done his work well, and that it was only fair to give him an order – with the usual commission – for a family spectre should such a thing be attainable.

It is one of my maxims to act promptly when once my mind is made up. Noon of the next day found me ascending the spiral stone staircase which leads to Mr Brocket's chambers, and admiring the succession of arrows and fingers upon the whitewashed wall, all indicating the direction of that gentleman's sanctum. As it happened, artificial aids of the sort were entirely unnecessary, as an animated flap-dance overhead could proceed from no other quarter, though it was replaced by a deathly silence as I groped my way up the stair. The door was opened by a youth evidently astounded at the appearance of a client, and I was ushered into the presence of my young friend, who was writing furiously in a large ledger – upside down, as I afterwards discovered.

After the first greetings, I plunged into business at once.

'Look here, Jack,' I said, 'I want you to get me a spirit, if you can.'

'Spirits you mean!' shouted my wife's cousin, plunging his hand into the waste-paper basket and producing a bottle with the celerity of a conjuring trick. 'Let's have a drink!'

I held up my hand as a mute appeal against such a proceeding so early in the day; but on lowering it again I found that I had almost involuntarily closed my fingers round the tumbler which my adviser had pressed upon me. I drank the contents hastily off, lest anyone should come in upon us and set me down as a toper. After all there was something very amusing about the young fellow's eccentricities.

'Not spirits,' I explained, smilingly; 'an apparition – a ghost. If such a thing is to be had, I should be very willing to negotiate.'

'A ghost for Goresthorpe Grange?' inquired Mr Brocket, with as much coolness as if I had asked for a drawing-room suite.

'Quite so,' I answered.

'Easiest thing in the world,' said my companion, filling up my glass again in spite of my remonstrance. 'Let us see!' Here he took down a large red note-book, with all the letters of the alphabet in a fringe down the edge. 'A ghost you said, didn't you? That's G. G – gems – gimlets – gas-pipes – gauntlets – guns – galleys. Ah, here we are. Ghosts. Volume nine, section six, page forty-one. Excuse me!' And Jack ran up a ladder and began rummaging among the pile of ledgers on a high shelf. I felt half inclined to empty my glass into the spittoon when his back was turned; but on second thoughts I disposed of it in a legitimate way.

'Here it is!' cried my London agent, jumping off the ladder with a crash, and depositing an enormous volume of manuscript upon the table. 'I have all these things tabulated, so that I may lay my hands upon them in a moment. It's all right – it's quite weak' (here he filled our glasses again). 'What were we looking up, again?'

'Ghosts,' I suggested.

'Of course; page 41. Here we are. "J.H. Fowler & Son, Dunkel Street, suppliers of mediums to the nobility and gentry; charms sold – love philtres – mummies – horoscopes cast." Nothing in your line there, I suppose.'

I shook my head despondently.

' "Frederick Tabb," ' continued my wife's cousin, ' "sole channel of communication between the living and the dead. Proprietor of the spirits of Byron, Kirke White, Grimaldi, Tom

Cribb, and Inigo Jones." That's about the figure!'

'Nothing romantic enough there,' I objected. 'Good heavens! Fancy a ghost with a black eye and a handkerchief tied round its waist, or turning summersaults, and saying, "How are you tomorrow?" ' The very idea made me so warm that I emptied my glass and filled it again.

'Here is another,' said my companion, ' "Christopher McCarthy; bi-weekly seances – attended by all the eminent spirits of ancient and modern times. Nativities – charms – abracadabras, messages from the dead." He might be able to help us. However, I shall have a hunt round myself to-morrow, and see some of these fellows. I know their haunts, and it's odd if I can't pick up something cheap. So there's an end of business,' he concluded, hurling the ledger into the corner, 'and now we'll have something to drink.'

We had several things to drink – so many that my inventive faculties were dulled next morning, and I had some little difficulty in explaining to Mrs D'Odd why is was that I hung my boots and spectacles upon a peg along with my other garments before retiring to rest. The new hopes excited by the confident manner in which my agent had undertaken the commission, caused me to rise superior to alcoholic reaction, and I paced about the rambling corridors and old-fashioned rooms, picturing to myself the appearance of my expected acquisition, and deciding what part of the building would harmonise best with its presence. After much consideration, I pitched upon the banqueting-hall as being, on the whole, most suitable for its reception. It was a long low room, hung round with valuable tapestry and interesting relics of the old family to whom it had belonged. Coats of mail and implements of war glimmered fitfully as the light of the fire played over them, and the wind crept under the door, moving the hangings to and fro with a ghastly rustling. At one end there was the raised dais, on which in ancient times the host and his guests used to spread their table, while a descent of a couple of steps led to the lower part of the hall, where the vassals and retainers held wassail. The floor was uncovered by any sort of carpet, but a layer of rushes had been scattered over it by my direction. In the whole room there was nothing to remind one of the nineteenth century; except, indeed, my own solid silver plate, stamped with the resuscitated family arms, which was laid out upon an oak table in the centre. This, I determined, should be the haunted room, supposing my wife's cousin to succeed in his negotiation with the spirit-mongers. There was nothing for it now but to wait patiently until I heard some news of the result of his inquiries.

A letter came in the course of a few days, which, if it was short, was at least encouraging. It was scribbled in pencil on the back of a playbill, and sealed apparently with a tobacco-stopper. 'Am on the track,' it said. 'Nothing of the sort to be had from any professional spiritualist, but picked up a fellow in a pub yesterday who says he can manage it for you. Will send him down unless you wire to the contrary. Abrahams is his name, and he has done one or two of these jobs before.' The letter wound up with some incoherent allusions to a cheque, and was signed by my affectionate cousin, John Brocket.

I need hardly say that I did not wire, but awaited the arrival of Mr Abrahams with all impatience. In spite of my belief in the supernatural, I could scarcely credit the fact that any mortal could have such a command over the spirit-world as to deal in them and barter them against mere earthly gold. Still, I had Jack's word for it that such a trade existed; and here was a gentleman with a Judaical name ready to demonstrate it by proof positive. How vulgar and commonplace Jorrocks' eighteenth-century ghost would appear should I succeed in securing a real mediaeval apparition! I almost thought that one had been sent down in advance, for, as I walked round the moat that night before retiring to rest, I came upon a dark figure engaged in surveying the machinery of my portcullis and drawbridge. His start of surprise, however, and the manner in which he hurried off into the darkness, speedily convinced me of his earthly origin, and I put him down as some admirer of one of my female retainers mourning over the muddy Hellespont which divided him from his love. Whoever he may have been, he disappeared and did not return, though I loitered about for some time in the hope of catching a glimpse of him and exercising my feudal rights upon his person.

Jack Brocket was as good as his word. The shades of another evening were beginning to darken round Goresthorpe Grange, when a peal at the outer bell, and the sound of a fly pulling up, announced the arrival of Mr Abrahams. I hurried down to meet him, half expecting to see a choice assortment of ghosts crowding in at his rear. Instead, however, of being the sallow-faced, melancholy-eyed man that I had pictured to myself, the ghost-dealer was a sturdy little podgy fellow, with a pair of wonderfully keen sparkling eyes and a mouth which was constantly stretched in a good-humoured, if somewhat artificial, grin. His sole stock-in-trade seemed to consist of a small leather bag jealously locked and strapped, which emitted a metallic chink upon being placed on the stone flags in the hall.

'And 'ow are you, sir?' he asked, wringing my hand with the utmost effusion. 'And the missus, 'ow is she? And all the others – 'ow's all their 'ealth?'

I intimated that we were all as well as could reasonably be expected, but Mr Abrahams happened to catch a glimpse of Mrs D'Odd in the distance, and at once plunged at her with another string of inquiries as to her health, delivered so volubly and with such an intense earnestness, that I half expected to see him terminate his cross-examination by feeling her pulse and demanding a sight of her tongue. All this time his little eyes rolled round and round, shifting perpetually from the floor to the ceiling, and from the ceiling to the walls, taking in apparently every article of furniture in a single comprehensive glance.

Having satisfied himself that neither of us was in a pathological condition, Mr Abrahams suffered me to lead him upstairs, where a repast had been laid out for him to which he did ample justice. The mysterious little bag he carried along with him, and deposited it under his chair during the meal. It was not until the table had been cleared and we were left together that he broached the matter on which he had come down.

'I hunderstand,' he remarked, puffing at a trichinopoly, 'that you want my 'elp in fitting up this 'ere 'ouse with a happarition.'

I acknowledged the correctness of his surmise, while mentally wondering at those restless eyes of his, which still danced about the room as if he were making an inventory of the contents.

'And you won't find a better man for the job, though I says it as shouldn't,' continued my companion. 'Wot did I say to the young gent wot spoke to me in the bar of the Lame Dog? "Can you do it?" says he. "Try me," says I, "me and my bag. Just try me." I couldn't say fairer than that.'

My respect for Jack Brocket's business capacities began to go up very considerably. He certainly seemed to have managed the matter wonderfully well. 'You don't mean to say that you carry ghosts about in bags?' I remarked, with diffidence.

Mr Abrahams smiled a smile of superior knowledge. 'You wait,' he said; 'give me the right place and the right hour, with a little of the essence of Lucoptolycus' – here he produced a small bottle from his waistcoat pocket – 'and you won't find no ghost that I ain't up to. You'll see them yourself, and pick your own, and I can't say fairer than that.'

As all Mr Abrahams' protestations of fairness were accompanied by a cunning leer and a wink from one or other of his wicked little eyes, the impression of candour was somewhat weakened.

'When are you going to do it?' I asked, reverentially.

'Ten minutes to one in the morning,' said Mr Abrahams, with decision. 'Some says midnight, but I says ten to one, when there ain't such a crowd, and you can pick your own ghost. And now,' he continued, rising to his feet, 'suppose you trot me round the premises, and let me see where you wants it; for there's some places as attracts 'em, and some as they won't hear of – not if there was no other place in the world.'

Mr Abrahams inspected our corridors and chambers with a most critical and observant eye, fingering the old tapestry with the air of a connoisseur, and remarking in an undertone that it would 'match uncommon nice.' It was not until he reached the banqueting-hall, however, which I had myself picked out, that his admiration reached the pitch of enthusiasm. ' 'Ere's the place!' he shouted, dancing, bag in hand, round the table on which my plate was lying, and looking not unlike some quaint little goblin himself. ' 'Ere's the place; we won't get nothin' to beat this! A fine room – noble, solid, none of your electro-plate trash! That's the way as things ought to be done, sir. Plenty of room for 'em to glide here. Send up some brandy and the box of weeds; I'll sit here by the fire and do the preliminaries, which is more trouble than you'd think; for them ghosts carries on hawful at times, before they finds out who they've got to deal with. If you was in the room they'd tear you to pieces as like as not. You leave me alone to tackle them, and at half-past twelve come in, and I lay they'll be quiet enough by then.'

Mr Abrahams' request struck me as a reasonable one, so I left him with his feet upon the mantelpiece, and his chair in front of the fire, fortifying himself with stimulants against his refractory visitors. From the room beneath, in which I sat with Mrs D'Odd, I could hear that, after sitting for some time, he rose up and paced about the hall with quick impatient steps. We then heard him try the lock of the door, and afterward drag some heavy article of furniture in the direction of the window, on which, apparently, he mounted, for I heard the creaking of the rusty hinges as the diamond-paned casement folded backward, and I knew it to be situated several feet above the little man's reach. Mrs D'Odd says that she could distinguish his voice speaking in low and rapid whispers after this, but that may have been her imagination. I confess that I began to feel more impressed than I had deemed it possible to be. There was something awesome in the thought of the solitary mortal standing by the open window and summoning in from the gloom outside the spirits of the nether world. It was with a trepidation which I could hardly disguise from Matilda that I observed that the clock was pointing to half-past twelve, and that the time had come for me to share the vigil of my visitor.

He was sitting in his old position when I entered, and there were no signs of the mysterious movements which I had overheard, though his chubby face was flushed as with recent exertion.

'Are you succeeding all right?' I asked as I came in, putting on as careless an air as possible, but glancing involuntarily round the room to see if we were alone.

'Only your help is needed to complete the matter,' said Mr Abrahams, in a solemn voice. 'You shall sit by me and partake of the essence of Lucoptolycus, which removes the scales from our earthly eyes. Whatever you may chance to see, speak not and make no movement, lest you break the spell.' His manner was subdued, and his usual cockney vulgarity had entirely disappeared. I took the chair which he indicated, and awaited the result.

My companion cleared the rushes from the floor in our neighbourhood, and, going down upon his hands and knees, described a half-circle with chalk, which enclosed the fireplace and ourselves. Round the edge of this half-circle he drew several hieroglyphics, not unlike the signs of the zodiac. He then stood up and uttered a long invocation, delivered so rapidly that it sounded like a single gigantic word in some uncouth guttural language. Having finished his prayer, if prayer it was, he pulled out the small bottle which he had produced before, and poured a couple of teaspoonfuls of clear transparent fluid into a phial, which he handed to me with an intimation that I should drink it.

The liquid had a faintly sweet odour, not unlike the aroma of certain sorts of apples. I hesitated a moment before applying it to my lips, but an impatient gesture from my companion overcame my scruples, and I tossed it off. The taste was not unpleasant; and, as it gave rise to no immediate effects, I leaned back in my chair and composed myself for what was to come. Mr Abrahams seated himself beside me, and I felt that he was watching my face from time to time, while repeating some more of the invocations in which he had indulged before.

A sense of delicious warmth and languor began gradually to steal over me, partly, perhaps, from the heat of the fire, and partly from some unexplained cause. An uncontrollable impulse to sleep weighed down my eyelids, while at the same time my brain worked actively, and a hundred beautiful and pleasing ideas flitted through it. So utterly lethargic did I feel that, though I was aware that my companion put his hand over the region of my heart, as if to feel how it were beating, I did not attempt to prevent him, nor did I even ask him for the reason of his action. Everything in the room appeared to be reeling slowly round in a drowsy dance, of which I was the centre. The great elk's head at the far end wagged solemnly backward and forward, while the massive salvers on the tables performed cotillons with the claret-cooler and the epergne. My head fell upon my breast from sheer heaviness, and I should have become unconscious had I not been recalled to myself by the opening of the door at the other end of the hall.

This door led on to the raised dais, which, as I have mentioned, the heads of the house used to reserve for their own use. As it swung slowly back upon its hinges, I sat up in my chair, clutching at the arms, and staring with a horrified glare at the dark passage outside. Something was coming down it – something unformed and intangible, but still a *something*. Dim and shadowy, I saw it flit across the threshold, while a blast of ice-cold air swept down the room, which seemed to blow through me, chilling my very heart. I was aware of the mysterious presence, and then I heard it speak in a voice like the sighing of an east wind among pine-trees on the banks of a desolate sea.

It said: 'I am the invisible nonentity. I have affinities and am subtle. I am electric, magnetic, and spiritualistic. I am the great ethereal sigh-heaver. I kill dogs. Mortal, wilt thou choose me?'

I was about to speak, but the words seemed to be choked in my throat; and, before I could get them out, the shadow flitted across the hall and vanished in the darkness at the other side, while a long-drawn melancholy sigh quivered through the apartment.

I turned my eyes towards the door once more, and beheld, to my astonishment, a very small old woman, who hobbled along the corridor and into the hall. She passed backward and forward several times, and then, crouching down at the very edge of the circle upon the floor, she disclosed a face the horrible malignity of which shall never be banished from my recollection. Every foul passion appeared to have left its mark upon that hideous countenance.

'Ha! ha!' she screamed, holding out her wizened hands like the talons of an unclean bird. 'You see what I am. I am the fiendish old woman. I wear snuff-coloured silks. My curse descends on people. Sir Walter was partial to me. Shall I be thine, mortal?'

I endeavoured to shake my head in horror; on which she aimed a blow at me with her crutch, and vanished with an eldritch scream.

By this time my eyes turned naturally toward the open door, and I was hardly surprised to see a man walk in of tall and noble stature. His face was deadly pale, but was surmounted by a fringe of dark hair which fell in ringlets down his back. A short pointed beard covered his chin. He was dressed in loose-fitting clothes, made apparently of yellow satin, and a large white ruff surrounded his neck. He paced across the room with slow and majestic strides. Then turning, he addressed me in a sweet, exquisitely modulated voice.

'I am the cavalier,' he remarked. 'I pierce and am pierced. Here is my rapier. I clink steel. This is a blood stain over my heart. I can emit hollow groans. I am patronised by many old Conservative families. I am the original manor-house apparition. I work alone, or in company with shrieking damsels.'

He bent his head courteously, as though awaiting my reply, but the same choking sensation prevented me from speaking; and, with a deep bow, he disappeared.

He had hardly gone before a feeling of intense horror stole over me, and I was aware of the presence of a ghastly creature in the room, of dim outlines and uncertain proportions. One moment it seemed to pervade the entire apartment, while at another it would become invisible, but always leaving behind it a distinct consciousness of its presence. Its voice, when it spoke, was quavering and gusty. It said: 'I am the leaver of footsteps and the spiller of gouts of blood. I tramp upon corridors. Charles Dickens has alluded to me. I make strange and disagreeable noises. I snatch letters and place invisible hands on people's wrists. I am cheerful. I burst into peals of hideous laughter. Shall I do one now?' I raised my hand in a deprecating way, but too late to prevent one discordant outbreak which echoed through the room. Before I could lower it the apparition was gone.

I turned my head toward the door in time to see a man come hastily and stealthily into the chamber. He was a sunburnt powerfully built fellow, with ear-rings in his ears and a Barcelona handkerchief tied loosely round his neck. His head was bent upon his chest, and his whole aspect was that of one afflicted by intolerable remorse. He paced rapidly backward and forward like a caged tiger, and I observed that a drawn knife glittered in one of his hands, while he grasped what appeared to be a piece of parchment in the other. His voice, when he spoke, was deep and sonorous. He said, 'I am a murderer. I am a ruffian. I crouch when I walk. I step noiselessly. I know something of the Spanish Main. I can do the lost treasure business. I have charts. Am able-bodied and a good walker. Capable of haunting a large park.' He looked toward me beseechingly, but before I could make a sign I was paralysed by the horrible sight which appeared at the door.

It was a very tall man, if, indeed, it might be called a man, for the gaunt bones were protruding through the corroding flesh, and the features were of a leaden hue. A winding-sheet was wrapped round the figure, and formed a hood over the head, from under the shadow of which two fiendish eyes, deep set in their grisly sockets, blazed and sparkled like red-hot coals. The lower jaw had fallen upon the breast, disclosing a withered, shrivelled tongue and two lines of black and jagged fangs. I shuddered and drew back as this fearful apparition advanced to the edge of the circle.

'I am the American blood-curdler,' it said, in a voice which seemed to come in a hollow murmur from the earth beneath it. 'None other is genuine. I am the embodiment of Edgar Allan Poe. I am circumstantial and horrible. I am a low-caste spirit-subduing spectre. Observe my blood and my bones. I am grisly and nauseous. No depending on artificial aid. Work with grave-clothes, a coffin-lid, and a galvanic battery. Turn hair white in a night.' The creature stretched out its fleshless arms to me as if in entreaty, but I shook my head; and it vanished, leaving a low, sickening, repulsive odour behind it. I sank back in my chair, so overcome by terror and disgust that I would have very willingly resigned myself to dispensing with a ghost altogether, could I have been sure that this was the last of the hideous procession.

A faint sound of trailing garments warned me that it was not so. I looked up, and beheld a white figure emerging from the corridor into the light. As it stepped across the threshold I saw that it was that of a young and beautiful woman dressed in the fashion of a bygone day. Her hands were clasped in front of her, and her pale proud face bore traces of passion and of suffering. She crossed the hall with a gentle sound, like the rustling of autumn leaves, and then, turning her lovely and unutterably sad eyes upon me, she said. 'I am the plaintive and sentimental, the beautiful and ill-used. I have been forsaken and betrayed. I shriek in the night-time and glide down passages. My antecedents are highly respectable and generally aristocratic. My tastes are aesthetic. Old oak furniture like this would do, with a few more coats of mail and plenty of tapestry. Will you not take me?'

Her voice died away in a beautiful cadence as she concluded, and she held out her hands as if in supplication. I am always sensitive to female influences. Besides, what would Jorrocks's ghost be to this? Could anything be in better taste? Would I not be exposing myself to the chance of injuring my nervous system by interviews with such creatures as my last visitor, unless I decided at once? She gave me a seraphic smile, as if she knew what was passing in my mind. That smile settled the matter. 'She will do!' I cried; 'I choose this one;' and as, in my enthusiasm, I took a step toward her I passed over the magic circle which had girdled me round.

'Argentine, we have been robbed!'

I had an indistinct consciousness of these words being spoken, or rather screamed, in my ear a great number of times without my being able to grasp their meaning. A violent throbbing in my head seemed to adapt itself to their rhythm, and I closed my eyes to the lullaby of 'Robbed, robbed, robbed.' A vigorous shake caused me to open them again, however, and the sight of Mrs D'Odd in the scantiest of costumes and most furious of tempers was sufficiently impressive to recall all my scattered thoughts, and make me realise that I was lying on my back on the floor, with my head among the ashes which had fallen from last night's fire, and a small glass phial in my hand.

I staggered to my feet, but felt so weak and giddy that I was compelled to fall back into a chair. As my brain became clearer, stimulated by the exclamations of Matilda, I began gradually to recollect the events of the night. There was the door through which my supernatural visitors had filed. There was the circle of chalk with the hieroglyphics round the edge. There was the cigar-box and brandy-bottle which had been honoured by the attentions of Mr Abrahams. But the seer himself – where was he? and what was this open window with a rope running out of it? And where, O where, was the pride of Goresthorpe Grange, the glorious plate which was to have been the delectation of generations of D'Odds? And why was Mrs D. standing in the grey light of dawn, wringing her hands and repeating her monotonous refrain? It was only very gradually that my misty brain took these things in, and grasped the connection between them.

Reader, I have never seen Mr Abrahams since; I have never seen the plate stamped with the resuscitated family crest; hardest of all, I have never caught a glimpse of the melancholy spectre with the trailing garments, nor do I expect that I ever shall. In fact my night's experiences have cured me of my mania for the supernatural, and quite reconciled me to inhabiting the humdrum nineteenth-century edifice on the outskirts of London which Mrs D. has long had in her mind's eye.

As to the explanation of all that occurred – that is a matter which is open to several surmises. That Mr Abrahams, the ghost-hunter, was identical with Jemmy Wilson, *alias* the Nottingham crackster, is considered more than probable at Scotland Yard, and certainly the description of that remarkable burglar tallied very well with the appearance of my visitor. The small bag which I have described was picked up in a neighbouring field next day, and found to contain a choice assortment of jemmies and centre-bits. Footmarks deeply imprinted in the mud on either side of the moat showed that an accomplice from below had received the sack of precious metals which had been let down through the open window. No doubt the pair of scoundrels, while looking round for a job, had overhead Jack Brocket's indiscreet inquiries, and promptly availed themselves of the tempting opening.

And now as to my less substantial visitors, and the curious grotesque vision which I had enjoyed – am I to lay it down to any real power over occult matters possessed by my Nottingham friend? For a long time I was doubtful upon the point, and eventually endeavoured to solve it by consulting a well-known analyst and medical man, sending him the few drops of the so-called essence of Lucoptolycus which remained in my phial. I append the letter which I received from him, only too happy to have the opportunity of winding up my little narrative by the weighty words of a man of learning:

Argentine D'Odd, Esq
The Elms, Brixton.

Arundel Street

Dear Sir: Your very singular case has interested me extremely. The bottle which you sent contained a strong solution of chloral, and the quantity which you describe yourself as having swallowed must have amounted to at least eighty grains of the pure hydrate. This would of course have reduced you to a partial state of insensibility, gradually going on to complete coma. In this semi-conscious state of chloralism it is not unusual for circumstantial and *bizarre* visions to present themselves – more especially to individuals unaccustomed to the use of the drug. You tell me in your note that your mind was saturated with ghostly literature, and that you had long taken a morbid interest in classifying and recalling the various forms in which apparitions have been said to appear. You must also remember that you were expecting to see something of that very nature, and that your nervous system was worked up to an unnatural state of tension. Under the circumstances, I think that, far from the sequel being an astonishing one, it would have been very surprising indeed to any one versed in narcotics had you not experienced some such effects. – I remain, dear sir, sincerely yours,

T. E. STUBE, MD

III

The Story of the Moor Road

E. and H. Heron

Flaxman Low, the ghost hunter who features in this next story has been called 'the first fully fledged occult detective' and certainly he is the earliest character in literature to make a speciality of supernatural investigations, appearing in over a dozen stories. These tales have been described as being 'derivative of Conan Doyle' and the Oxford-trained psychologist Low is undeniably similar to Sherlock Holmes in his painstaking methods and precise application of logic to even the most bizarre cases. As it says of him in a collected edition of the stories published in 1899, 'Flaxman Low is the first student in this field of inquiry who has had the boldness and originality to break free from old and conventional methods, and to approach the elucidation of so-called supernatural problems on the lines of natural law.'

The stories were the creation of a mother and son partnership, Kate Prichard *(1851-1913) and* Hesketh Prichard *(1876-1922) who published them under the pen-name, E. and H. Heron. Hesketh Prichard, a former big-game hunter and sportsman, was undoubtedly the more active writer of the two, though evidence suggests the idea for Flaxman Low may well have been his mother's who based him on 'one of the leading psychologists of the day.' Quite who this might have been, though, has proved impossible to establish. Hesketh Prichard actually made his reputation with a series of stories about a sadistic bandit called 'Don Q.' – who in his time was as popular with magazine readers as Sherlock Holmes and Captain Kettle – and in this Flaxman Low case introduces us to an elemental spirit capable of being every bit as nasty as that outlaw to anyone unfortunate enough to cross its path …*

'The medical profession must always have its own peculiar offshoots,' said Mr Flaxman Low, 'some are trades, some mere hobbies, others, again, are allied subjects of a serious and profound nature. Now, as a student of psychical phenomena, I account myself only two degrees removed from the ordinary general practitioner.'

'How do you make that out?' returned Colonel Daimley, pushing the decanter of old port invitingly across the table.

'The nerve and brain specialist is the link between myself and the man you would send for if you had a touch of lumbago,' replied Low with a slight smile. 'Each division is but a higher grade of the same ladder – a step upwards into the unknown. I consider that I stand just one step above the specialist who makes a study of brain disease and insanity; he is at work on the disorders of the embodied spirit, while I deal with abnormal conditions of the free and detached spirit.'

Colonel Daimley laughed aloud.

'That won't do, Low! No, no! First prove that your ghosts are sick.'

'Certainly,' replied Low gravely. 'A very small proportion of spirits return as apparitions after the death of the body. Hence we may conclude that a ghost is a spirit in an abnormal condition. Abnormal conditions of the body usually indicate disease; why not of the spirit also?'

'That sounds fair enough,' observed Lane Chaddam, the third man present. 'Has the Colonel told you of our spook?'

The Colonel shook his handsome grey head in some irritation.

'You haven't convinced me yet, Lane, that it is a spook,' he said drily. 'Human nature is at the bottom of most things in this world according to my opinion.'

'What spook is this?' asked Flaxman Low. 'I heard nothing of it when I was down with you last year.'

'It's a recent acquisition,' replied Lane Chaddam. 'I wish we were rid of it for my part.'

'Have you seen it?' asked Low as he relit his long pipe.

'Yes, and felt it!'

'What is it?'

'That's for you to say. He nearly broke my neck for me – that's all I can swear to.'

Low knew Chaddam well. He was a long-limbed, athletic young fellow, with a good show of cups in his rooms, and was one of the various short-distance runners mentioned in the Badminton as having done the hundred in level time, and not the sort of man whose neck is easy to break.

'How did it happen?' asked Flaxman Low.

'About a fortnight ago,' replied Chaddam, 'I was flight-shooting near the barn where the hounds killed the otter last year. When the light began to fail, I thought I would come home by the old quarry, and pot anything that showed itself. As I walked along the far bank of the burn, I saw a man on the near side standing on the patch of the sand below the reeds and watching me. As I came nearer I heard him coughing; it sounded like a sick cow. He stood still as if waiting for me. I thought it odd, because amongst the meres and water-meadows down there one never meets a stranger.'

'Could you see him pretty clearly?'

'I saw his outline clearly, but not his face, because his back was toward the west. He was tall and jerry-built, so to speak, and had a little head no bigger than a child's, and he wore a fur cap with queer upstanding ears. When I came close, he suddenly slipped away; he jumped behind a big dyke, and I lost sight of him. But I didn't pay much attention; I had my gun, and I concluded it was a tramp.'

'Tramps don't follow men of your size,' observed Low with a smile.

'This fellow did, at any rate. When I got across to the spot where he had been standing – the sand is soft there – I looked for his tracks. I knew he was bound to have a big foot of his own considering his height. But there were no footprints!'

'No footprints? You mean it was too dark for you to see them?' broke in Colonel Daimley.

'I am sure I should have seen them had there been any,' persisted Chaddam quietly. 'Besides, a man can't take a leap as he did without leaving a good hole behind him. The sand was perfectly smooth, because there had been a strong east wind all day. I looked about and seeing no marks, I went on to the top of the knoll above the quarry. After a bit I felt I was followed, though I couldn't see anyone. You remember the thorn bush that overhangs the quarry pool? I stopped there and bent over the edge of the cliff to see if there was anything in the pool. As I stooped I felt a point like a steel puncheon catch me in the small of the back. I kicked off from the quarry wall as well as I could, so as to avoid the broken rocks below, and I just managed to clear them, but I fell into the water with a flop that knocked the wind out of me. However, I held on to the gun, and, after a minute, I climbed to a ledge under the cliff and waited to see what my friend on top would do next. He waited, too. I couldn't see him, but I heard him – he coughed up there in the dusk, the most ghastly noise I ever heard. The Colonel laughs at me, but it was about as nasty a half-hour as I care to have. In the end, I swam out across the pool and got home.'

'I laugh at Lane,' said the Colonel, 'but all the same, it's a bad spot for a fall.'

'You say he struck you in the back?' asked Flaxman Low, turning to Chaddam.

'Yes, and his finger was like a steel punch.'

'What does Mrs Daimley say to this affair?' went on Low presently.

'Not a word to my wife or Olivia, my dear Low!' exclaimed Colonel Daimley. 'It would frighten them needlessly; besides, there would be an infernal fuss if we wanted to go flighting or anything after dark. I only fear for them, as they often drive into Nerbury by the Moor Road, which passes close by the quarry.'

'Do they go in for their letters every evening as they used to do?'

'Just the same. And they won't take Stubbs with them, in spite of my advice.' The Colonel looked disconsolately at Low. 'Women are angels, bless them! but they are the dickens to deal with because they always want to know why?'

'And now, Low, what have you to say about it?' asked Chaddam.

'Have you told me all?'

'Yes. The only other thing is that Livy says she hears someone coughing in the spinney most nights.'

'If all is as you say, Chaddam – pardon me, but in cases like this imagination is apt to play an unsuspected part – I should think that you have come upon a unique experience. What you have told me is not to be explained upon the lines of any ordinary theory.'

After this they followed the ladies into the drawing-room, where they found Mrs Daimley immersed in a novel as usual, and Livy looking pretty enough to account for the frequent presence of Lane Chaddam at Low Riddings. He was a distant cousin of the Colonel, and took advantage of his relationship to pay protracted visits to Northumberland.

Some years previous to the date of the above events, Colonel Daimley had bought and enlarged a substantial farmhouse which stood in a dip south of a lonely sweep of Northumbrian moors. It was a land of pale blue skies and far off fringes of black and ragged pine trees.

From the house a lane led over the wind-swept shoulder of the upland down to a hollow spanned by a railway bridge, then up again across the high levels of the moors until at length it lost itself in the outskirts of the little town of Nerbury. This Moor Road was peculiarly lonely: it approached but one cottage the whole way, and ran very nearly over the doorstep of that one – a deserted-looking slip of a place between the railway bridge and the quarry. Beyond the quarry stretched acres of marshland, meadows and reedy meres, all of which had been manipulated with such ability by the Colonel, that the duck shooting on his land was the envy of the neighbourhood.

In spite of its loneliness the Moor Road was much frequented by the Daimleys, who preferred it to the high road, which was uninteresting and much longer. Mrs Daimley and Olivia drove in of an evening to fetch their letters – being people with nothing on earth to do, they were naturally always in a hurry to get their letters – and they perpetually had parcels waiting for them at the station which required to be called for at all sorts of hours. Thus it will be seen that the fact of the quarry being haunted by Lane Chaddam's assailant, formed a very real danger to the inhabitants of Low Riddings.

At breakfast next day Livy said the tramp had been coughing in the spinney half the night.

'In what direction?' asked Flaxman Low.

Livy pointed to the window which looked on to the gate and the thick boundary hedge, the last still full of crisp ruddy leaves.

'You feel an interest in your tramp, Miss Daimley?'

'Of course, poor creature! I wanted to go out to look for him the other night, but they would not allow me.'

'That was before we knew he was so interesting,' said Chaddam. 'I promise we'll catch him for you next time he comes.'

And this was in fact the programme they tried to carry out, but although the coughing was heard in the spinney, no one even caught a glimpse of any living thing moving or hiding among the trees.

The next stage of the affair happened to be an experience of Livy's. In some excitement she told the assembled family at dinner that she had just seen the coughing tramp.

Lane Chaddam changed colour.

'You don't mean to say, Livy, that you went to search for him alone?' he exclaimed half-angrily.

Flaxman Low and the Colonel wisely went on eating oyster patties without taking any apparent notice of the girl's news.

'Why shouldn't I?' asked Livy quickly; 'but as it happens I saw him in Scully's cottage by the quarry this evening.'

'What?' said Colonel Daimley, 'in Scully's cottage. I'll see to that.'

'Why? Are you all so prejudiced against my poor tramp!'

'On the contrary,' replied Flaxman Low, 'we all want to know what he's like.'

'So odd-looking! I was driving home alone from the post when, as I passed the quarry cottage, I heard the cough. You know it is quite unmistakable; I looked up at the window and there he was. I have never seen anybody in the least like him. His face is ghastly pale and perfectly hairless, and he has such a little head. He stared at me so threateningly that I whipped up Lorelie.'

'Were you frightened, then?'

'Not exactly, but he had such a wicked face that I drove away as fast as I could.'

'I understood that you had arranged to send Stubbs for the letters?' said Colonel Daimley with some annoyance. 'Why can't girls say what they mean?'

Livy made no reply, and after a pause Chaddam put a question.

'You must have passed along the Moor Road about seven o'clock?'

'Yes, it was after six when I left the Post Office,' replied Livy. 'Why?'

'It was quite dark – how did you see the hairless man so plainly? I was round on the marshes all the evening, and I am quite certain there was no light at any time in Scully's cottage.'

'I don't remember whether there was any light behind him in the room,' returned Livy after a moment's consideration; 'I only know that I saw his head and face quite plainly.'

There was no more said on the subject at the time, though the Colonel forbade Livy to run any further risks by going alone on the Moor Road. After this the three men paraded the lane and lay in wait for the hairless tramp or ghost. On the second evening their watch was rewarded, when Chaddam came hurriedly into the smoking-room to say that the coughing could at that instant be heard in the hedge by the dining-room. It was still early, although the evening had closed in with clouds, and all outside was dark.

'I'll deal with him this time effectually!' exclaimed the Colonel. 'I'll slip out the back way, and lie in the hedge down the road by the field gate. You two must chivy him out to me, and when he comes along, I'll have him against the sky-line and give him a charge of No. 4 if he shows fight.'

The Colonel stole down the lane while the others beat the spinney and hedge. Flaxman Low very much chagrined at being forced to deal with an interesting problem in this rough and ready fashion. However, he saw that on this occasion at least it would be useless to oppose the Colonel's notions. When he and Chaddam met after beating the hedge they saw a tall figure shamble away rapidly down the lane towards the Colonel's hiding-place.

They stood still and waited for developments, but the minutes followed each other in intense stillness. Then they went to find the Colonel.

'Hullo, Colonel, anything wrong?' asked Chaddam on nearing the field gate.

The Colonel straightened himself with the help of Chaddam's arm.

'Did you see him?' he whispered.

'We thought so. Why did you not fire?'

'Because,' said the Colonel in a husky voice, 'I had no gun!'

'But you took it with you?'

'Yes.'

Flaxman Low opened the lantern he carried, and, as the light swept round in a wide circle, something glinted on the grass. It was the stock of the Colonel's gun. A little further off they came upon the Damascus barrels bent and twisted into a ball like so much fine wire. Presently the Colonel explained.

'I saw him coming and meant to meet him, but I seemed dazed – I couldn't move! The gun was snatched from me, and I made no resistance – I don't know why.' He took the gun-barrels and examined them slowly. 'I give in, Low, no human hand did that.'

During dinner Flaxman Low said abruptly: 'I suspect you have lately had an earthquake down here.'

'How did you know?' asked Livy. 'Have you been to the quarry?'

Low said he had not.

'It was such a poor little earthquake that even the papers did not think it worth while to mention it!' went on Livy. 'We didn't feel any shock, and, in fact, knew nothing about it until Dr Petterped told us.'

'You had a landslip though?' went on Low.

Livy opened her pretty eyes.

'But you know all about it,' she said. 'Yes, the landslip was just by the old quarry.'

'I should like to see the place to-morrow,' observed Low.

Next day, therefore, when the Colonel went off to the coverts with a couple of neighbours, whom he had invited to join him, Flaxman Low accompanied Chaddam to examine the scene of the landslip.

From the edge of the upland, looking across the hollow crowded with reedy pools, they could see in the torn, reddish flank of the opposite slope the sharp tilt of the broken strata. To the right of this lay the old quarry, and about a hundred yards to the left the lonely house and the curving road.

Low descended into the hollow and spent a long time in the spongy ground between the back of the quarry and the lower edge of the newly-uncovered strata, using his little hammer freely, especially about one narrow black fissure, round which he sniffed and pottered in absorbed silence. Presently he called to Chaddam.

'There has been a slight explosion of gas – a rare gas, here,' he said. 'I hardly hoped to find traces of it, but it is unmistakable.'

'Very unmistakable,' agreed Chaddam, with a laugh. 'You'd have said so had you been here when it happened.'

'Ah, very satisfactory indeed. And that was a fortnight ago, you say?'

'Rather more now. It took place a couple of days before my fall into the quarry pool.'

'Anyone ill near by – at that cottage for instance?' asked Low, as he joined Chaddam.

'Why? Was the gas poisonous? There's a man in the Colonel's employ named Scully in that cottage, who has had pneumonia, but he was on the mend when the landslip occurred. Since then he has grown steadily worse.'

'Is there anyone with him?'

'Yes, the Daimleys sent for a woman to look after him. Scully's a very decent man. I often go in to see him.'

'And so does the hairless man apparently,' added Low.

'No, that's the queer part of it. Neither he nor the woman in charge have ever seen such a person as Livy described. I don't know what to think.'

'The first thing to be done is to get the man from here at once,' said Low decidedly. 'Let's go in and see him.'

They found Scully low and drowsy. The nurse shook her head at the two visitors in a despondent way.

'He grows weaker day by day,' she said.

'Get him away from here at once,' repeated Low, as they went out.

'We might have him up at Low Riddings, but he seems almost too weak to be moved,' replied Chaddam doubtfully.

'My dear fellow, it's his only chance of life.'

The Daimleys made arrangements for the reception of Scully, provided Dr Thomson of Nerbury gave his consent to the removal. In the afternoon, therefore, Chaddam bicycled into Nerbury to see the doctor on the subject.

'If I were you, Chaddam,' said Low before he started, 'I'd be back by daylight.'

Unfortunately Dr Thomson was on his rounds, and did not return until after dark, by which time it was too late to remove Scully that evening. After leaving the doctor's house Chaddam went to the station to inquire about a box from Mudie's. The books having arrived, he took out a couple of volumes for Mrs Daimley's present consumption, and was strapping them on in front of his bicycle, when it struck him that unless he went home by the Moor Road he would be late for dinner.

Accordingly he branched off into the bare track which led over the moors. The twilight had deepened into a fine, cold night, and a moon was swinging up into a pale, clear sky. The spread of heather, purple in the daytime, appeared jet black by moonlight, and across it he could see the white ribbon of road stretching ahead into the distance. The scents of the night were fresh in his nostrils, as he ran easily along the level with the breeze behind him.

He soon reached the incline past Scully's cottage. Well away to the left lay the quarry pool like a blotch of ink under its shadowing cliff. There was no light in the cottage, and it seemed even more deserted-looking than usual.

As Chaddam flashed under the bridge, he heard a cough, and glanced back over his shoulder.

A tall, loose-jointed form he had seen once before, was rearing itself up upon the railway bridge. There was something curiously unhuman about the lank outlines and the cant of the small head with its prick-eared cap showing out so clearly against the lighter sky behind.

When Chaddam looked again, he saw the thing on the bridge fling up its long arms and leap down on to the road some thirty feet below.

Then Chaddam rode. He began to think he had been a fool to come, and he counted that he was a good mile from home. At first he fancied he heard footfalls, then he fancied there were none. The hard road flew under him, all thoughts of economising his strength were lost, his single aim was to make the pace.

Suddenly his bicycle jerked violently, and he was shot over into the road. As he fell, he turned his head and was conscious of a little, bleached, bestial face, wet with fury, not ten yards behind!

He sprang to his feet, and ran up the road as he had never run before. He ran wonderfully, but he might as well have tried to race a cheetah. It was not a question of speed, the game was in the hands of this thing with the limbs of a starved Hercules, whose bony knees seemed to leap into its ghastly face at every stride. Chaddam topped the slope with a sickening sense of his powerlessness. Already he saw Low Riddings in the distance, and a dim light came creeping along the road towards him. Another frantic spurt, and he had almost reached the light, when a hand closed like a vice on his shoulder, and seemed to fasten on the flesh. He rushed blindly on towards the house. He saw the door-handle gleam, and in another second he had pitched head foremost on to the knotted matting in the hall.

When he recovered his senses, his first question was; 'Where is Low?'

'Didn't you meet him?' asked Livy. 'I – that is, we were anxious about you as you were so late, and I was just going to meet you when Mr Low came downstairs and insisted on going instead.'

Chaddam stood up.

'I must follow him.'

But as he spoke the front door opened, and Flaxman Low entered, and looked up at the clock.

'Eight-twenty,' he said. 'You're late, Chaddam.'

Afterwards in the smoking-room he gave an account of what he had seen.

'I saw Chaddam racing up the road with a tall figure behind him. It stretched out its hand and grasped his shoulder. The next instant it stopped short as if it had been shot. It seemed to reel back and collapse, and then limped off into the hedge like a disappointed dog.'

Chaddam stood up and began to take off his coat.

'Whatever the thing is, it is something out of the common. Look here!' he said, turning up his shirt sleeve over the point of his shoulder, where three singular marks were visible, irregularly placed as the fingers of a hand might fall. They were oblong in shape, about the size of a bean, and swollen in purple lumps well above the surface of the skin.

'Looks as if someone has been using a small cupping glass on you,' remarked the Colonel uneasily. 'What do you say to it, Low?'

'I say that since Chaddam has escaped with his life, I have

only to congratulate him on what, in Europe certainly, is a unique adventure.'

The Colonel threw his cigar into the fire.

'Such adventures are too dangerous for my taste,' he said. 'This creature has on two occasions murderously attacked Lane Chaddam, and it would, no doubt, have attacked Livy if it had had the chance. We must leave this place at once, or we shall be murdered in our beds!'

'I don't think, Colonel, that you will be troubled with this mysterious visitant again,' replied Flaxman Low.

'Why not? Who or what is this horrible thing?'

'I believe it to be an Elemental Earth Spirit,' returned Low. 'No other solution fits the facts of the case.'

'What is an Elemental?' resumed the Colonel irritably. 'Remember, Low, I expect you to prove your theories so that a plain man may understand, if I am to stay on at Low Riddings.'

'Eastern occultists describe wandering tribes of earth spirits evil intelligences, possessing spirit as distinct from soul – all inimical to man.'

'But how do you know that the thing on the Moor Road is an Elemental?'

'Because the points of resemblance are curiously remarkable. The occultists say that when these spirits materialise, they appear in grotesque and uncouth forms; secondly, that they are invariably bloodless and hairless; thirdly, they move with extraordinary rapidity, and leave no footprints; and, lastly, their agility and strength is superhuman. All these peculiarities have been observed in connection with the figure on the Moor Road.'

'I admit that no man I have ever met with,' commented Colonel Daimley, 'could jump uninjured from a height of 30 ft., race a bicycle, and twist up gun-barrels like so much soft paper. So, perhaps you're right. But can you tell me why or how it came here?'

'My conclusions,' began Low, 'may seem to you far-fetched and ridiculous, but you must give them the benefit of the fact that they precisely account for the otherwise unaccountable features which mark this affair. I connect this appearance with the earthquake and the sick man.'

'What? Scully in league with the devil?' exclaimed the Colonel bluntly. 'Why, the man is too weak to leave his bed; besides, he is a short, thick-set fellow, entirely unlike our haunting friend.'

'You mistake me, Colonel,' said Low, in his quiet tones. 'These Elementals cannot take form without drawing upon the resources of the living. They absorb the vitality of any ailing person until it is exhausted, and the person dies.'

'Then they begin operations upon a fresh victim? A pleasant look-out to know we keep a well-attested vampire in the neighbourhood!'

'Vampires are a distinct race, with different methods; one being that the Elemental is a wanderer, and goes far afield to search for a new victim.'

'But why should it want to kill me?' put in Chaddam.

'As I have told you, they are animated solely by a blind malignity to the human race, and you happened to be handy.'

'But the earthquake, Low; where is the connection there?' demanded the Colonel, with the air of a man who intends to corner his opponent.

Flaxman Low lit one cigar at the end of another before he replied.

'At this point,' he said, 'my own theories and observations and those of the old occultists overlap. The occultists held that some of these spirits are imprisoned in the interior of the earth, but may be set free in consequence of those shiftings and disturbances which take place during an earthquake. This in more modern language simply means that Elementals are in some manner connected with certain of the primary strata. Now, my own researches have led me to conclude that atmospheric influences are intimately associated with spiritual phenomena. Some gases appear to be productive of such phenomena. One of these is generated when certain of the primary formations are newly exposed to the common air.'

'This is almost beyond belief – I don't understand you,' said the Colonel.

'I am sorry that I cannot give you all the links in my own chain of reasoning,' returned Low. 'Much is still obscure, but the evidence is sufficiently strong to convince me that in such a case of earthquake and landslip as has lately taken place here the phenomenon of an embodied Elemental might possibly be expected to follow, given the one necessary adjunct of a sick person in the near neighbourhood of the disturbance.'

'But when this brute got hold of me, why didn't it finish me off?' asked Chaddam. 'Or was it your coming that prevented it?'

Flaxman Low considered.

'No, I don't think I can flatter myself that my coming had anything to do with your escape. It was a near thing – how near you will understand when we hear further news of Scully in the morning.'

A servant entered the room at this moment.

'The woman has come up from the cottage, sir, to say that Scully is dead.'

'At what hour did he die?' asked Low.

'About ten minutes past eight, sir, she says.'

'The hour agrees exactly,' commented Low, when the man had left the room. 'The figure stopped and collapsed so suddenly that I believed something of this kind must have happened.'

'But surely this is a very unprecedented occurrence?'

'It is,' said Flaxman Low. 'Yet I can assure you that if you take the trouble to glance through the pages of the psychical periodicals you will find many statements at least as wonderful.'

'But are they true?'

Flaxman Low shrugged his shoulders.

'At any rate,' said he, 'we know this is.'

The Daimleys have spent many pleasant days at Low Riddings since then, but Chaddam – who has acquired a right to control Miss Livy's actions more or less – persists in his objection to any solitary expeditions to Nerbury along the Moor Road. For, although the figure has never been seen about Low Riddings since, some strange stories have lately appeared in the papers of a similar mysterious figure which has been met with more than once in the lonelier spots about North London. If it be true that this nameless wandering spirit, with the strength and activity of twenty men, still haunts our lonely roads, the sooner Mr Flaxman Low exorcises it the better.

IV

A Victim Of Higher Space

Algernon Blackwood

'By his friends John Silence was regarded as an eccentric, because he was rich by accident, and by choice – a doctor. That a man of independent means should devote his time to doctoring, chiefly doctoring to folk who could not pay, passed their comprehension entirely. The native nobility of a soul whose first desire was to help those who could not help themselves, puzzled them. After that, it irritated them, and, greatly to his own satisfaction, they left him to his own devices.' Such is the description of John Silence, 'Physician Extraordinary' given on the opening page of the collection of his adventures first published in 1908 – a book which E.F. Bleiler, the American authority on fantasy fiction has called, 'Probably the best single volume of 20th Century cases of an occult detective.'

The stories were written by Algernon Blackwood *(1869-1951), one of Britain's most famous supernatural writers, particularly in the field of occultism. He has explained how he came to create the redoubtable Dr Silence in these words. 'They were originally separate imaginative studies of various psychic themes,' he said, 'and it was on the suggestion of my publisher, Eveleigh Nash, that I grouped them under the common leadership of a single man, Dr Silence. The title was due to a chance question that Mr Nash put to his gifted reader, Maude Ffoulkes, as we sat at dinner one night discussing the stories and searching for a title and a name for the psychic doctor. Suddenly Nash turned to Mrs Ffoulkes and said, 'Didn't you have some ancestor or other with the name of Silence?' – and with one accord we all cried, 'Silence' – for it was just the kind of name we wanted.' Blackwood also explained that all the stories were based on real incidents which, of course, adds a special piquancy to the reading of them. The story which follows is rather special on two counts. Firstly, in that it deals with the case of a man who has the 'ghostly' ability to slip off into space and then reappear elsewhere. And, secondly, because it is the only John Silence adventure to have been written after that famous first book and, consequently, not included therein.*

'There's a hextraordinary gentleman to see you, sir,' said the new man.

'Why "extraordinary"?' asked Dr Silence, drawing the tips of his thin fingers through his brown beard. His eyes twinkled pleasantly. 'Why "extraordinary," Barker?' he repeated encouragingly, noticing the perplexed expression in the man's eyes.

'He's so – so thin, sir. I could hardly see 'im at all – at first. He was inside the house before I could ask the name,' he added, remembering strict orders.

'And who brought him here?'

'He came alone, sir, in a closed cab. He pushed by me before I could say a word – making no noise not what I could hear. He seemed to move very soft –'

The man stopped short with obvious embarrassment, as though he had already said enough to jeopardise his new situation, but trying hard to show that he remembered the instructions and warnings he had received with regard to the admission of strangers not properly accredited.

'And where is the gentleman now?' asked Dr Silence, turning away to conceal his amusement.

'I really couldn't exactly say, sir. I left him standing in the 'all –'

The doctor looked up sharply. 'But why in the hall, Barker? Why not in the waiting-room?' He fixed his piercing though kindly eyes on the man's face. 'Did he frighten you?' he asked quickly.

'I think he did, sir, if I may say so. I seemed to lose sight of him, as it were –' The man stammered, evidently convinced by now that he had earned his dismissal. 'He come in so funny, just like a cold wind,' he added boldly, setting his heels at attention and looking his master full in the face.

The doctor made an internal note of the man's halting description; he was pleased that the slight evidence of intuition which had induced him to engage Barker had not entirely failed at the first trial. Dr Silence sought for this qualification in all his assistants, from secretary to serving-man, and if it surrounded him with a somewhat singular crew, the drawbacks were more than compensated for on the whole by their occasional flashes of insight.

'So the gentleman made you feel queer, did he?'

'That was it, I think, sir,' repeated the man stolidly.

'And he brings no kind of introduction to me – no letter or anything?' asked the doctor, with feigned surprise, as though he knew what was coming.

The man fumbled, both in mind and pockets, and finally produced an envelope.

'I beg pardon, sir,' he said, greatly flustered; 'the gentleman handed me this for you.'

It was a note from a discerning friend, who had never yet sent him a case that was not vitally interesting from one point or another.

'Please see the bearer of this note,' the brief message ran, 'though I doubt if even you can do much to help him.'

John Silence paused a moment, so as to gather from the mind of the writer all that lay behind the brief words of the letter. Then he looked up at his servant with a graver expression than he had yet worn.

'Go back and find this gentleman,' he said, 'and show him into the green study. Do not reply to his question, or speak more than actually necessary; but think kind, helpful, sympathetic thoughts as strongly as you can, Barker. You remember what I told you about the importance of thinking, when I engaged you. Put curiosity out of your mind, and think gently, sympathetically, affectionately, if you can.'

He smiled, and Barker, who had recovered his composure in the doctor's presence, bowed silently and went out.

There were two different reception rooms in Dr Silence's house. One, intended for persons who imagined they needed spiritual assistance when really they were only candidates for the asylum, had padded walls, and was well supplied with various concealed contrivances by means of which sudden violence could be instantly met and overcome. It was, however, rarely used. The other, intended for the reception of genuine cases of spiritual distress and out-of-the-way afflictions of a psychic nature, was entirely draped and furnished in a soothing deep green, calculated to induce calmness and repose of mind. And this room was the one in which Dr Silence interviewed the majority of his 'queer' cases, and the one into which he had directed Barker to show his present caller.

To begin with, the arm-chair in which the patient was always directed to sit, was nailed to the floor, since its immovability tended to impart this same excellent characteristic to the occupant. Patients invariably grew excited when talking about themselves, and their excitement tended to confuse their thoughts and to exaggerate their language. The immobility of the chair helped to counteract this. After repeated endeavours to drag it forward, or push it back, they ended by resigning themselves to sitting quietly. And with the futility of fidgeting there followed a calmer state of mind.

Upon the floor, and at intervals in the wall immediately behind, were certain tiny green buttons, practically unnoticeable, which on being pressed permitted a soothing and persuasive narcotic to rise invisibly about the occupant of the chair. The effect upon the excitable patient was rapid, admirable, and harmless. The green study was further provided with a secret spyhole; for John Silence liked when possible to observe his patient's face before it had assumed that mask the features of the human countenance invariably wear in the presence of another person. A man sitting alone wears a psychic expression; and this expression is the man himself. It disappears the moment another person joins him. And Dr Silence often learned more from a few moments' secret observation of a face than from hours of conversation with its owner afterwards.

A very light, almost a dancing step followed Barker's heavy tread towards the green room, and a moment afterwards the man came in and announced that the gentleman was waiting. He was still pale and his manner nervous.

'Never mind, Barker,' the doctor said kindly; 'if you were not intuitive the man would have had no effect upon you at all. You only need training and development. And when you have learned to interpret these feelings and sensations better, you will feel no fear, but only a great sympathy.'

'Yes, sir; thank you, sir!' And Barker bowed and made his escape, while Dr Silence, an amused smile lurking about the corners of his mouth, made his way noiselessly down the passage and put his eye to the spy-hole in the door of the green study.

This spy-hole was so placed that it commanded a view of almost the entire room, and, looking through it, the doctor saw a hat, gloves, and umbrella lying on a chair by the table, but searched at first in vain for their owner.

The windows were both closed and a brisk fire burned in the grate. There were various signs – signs intelligible at least to a keenly intuitive soul – that the room was occupied, yet so far as human beings were concerned, it seemed undeniably empty. No one sat in the chairs; no one stood on the mat before the fire; there was no sign even that a patient was anywhere close against the wall, examining the Böcklin reproduction – as patients so often did when they thought they were alone – and therefore rather difficult to see from the spy-hole. Ordinarily speaking, there was no one in the room. It was unoccupied.

Yet Dr Silence was quite well aware that a human being *was* in the room. His sensitive system never failed to let him know the proximity of an incarnate or discarnate being. Even in the dark he could tell that. And he now knew positively that his patient – the patient who had alarmed Barker, and had then tripped down the corridor with that dancing footstep – was somewhere concealed within the four walls commanded by his spy-hole. He also realised – and this was most unusual – that this individual whom he desired to watch knew that he was being watched. And, further, that the stranger himself was also watching in his turn. In fact, that it was he, the doctor, who was being observed – and by an observer as keen and trained as himself.

An inkling of the true state of the case began to dawn upon him, and he was on the verge of entering – indeed, his hand already touched the door-knob – when his eye, still glued to the spy-hole, detected a slight movement. Directly opposite, between him and the fireplace, something stirred. He watched very attentively and made certain that he was not mistaken. An object on the mantelpiece – it was a blue vase – disappeared from view. It passed out of sight together with the portion of the marble mantelpiece on which it rested. Next, that part of the fire and grate and brass fender immediately below it vanished entirely, as though a slice had been taken clean out of them.

Dr Silence then understood that something between him and these objects was slowly coming into being, something that concealed them and obstructed his vision by inserting itself in the line of sight between them and himself.

He quietly awaited further results before going in.

First he saw a thin perpendicular line tracing itself from just above the height of the clock and continuing downwards till it reached the woolly fire-mat. This line grew wider, broadened, grew solid. It was no shadow; it was something substantial. It defined itself more and more. Then suddenly, at the top of the line, and about on a level with the face of the clock, he saw a small luminous disc gazing steadily at him. It was a human eye, looking straight into his own, pressed there against the spy-hole. And it was bright with intelligence. Dr Silence held his breath for a moment – and stared back at it.

Then, like someone moving out of deep shadow into light, he saw the figure of a man come sliding sideways into view, a whitish face following the eye, and the perpendicular line he had first observed broadening out and developing into the complete figure of a human being. It was the patient. He had apparently been standing there in front of the fire all the time. A second eye had followed the first, and both of them stared steadily at the spy-hole, sharply concentrated, yet with a sly twinkle of humour and amusement that made it impossible for the doctor to maintain his position any longer.

He opened the door and went in quickly. As he did so he noticed for the first time the sound of a German band coming in noisily through the open ventilators. In some intuitive, unaccountable fashion the music connected itself with the patient he was about to interview. This sort of prevision was not unfamiliar to him. It always explained itself later.

The man, he saw, was of middle age and of very ordinary appearance; so ordinary, in fact, that he was difficult to describe – his only peculiarity being his extreme thinness. Pleasant – that is, good – vibrations issued from his atmosphere and met Dr Silence as he advanced to greet him, yet vibrations alive with currents and discharges betraying the perturbed and disordered condition of his mind and brain.

There was evidently something wholly out of the usual in the state of his thoughts. Yet, though strange, it was not altogether distressing; it was not the impression that the broken and violent atmosphere of the insane produced upon the mind. Dr Silence realised in a flash that here was a case of absorbing interest that might require all his powers to handle properly.

'I was watching you through my little peep-hole – as you saw,' he began, with a pleasant smile, advancing to shake hands. 'I find it of the greatest assistance sometimes –'

But the patient interrupted him at once. His voice was hurried and had odd, shrill changes in it, breaking from high to low in unexpected fashion. One moment it thundered, the next it almost squeaked.

'I understand without explanation,' he broke in rapidly. 'You get the true note of a man in that way – when he thinks you saw very little. My case, as you of course grasp, Dr Silence, is extremely peculiar, uncomfortably peculiar. Indeed, unless Sir William had positively assured me –'

'My friend has sent you to me,' the doctor interrupted gravely, with a gentle note of authority, 'and that is quite sufficient. Pray, be seated, Mr –'

'Mudge – Racine Mudge,' returned the other.

'Take this comfortable one, Mr Mudge,' leading him to the fixed chair, 'and tell me your condition in your own way and at your own pace. My whole day is at your service if you require it.'

Mr Mudge moved towards the chair in question and then hesitated.

'You will promise me not to use the narcotic buttons,' he said, before sitting down. 'I do not need them. Also I ought to mention that anything you think of vividly will reach my mind. That is apparently part of my peculiar case.' He sat down with a sigh and arranged his thin legs and body into a position of comfort. Evidently he was very sensitive to the thoughts of others, for the picture of the green buttons had only entered the doctor's mind for a second, yet the other had instantly snapped it up. Dr Silence noticed, too, that Mr Mudge held on tightly with both hands to the arms of the chair.

'I'm rather glad the chair is nailed to the floor,' he remarked, as he settled himself more comfortably. 'It suits me admirably. The fact is – and this is my case in a nutshell – which is all that a doctor of your marvellous development requires – the fact is, Dr Silence, I am a victim of Higher Space. That's what's the matter with me – Higher Space!'

The two looked at each other for a space in silence, the little patient holding tightly to the arms of the chair which 'suited him admirably,' and looking up with staring eyes, his atmosphere positively trembling with the waves of some unknown activity; while the doctor smiled kindly and sympathetically, and put his whole person as far as possible into the mental condition of the other.

'Higher Space,' repeated Mr Mudge, 'that's what it is. Now, do you think you can help me with *that*?'

There was a pause during which the men's eyes steadily searched down below the surface of their respective personalities. Then Dr Silence spoke.

'I am quite sure I can help,' he answered quietly; 'sympathy must always help, and suffering always claims my sympathy. I see you have suffered cruelly. You must tell me all about your case, and when I hear the gradual steps by which you reached this strange condition, I have no doubt I can be of assistance to you.'

He drew a chair up beside his interlocutor and laid a hand on his shoulder for a moment. His whole being radiated kindness, intelligence, desire to help.

'For instance,' he went on, 'I feel sure it was the result of no mere chance that you became familiar with the terrors of what you term Higher Space; for higher space is no mere external measurement. It is, of course, a spiritual state, a spiritual condition, an inner development, and one that we must recognise as abnormal, since it is beyond the reach of the senses at the present stage of evolution. Higher Space is a mystical state.'

'Oh!' cried the other, rubbing his birdlike hands with pleasure, 'the relief it is to me to talk to someone who can understand! Of course what you say is the utter truth. And you are right that no mere chance led me to my present condition, but, on the other hand, prolonged and deliberate study. Yet chance in a sense now governs it. I mean, my entering the condition of higher space seems to depend upon the chance of this and that circumstance.' He sighed and paused a moment. 'For instance,' he continued, starting, 'the mere sound of that German band sent me off. Not that all music will do so, but certain sounds, certain vibrations, at once key me up to the requisite pitch, and off I go. Wagner's music always does it, and that band must have been playing a stray bit of Wagner. But I'll come to all that later. Only, first' – he smiled deprecatingly – 'I must ask you to send away your man from the spy-hole.'

John Silence looked up with a start, for Mr Mudge's back was to the door, and there was no mirror. He saw the brown eye of Barker glued to the little circle of glass, and he crossed the room without a word and snapped down the black shutter provided for the purpose, and then heard Barker shuffle away along the passage.

'Now,' continued the little man in the chair, 'I can go on. You have managed to put me completely at my ease, and I feel I may tell you my whole case without shame or reserve. You will understand. But you must be patient with me if I go into details that are already familiar to you – details of higher space, I mean – and if I seem stupid when I have to describe things that transcend the power of language and are really therefore indescribable.'

'My dear friend,' put in the other calmly, 'that goes without saying. To know higher space is an experience that defies description, and one is obliged to make use of more or less intelligible symbols. But, pray, proceed. Your vivid thoughts will tell me more than your halting words.'

An immense sigh of relief proceeded from the little figure half lost in the depths of the chair. Such intelligent sympathy meeting him half-way was a new experience, and it touched his heart at once. He leaned back, relaxing his tight hold of the arms, and began in his thin, scale-like voice.

'My mother was a Frenchwoman, and my father an Essex bargeman,' he said abruptly. 'Hence my name – Racine and Mudge. My father died before I ever saw him. My mother inherited money from her Bordeaux relations, and when she died soon after, I was left alone with wealth and a strange freedom. I had no guardian, trustees, sisters, brothers, or any connection in the world to look after me. I grew up, therefore, utterly without education. This much was to my advantage; I learned none of that deceitful rubbish taught in schools, and so had nothing to unlearn when I awakened to my true love – mathematics, higher mathematics and higher geometry. These, however, I seemed to know instinctively. It was like the memory of what I had deeply studied before; the principles were in my blood, and I simply raced through the ordinary stages, and beyond, and then did the same with geometry. Afterwards, when I read the books on these subjects, I understood how swift and undeviating the knowledge had come back to me. It was simple memory. It was simply re-collecting the memories of what I had known before in a previous existence and required no books to teach me.'

In his growing excitement, Mr Mudge attempted to drag the chair forward a little nearer to his listener, and then smiled faintly as he resigned himself instantly again to its immobility, and plunged anew into the recital of his singular 'disease.'

'The audacious speculations of Bolyai, the amazing theories of Gauss – that through a point more than *one* line could be drawn parallel to a given line; the possibility that the angles of a triangle are together *greater* than two right angles, if drawn upon immense curvatures – the breathless intuitions of Beltrami and Lobatchewsky – all these I hurried through, and emerged, panting but unsatisfied, upon the verge of my – my world, my higher space possibilities – in a word, my disease.

'How I got there,' he resumed after a brief pause, during which he appeared to be listening nervously for an approaching sound, 'is more than I can put intelligibly into words. I can only hope to leave your mind with an intuitive comprehension of the possibility of what I say.

'Here, however, came a change. At this point I was no longer absorbing the fruits of studies I had made before; it was the beginning of new efforts to learn for the first time, and I had to go slowly and laboriously through terrible work. Here I sought for the theories and speculations of others. But books were few and far between, and with the exception of one man – a "dreamer," the world called him – whose audacity and piercing intuition amazed and delighted me beyond description, I found no one to guide or help.'

'You, of course, Dr Silence, understand something of what I

am driving at with these stammering words, though you cannot perhaps yet guess what depths of pain my new knowledge brought me to, nor why an acquaintance with a new dimension of space should prove a source of misery and terror.'

Mr Racine Mudge, remembering that the chair would not move, did the next best thing he could in his desire to draw nearer to the attentive man facing him, and sat forward upon the very edge of the cushions, crossing his legs and gesticulating with both hands as though he saw into this region of new space he was attempting to describe, and might any moment tumble into it bodily from the edge of the chair and disappear from view. John Silence, separated from him by three paces, sat with his eyes fixed upon the thin white face opposite, noting every word and every gesture with deep attention.

'This room we now sit in, Dr Silence, has one side open to space – higher space. A closed box only *seems* closed. There is a way in and out of a soap bubble without breaking the skin.'

'You tell me no new things,' the doctor interposed gently.

'Hence, if higher space exists and our world borders upon it and lies partially in it, it follows necessarily that we see only portions of all objects. We never see their true and complete shape. We see three measurements, but not their fourth. The new direction is concealed from us, and when I hold this book and move my hand all round it I have not really made a complete circuit. We only perceive those portions of any object which exist in our three dimensions, the rest escapes us. But, once learn to see in higher space, and objects will appear as they actually are. Only they will thus be hardly recognisable_

'Now you may begin to grasp something of what I am coming to.'

'I am beginning to understand something of what you must have suffered,' observed the doctor soothingly, 'for I have made similar experiments myself, and only stopped just in time –'

'You are the one man in all the world who can understand, *and* sympathise,' exclaimed Mr Mudge, grasping his hand and holding it tightly while he spoke. The nailed chair prevented further excitability.

'Well,' he resumed, after a moment's pause, 'I procured the implements and the coloured blocks for practical experiment, and I followed the instructions carefully till I had arrived at an imaginative conception of four-dimensional space. The tessaract, the figure whose boundaries are cubes, I knew by heart. That is to say, I knew it and saw it mentally, for my eye, of course, could never take in a new measurement, nor my hands and feet handle it.

'So, at least, I thought,' he added, making a wry face. 'I had reached the stage, you see, when I could *imagine* in a new dimension. I was able to conceive the shape of that new figure which is intrinsically different to all we know – the shape of the tessaract. I could perceive in four dimensions. When, therefore, I looked at a cube I could see all its sides at once. Its top was not foreshortened, nor its farther side and base invisible. I saw the whole thing out flat, so to speak. Moreover, I also saw its contents – its in-sides.'

'You were not yourself able to enter this new world?' interrupted Dr Silence.

'Not then. I was only able to conceive intuitively what it was like and how exactly it must look. Later, when I slipped in there and saw objects in their entirety, unlimited by the paucity of our poor three measurements, I very nearly lost my life. For, you see, space does not stop at a single new dimension, a fourth. It extends in all possible new ones, and we must conceive it as containing any number of new dimensions. In other words, there is no space at all, but only a condition. But, meanwhile, I had come to grasp the strange fact that the objects in our normal world appear to us only partially.'

Mr Mudge moved farther forward till he was balanced dangerously on the very edge of the chair. 'From this starting point,' he resumed, 'I began my studies and experiments, and continued them for years. I had money, and I was without friends. I lived in solitude and experimented. My intellect, of course, had little part in the work, for intellectually it was all unthinkable. Never was the limitation of mere reason more plainly demonstrated. It was mystically, intuitively, spiritually that I began to advance. And what I learnt, and knew, and did is all impossible to put into language, since it describes experiences transcending the experiences of men. It is only some of the results – what you would call the symptoms of my disease – that I can give you, and even these must often appear absurd contradictions and impossible paradoxes.

'I can only tell you, Dr Silence ' – his manner became grave suddenly – 'that I reached sometimes a point of view whence all the great puzzle of the world became plain to me, and I understood what they call in the Yoga books "The Great Heresy of Separateness"; why all great teachers have urged the necessity of man loving his neighbour as himself; how men are all really *one*; and why the utter loss of self is necessary to salvation and the discovery of the true life of the soul.'

He paused a moment and drew breath.

'Your speculations have been my own long ago,' the doctor said quietly. 'I fully realise the force of your words. Men are doubtless not separate at all – in the sense they imagine.'

'All this about the very much higher space I only dimly, very dimly conceived, of course,' the other went on, raising his voice again by jerks; 'but what did happen to me was the humbler accident of – the simpler disaster – oh dear, how shall I put it –?'

He stammered and showed visible signs of distress.

'It was simply this,' he resumed with a sudden rush of words, 'that, accidentally, as the result of my years of experiment, I one day slipped bodily into the next world, the world of four dimensions, yet without knowing precisely how I got there, or how I could get back again. I discovered, that is, that my ordinary three-dimensional body was but an expression – a partial projection – of my higher four-dimensional body!

'Now you understand what I meant much earlier in our talk when I spoke of chance. I cannot control my entrance or exit. Certain people, certain human atmospheres, certain wandering forces, thoughts, desires even – the radiations of certain combinations of colour, and above all, the vibrations of certain kinds of music, will suddenly throw me into a state of what I can only describe as an intense and terrific inner vibration – and behold I am off! Off in the direction at right angles to all our known directions! Off in the direction the cube takes when it begins to trace the outlines of the new figure, the tessaract! Off into my breathless and semi-divine higher space! Off, *inside myself*, into the world of four dimensions!'

He gasped and dropped back into the depths of the immovable chair.

'And there,' he whispered, his voice issuing from among the cushions, 'there I have to stay until these vibrations subside, or until they do something which I cannot find words to describe properly or intelligibly to you – and then, behold, I am back again. First, that is, I disappear. Then I reappear. Only' – he sighed – 'I cannot control my entrance nor my exit.'

'Just so,' exclaimed Dr Silence, 'and that is why a few –'

'Why a few moments ago,' interrupted Mr Mudge, taking the words out of his mouth, 'you found me gone and then saw me return. The music of that wretched German band sent me off. Your intense thinking about me brought me back – when the band had stopped its Wagner. I saw you approach the peep-hole and I saw Barker's intention of doing so later. For me no interiors are hidden. I see inside. When in that state the content of your mind, as of your body, is open to me as the day. Oh dear, oh dear, oh dear!'

Mr Mudge stopped and mopped his brow. A light trembling ran over the surface of his small body like wind over grass. He still held tightly to the arms of the chair.

'At first,' he presently resumed, 'my new experiences were so vividly interesting that I felt no alarm. There was no room for it. The alarm came a little later.'

'Then you actually penetrated far enough into that state to experience yourself as a normal portion of it?' asked the doctor, leaning forward, deeply interested.

Mr Mudge nodded a perspiring face in reply.

'I did,' he whispered, 'undoubtedly I did. I am coming to all that. It began first at night, when I realised that sleep brought no loss of consciousness –'

'The spirit, of course, can never sleep. Only the body becomes unconscious,' interposed John Silence.

'Yes, we know that – theoretically. At night, of course, the spirit is active elsewhere, and we have no memory of where and how, simply because the brain stays behind and receives no record. But I found that, while remaining conscious, I also retained memory. I had attained to the state of continuous consciousness, for at night regularly, with the first approaches of drowsiness, I entered *nolens volens* the four dimensional world.

'For a time this happened frequently, and I could not control it; though later I found a way to regulate it better. Apparently sleep is unnecessary in the higher – the four dimensional – body. Yes, perhaps. But I should infinitely have preferred dull sleep to the knowledge. For, unable to control my movements, I wandered to and fro, attracted owing to my partial development and premature arrival, to parts of this new world that alarmed me more and more. It was the awful waste and drift of a monstrous world, so utterly different to all we know and see that I cannot even hint at the nature of the sights and objects and beings in it. More than that, I cannot even remember them. I cannot now picture them to myself even, but can recall only the *memory of the impression* they made upon me, the horror and devastating terror of it all. To be in several places at once, for instance –'

'Perfectly,' interrupted John Silence, noticing the increase of the other's excitement, 'I understand exactly. But now, please, tell me a little more of this alarm you experienced, and how it affected you.'

'It's not the disappearing and reappearing *per se* that I mind,' continued Mr Mudge, 'so much as certain other things. It's seeing people and objects in their weird entirety, in their true and complete shapes, that is so distressing. It introduced me to a world of monsters. Horses, dogs, cats, all of which I loved; people, trees, children; all that I have considered beautiful in life – everything, from a human face to a cathedral – appear to me in a different shape and aspect to all I have known before. Instead of seeing their partial expression in three dimensions, I saw them complete – in four. I cannot perhaps convince you why this should be terrible, but I assure you that it is so. To hear the human voice proceeding from this novel appearance which I scarcely recognise as a human body is ghastly, simply ghastly. To see inside everything and everybody is a form of insight peculiarly distressing. To be so confused in geography as to find myself one moment at the North Pole, and the next at Clapham Junction – or possibly at both places simultaneously – is absurdly terrifying. Your imagination will readily furnish other details without my multiplying my experiences now. But you have no idea what it all means, and how I suffer.'

Mr Mudge paused in his panting account and lay back in his chair. He still held tightly to the arms as though they could keep him in the world of sanity and three measurements, and only now and again released his left hand in order to mop his face. He looked very thin and white and oddly unsubstantial, and he stared about him as though he saw into this other space he had been talking about.

John Silence, too, felt warm. He had listened to every word and had made many notes. The presence of this man had an exhilarating effect upon him. It seemed as if Mr Racine Mudge still carried about with him something of that breathless higher-space condition he had been describing. At any rate, Dr Silence had himself advanced sufficiently far to realise that the visions of this extraordinary little person had a basis of truth for their origin.

After a pause that prolonged itself into minutes, he crossed the room and unlocked a drawer in the bookcase, taking out a small book with a red cover. It had a lock to it, and he produced a key out of his pocket and proceeded to open the covers. The bright eyes of Mr Mudge never left him for a single second.

'It almost seems a pity,' he said at length, 'to cure you, Mr Mudge. You are on the way to discovery of great things. Though you may lose your life in the process – that is, your life here in the world of three dimensions – you would lose thereby nothing of great value – you will pardon my apparent rudeness, I know – and you might gain what is infinitely greater. Your suffering, of course, lies in the fact that you alternate between the two worlds and are never wholly in one or the other. Also, I rather imagine, though I cannot be certain of this from any personal experiments, that you have here and there penetrated even into space of more than four dimensions, and have hence experienced the terror you speak of.'

The perspiring son of the Essex bargeman and the woman of Normandy bent his head several times in assent, but uttered no word in reply.

'Some strange psychic predisposition, dating no doubt from one of your former lives, has favoured the development of your "disease"; and the fact that you had no normal training at school or college, no leading by the poor intellect into the culs-de-sac falsely called knowledge, has further caused your exceedingly rapid movement along the lines of direct inner experience. None of the knowledge you have foreshadowed has come to you through the senses, of course.'

Mr Mudge, sitting in his immovable chair, began to tremble sightly. A wind again seemed to pass over his surface and again it set it curiously in motion like a field of grass.

'You are merely talking to gain time,' he said hurriedly, in a shaking voice. 'This thinking aloud delays us. I see ahead what you are coming to, only please be quick, for something is going to happen. A band is again coming down the street, and if it plays – if it plays Wagner – I shall be off in a twinkling.'

'Precisely. I will be quick. I was leading up to the point of how to effect your cure. The way is this: You must simply learn to block the entrances – prevent the *centres* acting.'

'True, true, utterly true!' exclaimed the little man, dodging about nervously in the depths of the chair. 'But how, in the name of space, can that be done?'

'By concentration. They are all within you, these centres, although outer causes such as colour, music, and other things lead you towards them. These external things you cannot hope to destroy, but once the entrances are blocked, they will lead you only to bricked walls and closed channels. You will no longer be able to find the way.'

'Quick, quick!' cried the bobbing figure in the chair. 'How is this concentration to be effected?'

'This little book,' continued Dr Silence calmly, 'will explain to you the way.' He tapped the cover. 'Let me now read out to you certain simple instructions, composed, as I see you divine, entirely from my own personal experiences in the same direction. Follow these instructions and you will no longer enter the state of higher space. The entrances will be blocked effectively.'

Mr Mudge sat bolt upright in his chair to listen, and John Silence cleared his throat and began to read slowly in a very distinct voice.

But before he had uttered a dozen words, something happened. A sound of street music entered the room through the open ventilators, for a band had begun to play in the stable mews at the back of the house – the March from *Tannhäuser*. Odd as it may seem that a German band should twice within the space of an hour enter the same mews and play Wagner, it was nevertheless the fact.

Mr Racine Mudge heard it. He uttered a sharp, squeaking cry and twisted his arms with nervous energy round the chair. A piteous look that was not far from tears spread over his white face. Grey shadows followed it – the grey of fear. He began to struggle convulsively.

'Hold me fast! Catch me! For God's sake, keep me here! I'm on the rush already. Oh, it's frightful!' he cried in tones of anguish, his voice as thin as a reed.

Dr Silence made a plunge forward to seize him, but in a flash, before he could cover the space between them, Mr Racine Mudge, screaming and struggling, seemed to shoot past him into invisibility. He disappeared like an arrow from a bow propelled at infinite speed, and his voice no longer sounded in the external air, but seemed in some curious way to make itself heard somewhere within the depths of the doctor's own being. It was almost like a faint singing cry in his head, like a voice of dream, a voice of vision and unreality.

'Alcohol, alcohol!' it cried faintly, with distance in it, 'give me alcohol! It's the quickest way. Alcohol, before I'm out of reach!'

The doctor, accustomed to rapid decisions and even more rapid action, remembered that a brandy flask stood upon the mantelpiece, and in less than a second he had seized it and was holding it out towards the space above the chair recently occupied by the visible Mudge. But, before his very eyes, and long ere he could unscrew the metal stopper, he saw the contents of the closed glass phial sink and lessen as though someone was drinking violently and greedily of the liquor within.

'Thanks! Enough! It deadens the vibrations ' cried the faint voice in his interior, as he withdrew the flask and set it back upon the mantelpiece. He understood that in Mudge's present condition one side of the flask was open to space and he could drink without removing the stopper. He could hardly have had a more interesting proof of what he had been hearing described at such length.

But the next moment – the very same moment it almost seemed – the German band stopped midway in its tune – and there was Mr Mudge back in his chair again, gasping and panting!

'Quick!' he shrieked, 'stop that band! Send it away! Catch hold of me! Block the entrances! Block the entrances! Give me the red book! Oh, oh, oh-h-h-h!!!'

The music had begun again. It was merely a temporary interruption. The *Tannhäuser* March started again, this time at a tremendous pace that made it sound like a rapid two-step, as though the instruments played against time.

But the brief interruption gave Dr Silence a moment in which to collect his scattering thoughts, and before the band had got through half a bar, he had flung forward upon the chair and held Mr Racine Mudge, the struggling little victim of Higher Space, in a grip of iron. His arms went all round his diminutive person, taking in a good part of the chair at the same time. He was not a big man, yet he seemed to smother Mudge completely.

Yet, even as he did so, and felt the wriggling form underneath him, it began to melt and slip away like air or water. The wood of the armchair somehow disentangled itself from between his own arms and those of Mudge. The phenomenon known as the passage of matter through matter took place. The little man seemed actually to be interfused with the other's being. Dr Silence could just see his face beneath him. It puckered and grew dark as though from some great internal effort. He heard the thin, reedy voice cry in his ear to 'Block the entrances, block the entrances!' and then – but how in the world describe what is indescribable?

John Silence half rose up to watch. Racine Mudge, his face distorted beyond all recognition, was making a marvellous inward movement, as though doubling back upon himself. He turned funnel-wise like water in a whirling vortex, and then appeared to break up somewhat as a reflection breaks up and divides in a distorting convex mirror. He went neither forward nor backwards, neither to the right nor the left, neither up nor down. But he went. He went utterly. He simply flashed away out of sight like a vanishing projectile.

All but one leg! Dr Silence just had the time and the presence of mind to seize upon the left ankle and boot as it disappeared, and to this he held on for several seconds like grim death. Yet all the time he knew it was a foolish and useless thing to do.

The foot was in his grasp one moment, and the next it seemed – this was the only way he could describe it – inside his own skin and bones, and at the same time outside his hand and all round it. It seemed mingled in some amazing way with his own flesh and blood. Then it was gone, and he was tightly grasping a mere draught of heated air.

'Gone! gone! gone!' cried a faint, whispering voice somewhere deep within his own consciousness. 'Lost! lost' lost!' it repeated, growing fainter and fainter till at length it vanished into nothing and the last signs of Mr Racine Mudge vanished with it.

John Silence locked his red book and replaced it in the cabinet, which he fastened with a click, and when Barker answered the bell he inquired if Mr Mudge had left a card upon the table. It appeared that he had, and when the servant returned with it, Dr Silence read the address and made a note of it. It was in North London.

'Mr Mudge has gone,' he said quietly to Barker, noticing his expression of alarm.

'He's not taken his 'at with him, sir.'

'Mr Mudge requires no hat where he is now,' continued the doctor, stooping to poke the fire. 'But he may return for it –'

'And the humbrella, sir.'

'And the umbrella.'

'He didn't go out *my* way, sir, if you please,' stuttered the amazed servant, his curiosity overcoming his nervousness.

'Mr Mudge has his own way of coming and going, and prefers it. If he returns by the door at any time remember to bring him instantly to me, and be kind and gentle with him and ask no questions. Also, remember, Barker, to think pleasantly, sympathetically, affectionately of him while he is away. Mr Mudge is a very suffering gentleman.'

Barker bowed and went out of the room backwards, gasping

and feeling round the inside of his collar with three very hot fingers of one hand.

It was two days later when he brought in a telegram to the study. Dr Silence opened it, and read as follows:

> Bombay. Just slipped out again. All safe. Have blocked entrances. Thousand thanks. Address Cooks, London. –
> Mudge

Dr Silence looked up and saw Barker staring at him bewilderingly. It occurred to him that somehow he knew the contents of the telegram.

'Make a parcel of Mr Mudge's things,' he said briefly, 'and address them Thomas Cook & Sons, Ludgate Circus. And send them there exactly a month from to-day, marked "To be called for." '

'Yes, sir,' said Barker, leaving the room with a deep sigh and a hurried glance at the waste-paper basket where his master had dropped the pink paper.

V

Case of the Haunting of Grange

Sax Rohmer

Sax Rohmer *(1883-1959) is, of course, famous as the creator of that evil Oriental villain, Fu Manchu, who has been immortalised in books, films and even comic strips. Yet Rohmer also wrote numerous other books of adventure, mystery and supernatural fiction, amongst which can be found the cases of Moris Klaw, a London antique dealer by profession but an authority and investigator of the occult. He is called in to solve seemingly impenetrable crimes, but posesses a special psychic ability to 'tune-in' his mind at the scene of the events and by so doing pick up from the ether the necessary clues to solve the mystery. For this reason he is known far and wide as 'The Dream Detective'.*

Rohmer, whose real name was Arthur Sarsfield Ward, had a life-long interest in the supernatural, and for several years belonged to the Order of the Golden Dawn, the most famous group of occult practitioners of the time. As a result of this association, many of his fantasy stories have a strong element of authenticity about them, although it is not unusual to find the most apparently supernatural cases which Dr Klaw investigates turn out to have a rational explanation. You are now invited to accompany 'The Dream Detective' on one of his strangest enquiries from the year 1920 …

A large lamp burned in the centre of the table; a red-shaded candle stood close by each diner; and the soft light made a brave enough show upon the snowy napery and spotless silver, but dispersed nothing of the gloom about us. The table was a lighted oasis in the desert of the huge apartment. One could barely pick out the suits of armour and trophies which hung from distant panelled walls, and I started repeatedly when the butler appeared, silent, at my elbow.

Of the party of five, four were men – three of them (for I venture to include myself) neatly groomed and dressed with care in conventional dinner fashion. The fourth was a heavy figure in a dress-coat with broad satin lapels such as I have seen, I think, in pictures of Victorian celebrities. I have no doubt judging from its shiny appearance, that it was the workmanship of a Victorian tailor. The vest was cut high and also boasted lapels; the trousers, though at present they were concealed beneath the table, belonged to a different suit, possibly a mourning suit, and to a different sartorial epoch.

The woman, young, dark and exceedingly pretty, wore a gown of shimmering amber, cut with Parisian daring. Her beautiful eyes were more often lowered than raised, for Sir James Leyland, our host, was unable to conceal his admiration; his face, tanned by his life in the Bush, was often turned to her. Clement Leyland, the baronet's cousin, bore a striking resemblance to Sir James, but entirely lacked the latter's breezy manner. I set him down for a man who thought much and said little.

However, conversation could not well flag at a board boasting the presence of such a genial colonial as Sir James, and such a storehouse of anecdotal oddities as Moris Klaw. Mr Leyland and myself, then, for the most part practised the difficult art of listening; for Isis Klaw, I learned, could talk almost as entertainingly as her father.

'I am so glad,' said Moris Klaw, and his voice rumbled thunderously about the room, 'that I have this opportunity to visit Grange.'

'It certainly has great historic interest,' agreed Sir James. 'I had never anticipated inheriting the grand old place, much less the title. My uncle's early death, unmarried, very considerably altered my prospects; I became a landed propietor who might otherwise have become a Murrumbidgee whaler!'

He laughed, light-heartedly, glancing at Isis Klaw, and from her to his cousin.

'Clem had everything in apple-pie order for me,' he added, 'including the family goblin!'

'Ah! that family goblin!' rumbled Moris Klaw. 'It is him I am after, that goblin!'

The history of Grange, in fact, was directly responsible for Moris Klaw's presence that night. An odd little book, *Psychic Angles*, had recently attracted considerable attention amongst students of the occult, and had proved equally interesting to the general public. It dealt with the subject of ghosts from quite a new standpoint, and incidentally revealed its anonymous author as one conversant apparently with the history of every haunted house in Europe. Few knew that the curio-dealer of Wapping was the author, but as Grange was dealt with in *Psychic Angles*, amongst a number of other haunted homes of England, a letter from Sir James Leyland, forwarded by the publisher, had invited the author to investigate the latest developments of the Leyland family ghost.

I had had the privilege to be associated with Moris Klaw, in another case of apparent haunting – that which I have dealt with in an earlier paper; the haunting of The Grove. He had courteously invited me, then, to assist him (his own expression) in the inquiry at Grange. I welcomed the opportunity; for I was anxious to include in my annals at least one other case of the apparent occult.

'We shall without delay,' continued the eccentric investigator, 'endeavour to meet him face to face – this disturber of the peace. Sir James, it is with the phenomena you call ghosts the same as with valuable relics, with jewels, with mummies – ah, those mummies! – with beautiful women!'

'To liken a beautiful woman to a relic,' said Sir James, 'would be – well –' he glanced at Isis, 'hardly complimentary!'

'It would be true!' Moris Klaw assured him impressively. 'Nature, that mystic process of reproduction, wastes not its models. Sir James, all beauty is duplicated. Look at my daughter, Isis,' (Sir James readily obeyed.) 'You see her, yes? And what do you see?'

Isis lowered her eyes, but, frankly, I was unable to perceive any evidence of embarrassment in this singularly self-possessed girl.

'Perhaps,' resumed her father, 'I could tell you what you see; but I will only tell you what it is you *may* see. You may see a beauty of your Regency or a favourite of your Charles; the daughter of a Viking, an ancient British princess; the slave of a Caesar, the dancer of a Pharaoh!'

'You believe in reincarnation?' suggested Clement Leyland, quietly.

'Yes, certainly, why not, of course!' rumbled Moris Klaw. 'But I do not speak of it now, not I; I speak of Nature's reproduction; I tell you how Nature wastes nothing which is beautiful. What has the soul to do with the body? I tell you how the reproduction goes on and on until the mould, the plate, the die, has perished! So is it with ghosts. You write me that your goblin has learned some new tricks. I answer, your goblin can never learn new tricks; I answer this is not he, it is another goblin! Nature is conservative with her goblins as with her beautiful women; she does not disfigure the old model with alterations. What! Chop them about! Never! she makes new ones.'

Clement Leyland smiled discreetly, but Sir James was evidently interested.

'Of course I've read *Psychic Angles*, Mr Klaw,' he said, 'consequently your novel theories do not altogether surprise me. I gather your meaning to be this: a haunted house is haunted in exactly the same way generation after generation? Any new development points to the presence of a new force or intelligence?'

'It is exactly quite so,' Moris Klaw nodded sympathetically. 'You have the receptive mind, Sir James; you should take up ghosts; they would like you. There is a scientific future for the sympathetic ghost-hunter – for I will whisper it – these poor ghosts are sometimes so glad to be hunted! It is a lonely life, that of a ghost!'

'The Grange ghost,' Sir James assured him, 'is a most gregarious animal. He doesn't go in for lonely groanings in the chapel or anything of that kind; he drops into the billiard-room frequently, he's often to be met with right here in the dining-room, and of late he's been sleeping with me regularly!'

'So I hear,' rumbled Moris Klaw; 'so I hear. It is quaint, yes, proceed, my friend.'

Isis Klaw sat with her big eyes fixed upon Sir James as he continued:

'The traditional ghost of Grange was a grey monk, who on certain nights – I forget the exact dates – came out from the chapel beyond the orchard carrying a long staff, walked up to a buttress of the west wall and disappeared at the point where formerly there was a private entrance. In fact there used to be a secret stair opening at that point and communicating with a room built by a remote Leyland of the eighth Henry's time – a notorious *roué*. The last Leyland to use the room was Sir Francis, an intimate of Charles II. The next heir had the wing rebuilt, and the ancient door walled up.'

'Yes, yes,' said Moris Klaw. 'I know it all, but you tell it well. This is a most interesting house, this Grange. I have recorded him, the grey monk, and I learn with surprise how another spook comes poaching on his preserves! Tell us now of these new developments, Sir James.'

Sir James cleared his throat and glanced about the table.

'Please smoke,' said Isis; 'because I should like to smoke, too!'

'Yes, yes!' agreed Moris Klaw. 'Remain, my child, we will all remain; do not let us move an inch. This banqueting-hall is loaded with psychic impressions. Let us smoke and concentrate our minds upon the problem.'

Coffee and liqueurs were placed upon the table and cigarettes lighted. In deference to the presence of Isis, I suppose, no cigars were smoked; but the girl lighted an Egyptian cigarette proffered by Sir James with the insouciance of an old devotée of my Lady Nicotine. The butler having made his final departure, we were left – a lonely company in our lighted oasis – amid the shadow desert of that huge and ghostly apartment.

'All sorts of singular things have happened,' began Sir James, 'since my return from Australia. Of course I cannot say if these are recent developments, because my uncle, for seven or eight years before his death, resided entirely in London, and Grange was in charge of the housekeeper. It is notorious, is it not, that housekeepers and such worthy ladies never by any chance detect anything unseemly in family establishments with which they are associated? Anyway, when I was dug up out of the Bush, and all the formalities were through, good old Clement here set about putting things to rights for me and I arrived to find Grange a perfect picture from floor to roof. New servants engaged, too, though the housekeeper and the butler, who have been in the family for years, remained, of course, with some other old servants. As I have said, everything was in apple-pie order.'

'Including the ghost!' interpolated his cousin, laughing.

'That's the trouble,' said Sir James, banging his fist upon the table; 'the very first night I dined in this room there was a most uncanny manifestation. Clement and I were sitting here at this very table; we had dined – not unwisely, don't think that – and were just smoking and chatting, when –'

He ceased abruptly; in fact the effect was similar to that which would have resulted had a solid door suddenly been closed upon the speaker. But the stark silence which ensued was instantly interrupted. My blood seemed to freeze in my veins; a horrid, supernatural dread held me fast in my chair.

For, echoing hollowly around and about the huge, ancient apartment, rolled, booming, a peal of demoniacal laughter! From whence it proceeded I was wholly unable to imagine. It seemed to be all about, above us, and beneath us. It was mad, devilish, a hell-sound impossible to describe. It rose, it fell, it rose again – and ceased abruptly.

'My God!' I whispered, "What was it?'

II

In the silence that followed the ghostly disturbance we sat around the table listening. Sir James was the first to speak.

'A demonstration, Mr Klaw!' he said. 'This sort of thing happens every night!'

'Ah!' rumbled Moris Klaw, 'every night, eh? That laughing? You have investigated – yes – no?'

'I tried to investigate,' explained the baronet, 'but quite frankly I didn't know where to begin.'

We were all recovering our composure somewhat, I think.

'You hear that laughter nowhere but in this room?' asked Klaw.

'I have always heard it when we have been seated at this table,' was the reply; 'at no other time, but it can be heard clearly beyond the room. The servants have heard it. Excepting the housekeeper and the butler, they are leaving almost immediately.'

'Ah! *canaille!*' grunted Moris Klaw, 'fear-pigs! It is always so, these servants. So you have not located the one that laughs, no?'

'No,' answered Sir James; 'and he doesn't stop at laughing – does he, Clem?'

Clement Leyland shook his head. He looked even paler than usual, I thought, and the uncanny incident seemed to have disturbed him greatly.

'What else?' rumbled Moris Klaw. 'The Grey monk is forgetting his manners. He becomes rude, eh – that grey monk?'

'The house has practically become uninhabitable,' said the baronet, bitterly. 'None of the usual phenomena are missing. We have slamming doors, phantom footsteps, and, if the servants are to be believed, half the forces of hell loose here at night!'

'But your *own* experiences?' interrupted Klaw.

'My own experiences in brief amount to this: I rarely sit at this table at night without hearing that beastly laughter, at least once. I never go into the billiard-room, which opens out under the gallery yonder, without feeling a cold wind blowing upon my face or head, even in perfectly still weather, or with all the windows closed. To the left of the billiard-room, and opening out of it, is a third centre of these disturbances. It's the gun-room, and guns have been fired there in the night with the door locked, on no fewer than five occasions!'

Moris Klaw, from a tail pocket of his coat, produced a cylindrical scent-spray and squirted verbena upon his high, yellow forehead.

'It grows exciting, this,' he said. 'I require the cool brain.'

'Finally,' added Sir James, 'the only other point worth mentioning is the ghostly voice which regularly wakes me from my sleep at night.'

'A voice,' rumbled Klaw, 'what voice and what does it say, that voice?'

'I won't repeat what it says!' replied the baronet, glancing at Isis; 'but it offers obscene suggestions, or that is the impression I have of it – a low filthy mumbling; if you can follow me, the voice of something dead and infinitely evil.'

Moris Klaw stood up.

'This intelligence,' he rumbled, 'a living or a dead one, has thoughts then, and thoughts, Sir James, are things. I shall sleep in one of the centres of its activity to-night, perhaps here, perhaps in the billiard-room or the gun-room. Isis, my child, bring for me my odically sterilised pillows. This is a charming case and worthy of the subtle method.'

He placed his hands upon the shoulders of Sir James Leyland, who stood facing him.

'Evil thoughts live, Sir James,' he said. 'I cannot explain to you how hard it is to slay them. Few good thoughts survive; but such an ancient abode as this' – he waved his long hands characteristically about him – 'is peopled with thought-forms surviving from the dark ages. I have opened the inner eye, my friend. Mercifully, perhaps, the inner eye is closed in most of us; in some it is blind. But I have opened that eye and trained it. As I sleep' – he lowered his voice oddly – 'those thought-things come to me. It is an uncomfortable gift, yes; for here in Grange I shall find myself tonight in evil company. Murders long forgotten will be accomplished again before that inner eye of mine! I shall swim in blood! Assassins will come stealing to me, murdered ones will scream in my ears, the secret knife will flash, the honest axe do its deadly work; for in the moment of such deeds two imperishable thought-forms are created: the thought-form of the slayer, strong to survive, because a blood-lustful thought, a revengeful thought; and the thought of the slain, likewise a long-surviving thought because a thought of wildest despair, a final massing of the mental forces greater than any generally possible in life, upon that last awful grievance.'

He paused, looking around him.

'From the phantom company,' he said, 'I must pick out that one whose thought is of laughter, of firing guns, and of evil whisperings. What a task! Wondrous is the science of the mental negative!'

The meeting broke up, then, and Isis Klaw, having brought from a large case, which formed part of her father's luggage, two huge red cushions, bade us good-night and retired to her own room. Moris Klaw, with a cushion swinging in each hand, went shuffling ungainly from room to room like some strange animal seeking a lair.

'Do I understand,' Clement Leyland whispered to me, 'that your friend proposes to sleep down here?'

'Yes,' I replied, smiling at his evident wonderment; 'such is his method of investigation, eccentric, but effective.'

'It is really effective, then? The experiences given in *Psychic Angles* are not fabulous?'

'In no way. Moris Klaw is a very remarkable man. I have yet to meet the mystery which is beyond him.'

Moris Klaw's rumbling voice, which frequently reminded me of the rolling of casks in a distant cellar, broke in upon our conversation –

'Here is the ideal spot; here upon this settee by the door of the gun-room I am in the centre of these psychic storms which nightly arise in Grange.'

'If you are determined to remain here, Mr Klaw,' said Sir James, 'I shall not endeavour to dissuade you, of course; but I should prefer to see you turn into more comfortable quarters.'

'No, no,' was the reply; 'it is here I shall lay down my old head, it is here I shall lie and wait for him, the one who laughs.'

Accordingly, since the hour grew late, we left this novel ghost-hunter stretched out upon the settee in the billiard-room; and as I knew his objection to any disturbance, I suggested to Sir James that we should retire out of earshot for a final smoke ere seeking our separate apartments.

We sat chatting for close upon an hour, I suppose. Then Clement Leyland left us, saying that he had had a heavy day.

'Clement's been working real hard,' the baronet confided to me. 'In the circumstances, as I think I told you, I have decided to abandon Grange, and we are having the old Friars House, a mile from here, but on part of the estate, restored. It hasn't been inhabited for about three generations, and it's very much older than Grange; part of it dates back to King John. Perhaps I can get servants to stop there, though, and it's quite impossible to keep up Grange without a staff. Clement has been superintending the work over there all day; he's one of the best.'

A few moments later we parted for the night. I left Sir James at the door of his room, which had formerly opened off the balcony overlooking the banqueting-hall. That door was now walled up, however, and the entrance was from the corridor beyond. The room allotted to me was upon the opposite side of the same corridor and farther to the north.

I felt particularly unlike sleep. The extremely modern furniture of my room could not rob the walls, with their small square panelling, of the air of hoary antiquity which was theirs. The one window, deep set, and overlooking an extensive orchard, was such as might have formed the focus for cavalierly glance, was such as might have framed the head of a romantic maid of Stuart days. And with it all was that gloomy air that had a more remote antiquity, that harked back to darker times than those of the Merry Monarch: the air of ghostly evil, the cloud from which proceeded the devilish laughter, the obscene whisperings.

Where the shadows of the trees lay beneath me on the turf, I could fancy a grey cowled figure flitting across the lighted patches and lurking, evilly watching, amid the pools of darkness. Sleep was impossible. Moris Klaw, to whom such fears as mine were utterly unknown, might repose, nay, was actually reposing, in the very vortex of this psychical storm; but I was otherwise constituted. I had been with him in many cases of dark enough evil-doing, but this purely ghostly menace was something that sapped my courage.

Grange stood upon rather high ground, and in a north-easterly direction, peeping out from the trees of a wooded slope, showed a grey tower almost like a giant monkish figure under the moon. I watched it with a vague interest. It was Friars House, to which the baronet projected retreat from the haunted Grange. Lighting my pipe, I leaned from the window, idly watching that ancient tower and wondering if more evil deeds had taken place within it – long as it had there amid the trees – than those which had left their mark ghostly upon Grange.

The night was very beautiful and very still. Not the slightest sound could I detect within or without the house. How long I had lounged there in this half dreamy, but vaguely fearful, mood I cannot say, but I was aroused by a tremendous outcry. Loud it broke in upon the silence of the night, broke in on my mood with nerve-racking effect. My pipe dropped upon the floor, and taking one step across the room I stood there, rooted to the spot with indefinable horror.

'Father!' it came in a piercing scream, and again: 'Father! O God! save him! save him!'

III

The voice was that of Isis Klaw!

Whenever I accompanied her father upon any of his inquiries I came armed, and now with a magazine pistol held in my hand I leapt out into the corridor and turned toward the stair. A door slammed open in front of me and Sir James Leyland also came running out, pulling on his dressing-gown as he ran. One quick glance he gave me; his face was very pale; and together we went racing down the stairs into the hall patched with ghostly moonlight.

'You heard it?' he breathed, hoarsely. 'It was Miss Klaw! What in God's name has happened? Where is she?'

But even as he asked the question, and as we pressed on into the billiard-room, it was answered. For Isis Klaw, with a dressing-gown thrown over her night apparel, was kneeling beside the settee upon which her father lay!

'What has happened? What has happened?' groaned Sir James. Then, as we approached together: 'Mr Klaw! Mr Klaw!' he cried.

'All right, my friend!' came the rumbling voice, and to my inestimable relief, Moris Klaw sat up and looked around upon us, adjusting his pince-nez to the bridge of his massive nose: 'I live! It has saved me, the Science of the Mind!'

Isis Klaw bowed her head upon the red cushion, and I saw that she was trembling violently. It was the first time I had known her to lose her regal composure, and, utterly mystified, I wondered what awful danger had threatened Moris Klaw.

'Thank Heaven for that!' said the baronet, earnestly.

Approaching footsteps sounded now, and a group of frightened servants, headed by the butler, appeared at the door of the billiard-room. Through them came pressing Mr Clement Leyland. His face was ghastly, showing a startling white against the dull red of the dressing-gown he wore.

'James!' he said, huskily. 'James! that awful screaming! What was it? What has occurred?'

I knew that he slept in the west wing and that he must have

been unable to distinguish the words which Isis had cried. Thus heard, the shrill scream must have sounded even more terrifying.

Moris Klaw raised his hand protestingly.

'No fuss, dear friends,' he implored, in rumbling accents, 'no wonderings and botherings. They so disturb the nerves. Let us be calm, let us be peaceful.' He laid his hand upon the head of the girl who knelt beside him. 'Isis, my child, what a delicate instrument is the psychic perception! You knew it, the danger to your poor old father, to the poor old fool who lies here waiting to be slaughtered! Almost you knew it before I knew it myself!'

'For God's sake, Mr Klaw,' said Clement Leyland, shakily, 'what has happened? Who, or what, came to you here? What occasioned Miss Klaw's terror?'

'My friend,' replied Klaw, "you ask me conundrum-riddles. Some dreadful thing haunts this Grange, some deadly thing. The man has not lived who has not tasted fear, and I, the old foolish, have lived indeed to-night! I fail, my friend. There is some evil intelligence ruling this Grange, which I cannot capture upon my negative' – he tapped his brow characteristically – 'to attempt it would be to die. It is too powerful for me. Grange is unclean, Sir James. You will leave Grange without delay; it is I, the old experienced who knows, that warns you. Fly from Grange. Take up your residence, to-morrow, at Friars House!'

No further explanation would be vouchsafe.

'I am defeated, my friends!' he declared, shrugging resignedly.

Accordingly, Isis, her beautiful face deathly pale and her great eyes feverishly bright, returned to her room. She covered her face with her hands as she passed to the door. Moris Klaw accepted the use of an apartment next to mine, and we all sought our couches again in states of varying perturbation.

That there was some profound mystery underlying these happenings of the night was evident to me. Moris Klaw and Isis Klaw were keeping something back. They shared some dark secret and guarded it jealously; but with what motive they acted in this fashion was a problem that defied my efforts at solution.

The morning came, and brought a haggard company to the breakfast table. Few, if any, beneath the roof of Grange, had known sleep that night, although, so far as I could gather, there had been no manifestations of any kind.

Moris Klaw talked incessantly about the fauna of the Sahara Desert, and so monopolised the conversation with his queer anecdotes of snakes and scorpions, that no other topic found entrance.

After breakfast the whole party, in Sir James's car, drove over to Friars House; and despite the up-to-date furniture and upholstery, I found it a very gloomy residence. Stripped of its ghostly atmosphere, Grange had been quite a charming seat for any man; but this dungeonesque place, with its lichened tower that had dominated the valley when John signed Magna Charta, with its massive walls and arrow-slit windows, its eccentrically designed apartments and crypt-like smell, was altogether too archaic to be comfortable.

Moris Klaw, standing in the room which had been fitted up as a library, removed his flat-topped brown bowler and fumbled for his scent-spray.

'This place,' he said, 'smells abominably of dead abbots!'

He squirted verbena upon himself and upon Isis. He replaced the scent-spray in the lining of the hat, and was about to replace the hat on his head, when he paused, staring straight up at the ceiling reflectively.

'My notes!' he said abruptly; 'I have left those notes in my valise. I must have them. Curse me, for an old foolish! Sir James, you will show Isis this charming old tower in my absence? Do I intrude? But I would borrow the car and return to Grange for my notes!'

'Not a bit!' replied the baronet readily. 'Clement can go with you!'

'No, no! Certainly no! I could not think of it! My old friend, Mr Searles, may come if he so likes; if not, I go alone.'

Naturally I agreed to accompany him; and leaving the others at the ancient gateway, we set off in Sir James's car back to Grange. Down into the valley we swept and up the slope to Grange, Moris Klaw sitting muttering in his beard, but offering no remark and patently desirous to avoid conversation.

'Come, my friend,' he said, as the car drew up before the

house, 'and I will show you what my mental negative recorded to me last night, just before the great danger came.'

He led the way into the billiard-room, curtly directing the butler to leave us. When we were alone –

'You will note something,' he rumbled, swinging his arm vaguely around in the direction of the banqueting-hall. 'What you will note is this: the laughter – where is it heard? It is heard here, in the gun-room on my right, in the banquet-room before me. Great is the science of the mind! I will now test my negative.'

I followed him with wondering gaze as he stepped into the deep old-fashioned fireplace which formed one of the quaintest features of the room. He bent his tall figure to avoid striking his head upon the stonework, and placed the historic brown bowler upon one of the settles.

'Perhaps I cannot find it,' came his rumbling voice; 'my negative was fogged by assassinations, murderous sieges, candle-light duels, and other thought-forms of the troubled past; but I may triumph – I may triumph!'

He was standing on a settle with his head far up the chimney, and presently a faint grating sound proceeded from that sooty darkness.

'I have it!' he rumbled, triumphantly. 'And in my pocket reposes the electric lamp. I ascend; you, my good friend, will follow.'

True enough he scrambled upwards, and to my unspeakable amazement disappeared in the chimney. Filled with great wonder I followed and saw him standing in a recess high above my head, a recess which he must have opened in some way unknown to me. He extended a long arm and grasped my hand in his.

'Up!' he cried, exerted his surprising strength, and jerked me up beside him with as little effort as though I had been a child.

He pressed the button of a torch which he held and I saw that we stood upon an exceedingly steep and narrow wooden stair.

'It is in the thickness of the wall between the panellings,' he whispered, solemnly; 'a Jacobite hiding-place. Sir James knows nothing of it, for has he not spent his life in the Bush.'

He mounted the stair.

'On the right,' his voice came back to me, 'the gun-room, the billiard-room! On the left the banquet-room. From here comes the laughter – from here comes the danger.'

Still he ascended and I followed. The narrow stair terminated in a dusty box-like apartment no more than six feet high by six feet square. Moris Klaw, ducking his head grotesquely, stood there shining the light about him. From the floor he took up a square wooden case, and waved to me to descend again.

'No exit,' he said; 'no exit. Sir James's bedroom is upon the further side, but, as I had anticipated, there is no exit.'

We returned the way we had come; clearly there was no other. Beneath his caped coat Moris Klaw jealously concealed the case which he had discovered in the secret chamber. I was filled with intense curiosity; but Moris Klaw, having gone to his room, asking me to await him outside in the drive, returned ultimately, without the case, but carrying a huge notebook, and intimated that he was prepared to re-enter the waiting car.

Behind the pebbles of his pince-nez, his strange eyes gleamed triumphantly.

'We triumph,' he said. 'The haunting of Grange succumbs to the Science of the Mind!'

IV

We all had lunch at Friars House, but were by no means a jovial party. Sir James seemed worried and pre-occupied, and Clement Leyland even more reticent than usual. Moris Klaw talked, certainly, but his conversation turned entirely upon the subject of the Borgias, concerning which notorious family he was possessed of a stock of most unsavoury anecdote. So realistic were his gruesome stories, delivered in that rumbling whisper, wholly impossible to describe or imitate, that every mouthful of food which I swallowed threatened to choke me.

Afterwards we wandered idly about the beautiful old grounds, which bore ineffaceable marks of monkish cultivation. Sir James, who was walking ahead with Moris Klaw and Isis, suddenly turned and waited for me. I had been examining a sundial with much interest, but I now walked on and joined our host.

'Mr Searles,' he said, 'may I press you to remain here over the week-end?'

'That's very good of you,' I replied. 'I think I could manage it, and I should enjoy the stay immensely.'

I concluded that Moris Klaw also was remaining, and consequently was surprised when a short time later he drew me aside into a rose-covered arbour, and announced that he was leaving by the four o-clock train.

'But I shall be back in the morning, Mr Searles,' he assured me, wagging his finger mysteriously. 'I shall be back in the morning!'

'And Miss Klaw?'

'She, too, goes by the four o'clock train and will not be returning – for the present.'

'I understand that Sir James is taking up his residence here at Friars House from now onward?'

'It is so, my friend; he deserts Grange. The servants come over here to-day. Is he not well advised? Mr Clement has all along recommended that this shall be his residence. He was against it, the idea of inhabiting Grange, from the first. He is wise, that Mr Clement. He has lived in these parts so long. He knows that Grange is haunted, is uninhabitable.'

Later, then, Moris Klaw and Isis took their departure; and just as the car was about to drive off my eccentric friend removed his brown bowler, and sprayed his bald brow with verbena. He bent to me:

'Day and night,' he whispered, huskily, 'do not lose sight of him, Sir James! Above all, allow him not to *explore!*'

With that the car drove off, and I stood looking after it, wondering, utterly mystified. On the steps behind me stood Clement Leyland and his cousin. The latter's gaze followed the course of the car along the picturesque winding road until it became lost from view. I thought I heard him sigh.

Ensued an uneventful day and night. Life was pleasant enough at Friars House, if a trifle dull; and Sir James seemed unsettled, whilst his disquietude was reflected in his cousin. The latter, now that his active labours in preparing this new residence for the baronet were checked, seemed a man at a loss what to do with himself. His was one of those quietly ardent temperaments, I divined, and idleness palled upon him. Apparently he had no profession, and although I presumed that he had some residence of his own in the neighbourhood, he, apparently, was prepared indefinitely to prolong his stay at Friars House. I think his companionship was welcome to Sir James, for the latter was yet strange to the new duties of a landed gentleman.

The next morning brought Moris Klaw, and I learned with ever-growing surprise that he had made arrangements to spend the following week beneath the hospitable roof of Friars House.

I have nothing to record of interest up to the time I left; but often during the ensuing six days the problem of the haunting of Grange, and the mystery of Moris Klaw's protracted visit to Friars House came between me and my work. Then on the Saturday morning arrived a telegram –

> Can you join us for week-end – car will meet 2.30. Wire reply. Best wishes. –
>
> LEYLAND

I determined to accept the invitation; for respecting the nature of Moris Klaw's business at Friars House – and that he had some other motive than ordinary in sojourning there I was persuaded – my curiosity knew no bounds. Accordingly I packed my grip, and at about five o'clock on a delightful afternoon found myself taking tea in a cloister-like apartment of the former Friary.

'Grange,' said Sir James, in answer to a question of mine, 'is shut up.'

'It is shut, yes,' rumbled Moris Klaw. 'What a pity! What a pity!'

In the course of the day occurred incidents which I have since perceived to have been significant. I will pass over them, however, and hasten to what I may term the catastrophe of this very singular case.

Four of us sat down to dinner in an apartment which clearly had been the ancient refectory of the monks. Clement Leyland, who had arrived barely in time to dress, looked haggard and worried. I determined that he had some private troubles of his own, and beneath his quiet geniality I thought I could detect a sort of brooding gloom. His pale, clean-shaven face, so like, yet so unlike, that of his cousin, was a mask that ill repaid study; yet I knew that the real Clement Leyland was a stranger to me, perhaps to all of us.

I was most anxious to learn if Moris Klaw had divulged the secret of the hidden chamber at Grange to Sir James; and I was unspeakably curious concerning the box of which I had had but a glimpse – the box that he had found there. But he baffled my curiosity at every point.

Have you experienced that sense of impending calamity which sometimes heralds tragic things? It was with me that night, throughout dinner; and afterwards, when we entered the library and sat over our cigars, it grew portentously. I felt that I stood upon the brink of a precipice. And literally I was not in great error. Moris Klaw, to the evident discomfort of Sir James, brought the conversation around to the subject of the haunting. I observed him to glance at his watch, with a rather odd expression upon his vellum-hued face.

'Is it not singular,' he said, 'how poor spectres are confined, like linnets, to their cages? They seem, these spooks, never to roam. That laughing demon of Grange – look at him. He remains in that empty, desolate house; he –'

There was a dreadful interruption.

Commencing with a sort of guttural rattle, out upon the cloisteresque stillness burst a peal of wicked laughter!

It rang throughout the room; it poured fear into my every fibre. It died away – and was gone.

Sir James, clutching the leather-covered chair-arms, looked like a man of stone. I was frankly terrorised. Moris Klaw stood behind me, by a bookcase; him I could not see. But Clement Leyland's face I can never forget. It was positively deathlike. His eyes seemed starting from their sockets, and his teeth chattered horribly.

'God in Heaven!' he whispered, brokenly. 'What is it? O God! What is it! Take it away – take it away!'

Then Moris Klaw spoke, slowly –

'It is for *you* to take it away, Mr Leyland!'

Clement Leyland rose from his seat; he swayed like a

drunken man, and there was madness in the glaring eyes that he turned in Klaw's direction.

'You – you –' he gasped.

'I – I –' rumbled Moris Klaw sternly, and took a step forward – 'I have entered the Jacobite hiding-place at Grange, and there I found a box! Ah! you glare! glare on, my friend! I returned that box to where I found it; but first I examined its contents! What! that demon laughter frightens you! Then descend, Mr Leyland, descend and bring him out – the one who laughs!'

Rigidly, Sir James sat in his chair; I, too, seemed to be palsied. But at sight of the next happening we both stood up. Moris Klaw stamped heavily upon the oaken floor in a deep recess; then applied his weight to a section of the seemingly solid stone wall.

It turned, as on a pivot, revealing a dark cavity.

He stood there, a bizarre figure, pointing down into the blackness.

'Descend, my friend!' he cried. 'The one who laughs is upon the seventh step!'

'*The seventh step!*'

In a whisper the words came from Clement Leyland. A draft of damp, cavernous air blew into the library out of the opening.

'Descend, my friend!'

Remorselessly, Moris Klaw repeated the words. In the centre of the room, Clement Leyland, a pitiable sight, stood staring – and hesitating. Suddenly his cousin spoke.

'Don't go, Clement!' he whispered.

The other turned to him, dazedly.

'Don't go – down that place. But – O God! I understand at last, or partly … *Quit!* I give you half an hour!'

Sir James sank back into his chair and buried his face in his hands; Moris Klaw never moved from where he stood by the cavity. But Clement Leyland with bowed head, walked from the room.

In the silence that followed his going –

'Await me, gentlemen,' rumbled Klaw; 'I descend for the laughter!'

He stepped into the opening.

'One,' he counted, 'two – three – four – five –' his voice came up to us from the depths, '*six!*'

We heard him ascending. Walking into the library he placed upon the table beside Sir James a very large and up-to-date gramophone!

'The laughter!' he explained, simply. 'That night, my friends, when first I slept at Grange, I secured, among a host of other dreadful negatives, the negative of one who lurked in a secret hiding-place. I saw him come creeping from the chimney-corner, bearing a great mace which I recognised for one that had hung in the hall! Almost, the Science of the Mind betrayed me; for I mistook him for a thought-form! But the mind of Isis is *en rapport* with the mind of her poor old father. In her dreams she saw my peril, and she it was who, screaming, saved me! – saved me from the murderer with the mace!'

Sir James made no sign. Moris Klaw continued –

'I gathered, then, that the one who sometimes lurked in the Jacobite hiding-place and who, somehow, made the demon laughter, and the other phenomena, sought *one* end. It was to cause you to leave Grange and to live in Friars House! Beyond so far, my science could not show me. I assisted, therefore, the project of the lurker; and came myself, too, in order to watch, my friend, to guard and to spy!

'His gramophone I found, examined, and replaced. It had a clockwork attachment, very ingenious, which both started and stopped it; there was little or no scraping. To-night, from his room, unknown to him, I removed the instrument from its case, which lay hidden at the bottom of his trunk. Yes! I stole his key! I am the old fox! Why did he bring it here? I cannot reply. Perhaps he meant again to use it; his future projects are dark to me, but their object is all too light.'

Sir James groaned.

'Old Clem!' he whispered, 'and how I trusted him!'

'He did not quite believe in my science,' resumed Moris Klaw, 'but he did not know that, hidden, I slept almost beside him as he sat, planning, in this very room! From his own bad mind I secured my second negative; and it showed me the death-trap of some bad old son of Mother Church! At Grange there was but the Jacobite hiding-place, but here was the devilry of feudal times! I returned to London. Why? To learn if my suspicions were well founded. Yes! You may, or may not, be aware; but if you die childless, the wicked Clement inherits Grange!'

'I knew that,' whispered Sir James.

'Ah! you knew? *So*. I returned to here, for, even at that time, I suspected that your *accidental* death was the object of removal! Then I secured it, my second negative. Biding my time, I explored that death-smelling place. Its wicked machinery had been *freshly oiled!* Ah! he knew its secrets well, the old house that he hoped to inherit!

'One night, all innocent, as you sat here, with other guests, he would have blundered upon that doorway! And *you*, the host, would have led the search-party! But I saw that he feared to move whilst I remained, and so I played the ghost upon him with his own spook!'

Sir James Leyland looked up. His bronzed face was transformed with emotion.

'Mr Klaw,' he said, huskily, 'why did you lay so much emphasis upon the words, "the seventh step"?'

Moris Klaw shrugged, replying simply:

'Because *there is no seventh step – only the mouth of a well!*'

Sleuth: Mr Psyche

VI

The Telepather

Henry A. Hering

Not all ghost hunters were the reserved and slightly forbidding figures we have met in the past few stories. There were occasionally more jovial characters such as Henry Hering's occultist Mr Psyche, of 'Psyche & Co – Ghosts and Spectre Purveyors' who delighted readers of the Windsor *magazine in the late 1920's. In introducing him in the first of a series of cases in 1927, Hering wrote, 'There are many curious trades and occupations in England, and there are many merchants of great respectability; but no merchant is more eminent or carries on a stranger business than does Psyche of Archipelago Street, Soho. He sells liquid air, buys, sells or exchanges ghosts of repute, stocks old and decayed brains with new ideas, and has many other out-of-the-way branches of trade.'*

The intriguing Psyche may well be the most interesting of the literary creations of Henry Augustus Hering *(1864-1932), but it is the stories of* The Burglars' Club *which he wrote in 1906 which established his reputation. Mystery and the supernatural were, though, clearly an abiding interest as the following story of Mr Psyche and his strange machine for communicating with the world of spirits clearly demonstrates ...*

*

> *A middle-aged New Yorker jeweller, without any Art training, is painting exquisite pictures under the telepathic influence of a deceased artist.* – Daily Paper.

'Mr Psyche,' said the caller, 'I have come for your assistance. My name is Banwell. I am a bookseller in Pitt Alley, Cornhill.'

Psyche the occultist bowed, for literature appealed to him.

'Will you kindly step this way, Mr Banwell?' he asked politely.

'Do you remember the name of Aylmer Lupton?' asked Mr Banwell as he sat down in the consulting room.

'I seem to know it,' said the occultist. 'A poet, I believe?'

'He was a painter – an Associate of the Royal Academy,' Mr Banwell replied. 'He was a man of singular fascination, as those people often are,' he added regretfully. 'It seems scarcely credible to me now, but I lent him money, a great deal of money, on very little security. I lent him five thousand pounds, and now he is dead.'

'You have my sincere sympathy,' said Mr Psyche.

'Thank you. His house and his insurance policies were mortgaged to me, and he has left me his furniture and what pictures he had on hand; but all these don't tot up to more than a couple of thousands. He still owes me three thousand pounds, and I must have the money, Mr Psyche. I can't afford to lose it.'

'But how can you get money from a dead man?' asked Psyche.

'That is precisely what I came here to learn,' said the bookseller, 'and I am sure you can help me. You may have come across Lupton's ghost in the way of business, and I should very much like to be placed in communication with it, if you have. He could put me up to a soft thing somewhere, I'm sure – a gold mine, for instance. He must know of things we are quite ignorant of here, for he is certainly under a great obligation to me.'

'We have not come across Mr Lupton's ghost as yet,' said Mr Psyche gravely. 'In fact, I may tell you our ghost department is not what is used to be. People are indifferent to apparitions nowadays, in this country, at any rate, and ghosts are so sensitive that they don't go where they are not wanted – consequently we see very little of them. I rarely have an application from one. They do better in the Colonies. In Australian and Canadian up-country districts they are much in demand, I believe. You see the evenings are long and dull there, and people are glad to have a little excitement. But if by any chance I do hear of Mr Lupton's ghost, I will try to arrange an appointment for you.'

'But,' said the bookseller, getting up and pacing the room, 'I want something definite, and that at once. You surely must be able to communicate with the departed in the regular way of business. You have a medium?'

'We have several,' Mr Psyche replied, 'and they are at your service; but mediums are only good when they are fresh and impressionable. Two years at the business seems quite enough to exhaust their powers, with the result that they colour their communications with their own individuality. Frankly, I am disappointed with the recent working of my mediums.'

Mr Psyche was hardly himself that day. Once he had had the monopoly of the occult market, but now competition was keen, and the trend of prices was downward. Moreover, duties were threatened on sundry of his importations, and as they might fairly be scheduled under the head of luxuries, he knew the toll would be heavy. A parcel of novelties, too, had just gone down in the Dead Sea. Therefore he had some cause for depression. Suddenly his face cleared. 'This is not a case for a medium,' he said. 'It is one for my Telepather.'

'Ah,' said Mr Banwell, 'Who's he?'

'It isn't a man; it's a machine,' explained Mr Psyche, 'a machine invented by an adept in Thibet for establishing communication with the spirits of the departed. The unreliability of mediums is recognized even in the Home of Occultism, and this machine is intended to do their work, and do it more perfectly. I have only recently acquired it, and as yet have not made use of its services, since the communications desired by my clients with their departed friends have been of a purely sentimental character, and for this purpose a medium is quite able to satisfy them. But you have an important business matter to discuss, so I shall be happy to place my Telepather at your disposal. Come this way, please.'

Mr Psyche led the bookseller along a dark and narrow passage, and at the end unlocked the door of a small room. On a table in the centre was a box about two feet square. The occultist took off the cover with extreme care, and exposed to view a very curious-looking machine. It was like no other machine that Mr Banwell had ever seen. It was a medley of wheels and drums, and from a central cylinder projected a tangle of wires, the extremities of which fell loosely down when the cover was removed. Two strands coated with green silk ended in metal holders. There were dials on which were mysterious markings, six drums, and six funnelled orifices pointing in as many directions.

Mr Banwell examined it with much interest. 'How does the thing work?' he asked.

'I can't explain its mechanism,' said Mr Psyche, 'but all you have to do is to grasp these handles, and concentrate your thoughts on the person with whom you wish to communicate. It is necessary for the success of the experiment to have surroundings in harmony with the person sought. In your case the Telepather ought to be put in the studio of the dead artist, where his personality will still be the dominating influence. The room in which he worked will yet contain remnants of his psychic aura, and this will place the instrument in touch with him. Armed with that clue it will track him on the psychic plane pretty much as a bloodhound traces a criminal on this. The success of the experiment, however, depends chiefly on the intensity of your concentration on the subject. I gather that will not be wanting?'

'Lupton owes me £3,000,' said Mr Banwell, 'and I need it badly. I can concentrate intensely on that thought without the slightest effort.'

'Good,' said the occultist, rubbing his hands together. 'You say the house is in your possession?'

'It is. I am trying to let it furnished, but at present no one is in it.'

'Good again,' said Psyche. 'As a rule I let my manager superintend such matters, but as I wish to have personal experience of the working of the Telepather I will conduct the experiment myself. We can start at once if it suits you. There is a preliminary fee,' he added.

'How much?' inquired Mr Banwell.

Psyche reflected. 'I will only charge you five guineas. If you get into contact with Mr Lupton there will be an additional twenty guineas to pay, and if you get your money back, a further sum of one hundred guineas. For the latter fee I will also include a communication to another departed friend.'

Mr Banwell pulled out his purse. 'Here is your preliminary fee,' he said, handing over the money. 'I shan't trouble any other friend with a communication. Mr Lupton is the only dead man I hanker after, but I want him badly.'

Two hours after they drove up to the house on Muswell Hill lately occupied by Aylmer Lupton the artist, and Mr Psyche himself carried the Telepather into the studio. This was a large apartment with a good light, comfortably and even luxuriously furnished. There were rich rugs and draperies, bronzes and casts. There was a fine baronial fireplace and an oak gallery. Two or three large easels and a quantity of canvases, sketchbooks, portfolios, colour-boxes, palettes and brushes testified to the industry of the deceased artist.

Psyche remarked on the luxury of the place. 'It was paid for in my money,' said Mr Banwell. 'And you should see my own room,' he added bitterly. 'Over the shop – horse-hair and antimacassars. The contrast with this won't bear thinking of.'

'We have all got to learn from sad experience, and I myself once lost as much as you through an Italian nobleman,' said Mr Psyche gently, as he placed the Telepather on a side table, and removed the cover. 'Now will you kindly pull up a chair, sit down, and take hold of the two metal holders? Grasp them tightly, as you would the handles of an ordinary electric battery. Concentrate your thoughts for all you are worth on Aylmer Lupton – on the promises he made – on the money he owes you.'

Mr Banwell sat down and gripped the holders. 'I will leave you,' said Psyche, 'so that my individuality shall not be a disturbing influence.'

Half an hour later he returned. 'Any results?' he asked.

'None whatever,' said Mr Banwell gloomily.

'Don't be discouraged,' said the occultist. 'The instrument may still be charged with the personality of the last user. Concentrate. Concentrate. This is generally difficult, and in your case I fancy the thought of the money may be stronger than that of the man himself. I find poetry a great help in concentration – even the mechanical repetition of it. I have put down a few lines on the situation which may be of some use,' modestly producing a piece of paper from which he read:

Aylmer Lupton, artist rare,
Aylmer Lupton, A.R.A.
I am Banwell calling you,
Answer make without delay.

Golden pounds you owe to me,

Thousands three of them there are,
Let me have my thousands back
Or I'll haunt you, near or far.

'Don't you think the last line a bit strong?' said Banwell.

'You can't put it strong enough with spirits,' explained Mr Psyche. 'They'll hedge if at all possible, but if they see you're in earnest they'll come to terms. There's nothing a spirit dislikes so much as someone from down here following it, and the best way to deal with Lupton is to let him know we mean business. Ah!'

The exclamation was caused by a convulsive movement of one of the wires. A tremor ran along its length. It lifted itself drowsily, and commenced to paw the air with its feelers. A tremor ran down the second wire, and then it, too, raised itself and waved slowly in the air.

'Bravo, bravo,' cried Mr Psyche. 'Concentrate! Concentrate! The Telepather is moving!'

Another strand rose, and still another, till at last all the wires were in motion. Gradually their movements increased in rapidity. Now the first one was whirling round, licking the air to the left, to the right, above and below. Gradually the others quickened their action, and soon all the wires were lashing round in every direction, like so many angry snakes.

'Concentrate! Concentrate!' repeated Psyche, as he put the verses in front of Mr Banwell, who repeated:

Aylmer Lupton, artist rare,
Aylmer Lupton, A.R.A.
I am Banwell calling you,
Answer make without delay.

The whirling of the wires increased, and from the Telepather came a gurgling sound as if the machine were waking to a living intensity. Its antennae shot out madly. They flicked Banwell in the face and across his hands. Still he hung on to the metal holders and recited Mr Psyche's verses.

Suddenly a change came over the wires. From moving in all directions, one by one they assumed a common course. One by one they turned to the same quarter – towards the big light of the room.

'Good, good,' said Mr Psyche, rubbing his hands. 'They're tracking him.' He consulted a compass on his watch-chain. 'He's gone north. They're after him, and they'll find him. I'll leave you to work it out with the Telepather.'

When he came back the wires were interlocked and rigid. They were fixed at an angle of forty-five degrees, pointing direct to the window. Mr Banwell was showing signs of exhaustion.

'That will do for the present,' said Psyche. 'We've got into communication, and that's a fine day's work. It's equal to my most sanguine expectations.'

'That's all very well,' said Banwell, 'but I don't see any particular results.'

'My dear sir,' protested Mr Psyche, 'these things are not worked like trade. You can't pay your money, and get what you want over the counter, so to speak. The Telepather has obviously tracked its object, and most probably will have delivered your message. Mr Lupton's ghost will be surprised and annoyed, and possibly frightened at being followed, and will be inclined to do something for you, if only to get rid of you. We shall have to give it no rest till it sends a satisfactory reply. But we have probably done enough for to-day. I will leave the instrument with you on the understanding that you are not to touch it till I come in the morning, when we will repeat the communication. I suggest that you pass as much time as possible in this room. Take your meals here if you can, and above all, sleep here.'

With this, Mr Psyche departed for Soho. The day waned, and darkness finally settled on Muswell Hill. No one could have guessed that anything unusual was occurring there. Milkmen, postmen, and lamplighters went their customary rounds. People came home. Meals were eaten. Some men made love: others made strife – just as in any other suburb of London that night. Then lights were extinguished one by one, and Muswell Hill became inert. On a studio floor, Banwell, the bookseller of Pitt Court, Cornhill, slept and snored; but on a table the Telepather still reared its mystic wires to the north.

On the following day when Mr Psyche returned, the bookseller opened the door with palette and paint-brushes in hand.

'Ah, Mr Banwell,' said the occultist, 'I did not know you were an artist.'

'I didn't know it myself,' said Banwell sheepishly, 'but as I had nothing to do I thought I might as well pass the time painting. What do you think of the result?' he asked, pointing to a picture on an easel.

Mr Psyche looked at it critically. 'It's very good,' he said at last. 'But surely you have not done all that?'

'Not all,' Banwell replied, 'but I did the cardinal and the lady.'

'Hum, I congratulate you,' said Mr Psyche. 'For a bookseller I think it wonderful. But now to business, for I must get back by noon. Have you had any communication from Mr Lupton?'

'None whatever,' said Banwell.

'Perhaps not directly – but indirectly? Don't you feel different in any way? How do your thoughts run?'

'I feel all right,' said Mr Banwell. 'In fact, now I come to think of it, I feel especially right. My brain is clearer than usual – or is it my eyes that are so? I see things differently, somehow. The world looks pleasanter and more vivid. I can see pictures everywhere – I can even see one in you. You don't know what a picture you make with that shiny hat of yours against the drapery. You're positively chic. Hold on a minute.'

He took up a sketch-block and a crayon, and began to draw – to draw rapidly. His hand moved across the paper in a businesslike manner. In five minutes he scrawled a signature, and presented the block with a flourish to Psyche.

The occultist looked at it. 'Wonderful!' he exclaimed. 'You're an artist.'

Mr Banwell looked extremely gratified. 'I think you're right,' he said. 'I never knew it before, but now I feel I am one. It must be my surroundings that have brought it out.'

'It's more than that,' replied Mr Psyche solemnly. 'Look at the writing on the wall.'

The bookseller looked round. 'I spoke metaphorically,' said Psyche, returning the block. 'Look at the name you've put to your sketch.'

'Why, I've signed it "Aylmer Lupton!" ' exclaimed Banwell. 'I don't know how I came to do it.'

'I congratulate you; I congratulate myself on the entire success of the experiment,' said Mr Psyche with a little pomp and circumstance. 'It is most gratifying.'

'I don't follow you,' said Banwell. 'Please explain.'

'Explain? Your own handwriting explains,' replied Mr Psyche, pointing to the drawing. 'This is Lupton's answer. He can't put your money down for you, and he doesn't see his way to allocate you an actual gold mine; but he can work out his own individuality through you. In other words, he can make you paint his pictures for him. I've inquired about him, and find his work is in great demand. You can satisfy that demand. There's your gold mine for you. This is really fine. The Telepather has more than fulfilled its warranty, and I shall now feel justified in ordering the few additional parts suggested by the adept in Thibet – and another machine as well.'

In his professional gratification Mr Psyche paced the room, rubbing his hands joyfully. Suddenly he stopped.

'As the machine is here,' he said, 'you'd better have another hour at it. That will serve to clinch matters and keep Lupton up to the scratch if he has any intention of hedging.'

Once more Mr Banwell sat down and grasped the handles of the Telepather. A happy contented buzz came from the machine, and a happy, contented smile covered the bookseller's face. Mr Psyche went into the garden, and when he again entered the room Banwell had left the machine and was standing before another easel with a new canvas in front of him, sketching an outline with masterly strokes.

'I could not help it,' he explained apologetically. 'The impulse was too strong.'

Mr Psyche fitted the top to his Telepather. 'A complete success. Most satisfactory,' he said. 'I shall give my mediums notice to leave when I get back to the shop. I expect there'll be another outcry about the displacement of labour by machinery, but it can't be helped. The Telepather will do the work much better and more economically. Perhaps you'll let me have my further fee now,' he continued to Banwell – 'twenty guineas according to our agreement, since communication has been established with Mr Lupton.'

Banwell nodded, pulled out his cheque-book and made out a cheque for the amount.

'One word of advice,' said the occultist, as he folded it up and put it in his pocket-book. 'From my long experience I suggest that you do not altogether neglect your bookselling business. Art is all very well in its way, but a snug little shop is probably more dependable in the long run.'

Mr Banwell waved his brush disdainfully. 'When I think of the years I've wasted in trade,' he said, 'I'm ashamed of myself.' Then he turned to his easel again.

Mr Psyche watched him for a few minutes, and then put on his hat. He took up the Telepather, and left the artist at his work.

A month passed. In all that time, Mr Banwell, despite the warning of the occultist, only paid one visit to his shop. On that occasion he wore a wide-brimmed felt hat and a velvet jacket. A black cravat tied in a bunching bow adorned his neck, and there was a little uncertainty as to the existence of a collar. At first the assistant left in charge of the shop did not recognise him.

'Oh, good-morning, sir,' he gasped at length, as the identity of the caller dawned upon him. 'Glad to see you, sir, at last. There's a great deal to talk about. You didn't let me know what to reply to W. H. Smith and Son, and I'm afraid they've gone to law. Then there's that matter of Britton's to settle, and Motte writes that –'

'Don't worry me with such sordid trifles, Dufton,' said Mr Banwell. 'I'm not in a mood to attend to them. I want a nice present for a lady.'

'For a lady, sir!' said the assistant with marked surprise, for Mr Banwell had hitherto been regarded as an avoider of the sex.

'For a lady,' repeated the bookseller. 'You wouldn't expect me to buy one for a canary, would you? What can you recommend?'

'Here's a new edition of the late Lord Tennyson, sir,' said the assistant, 'but perhaps the edition de luxe of Ella Wheeler Wilcox would suit better,' pointing to a fair array of volumes in an artistic case.

'Hum,' reflected Mr Banwell, glancing from one to the other of the proffered wares. 'The edition de luxe of Miss Wilcox will do,' he said at last. 'Book it to me – Banwell, Muswell Hill –

you have the address. Oh, and Dufton, I ought to tell you I'm giving up the shop as soon as I can. If you hear of a likely purchaser let me know, but don't worry me with details. I can't bear too many crude facts. I'm living in another atmosphere.'

With this and a jaunty nod, Mr Banwell swept out of the shop.

The assistant stared after him, and then went to the door and watched him out of sight. 'Oh, he's dotty,' he said when he came back. 'Clean dotty. I've run straight, so far, but this temptation is more than I can stand. I will not be responsible for the consequences. "A nice present for a lady!" Oh, golly!'

When Mr Psyche called at Muswell Hill a fortnight later, he was ushered into the drawing-room, and, a few minutes later, an astonishing figure entered. It was a comely lady of the Georgian period, with hooped dress, powdered hair and patches.

'I beg your pardon,' said Mr Psyche as this apparition sat down. 'I came to see Mr Banwell. Is he at home?'

'He is,' replied the lady, 'and, what's more, he's likely to be for some time ahead. He's my husband,' she exclaimed.

'Indeed!' exclaimed Mr Psyche. 'I didn't know he was a married man.'

'He didn't know it himself a week ago,' said the lady with much cheerfulness. 'We were married last Thursday. I'm glad you've called. We've had a lot of talk durin' our 'oneymoon, and he's told me a cock-an'-bull tale about you and a machine or an animal called a telepanther. I say, is Banny all there?' and she tapped her head significantly.

'I look upon him as a very intelligent tradesman,' replied Psyche.

'And an artist,' added Mrs Banwell.

'Certainly an artist. Taking him all round, I should say his present mental equipment is far above the ordinary.'

'I'm a model,' continued the lady. 'I sat for Aylmer Lupton, and when I called the other week I found Banny here instead. I bowled him over straight away at my first sittin'. Lucky he fell in with me, for I can look after him. Some others I won't name would just have bled him dry. Well, I fancy I know somethin' about Art, and Banny's pictures are just as good as Lupton's. I can't tell one from t'other.'

'I should expect that to be the case,' said Mr Psyche.

'They're worth two 'undred apiece.'

'Very gratifying,' murmured the occultist.

'They are. And he's got orders for as many as he can bring. He does one a week.'

'I am glad to hear it. There is a little account I have against your husband for one hundred guineas which I shall now be justified in presenting,' said Mr Psyche, unbuttoning his coat and producing a paper from his pocket.

The lady ignored his movements. 'Two 'undred a week is ten thousand four 'undred a year,' she said.

'All about that,' admitted Mr Psyche, 'but you must make allowances for wear and tear – I mean holidays or illnesses. A man cannot work like a machine.'

'Banny does. He works just like a machine. Directly he's finished one canvas he takes up another.'

'Re-markable,' said Mr Psyche.

'I shall keep him up to it,' said the lady. 'Ten thousand a year! Think of that! The old country isn't played out when a little snip of a chap like Banny can make ten thousand a year.'

'The country is far from being played out, madam,' said Mr Psyche, who was in an optimistic frame of mind that day. 'I was never one of those who regarded the outlook in that light. In my business, although we have undoubtedly lost ground in some directions, such as ghosts and apparitions generally, yet in others – psychic thought and clairvoyancy, for instance – we have more than held our own. I could give you some statistics conclusively proving that we are still far ahead of our nearest competitors in these respects.'

'My hat!' exclaimed the lady. 'How you do talk. Well, you can't see Banny to-day. He's paintin', and I must get back now. I'm sittin' for Mary Antoinette.'

'At any rate, I suppose he can give me a cheque for this,' said Mr Psyche, tendering his account.

'It's a lot o' money,' Mrs Banwell remarked as she looked at the document. 'Shall I tell him you'll settle for eighty quid, spot cash?'

'The agreement was for a hundred guineas – not quids,' said Mr Psyche stiffly, 'so I am afraid I cannot reduce the amount. Whatever income Mr Banwell is now making from Art is undoubtedly owing to my services, so if there were any alteration in my honorarium I should expect an increase rather than a decrease in the amount.'

'You do talk,' said the lady admiringly. 'It's as good as a recitation. Well, I'll have a word with Banny.'

Ten minutes later Mr Psyche left the house on Muswell Hill the richer by one hundred guineas.

Weeks, and even months passed, and the incident had become but a pleasing memory to the occultist, when one day he received a telegram: 'Bring Telepather at once. Same terms. Waiting. – *Banwell.*'

Somewhat surprised by the urgency of the message Mr Psyche proceeded to Muswell Hill. Banwell, red-eyed and dishevelled, met him in the doorway. Behind him with folded arms and puckered lips loomed his wife.

'What's the matter?' inquired Mr Psyche.

'I can't paint,' said Banwell.

'He can't even draw,' snapped the lady.

'Dear me, how's that?' inquired the occultist.

Banwell shook his head lugubriously. 'I finished a Lupton last week, as good as any I've done, and it went to my usual customer for £200. Since then I've tried to start another, but I can't think of a subject, and I can't even draw a cow. Come and look at my attempts.'

Mr Psyche looked at them. They were puerile efforts, suitable for a person of no artistic gifts whatever. 'You certainly can't draw cows,' said Mr Psyche at last.

'And what's more, I don't want to,' Banwell rasped. 'I don't know what I'm doing here at all. I don't feel at home in this place. I wanted to go to business this morning, but Maria wouldn't let me. She insisted on sending that wire for you to come.'

'And now you've got here, you'd better get to work,' said the lady. 'I understand you'll want a fiver in advance,' handing over a bank note.

'Guineas, madam,' said Mr Psyche. 'Thank you,' as a further five shillings were produced. 'Now I propose to repeat what I did before with such excellent results. Our previous experiment was so eminently successful that there is hardly room to doubt the result of this. If Mr Banwell will kindly sit down and concentrate his thoughts on Mr Lupton, and say the poetry I composed, no doubt all will turn out well and he'll start painting again as merrily as ever. The connection will probably require renewing from time to time. I blame myself for not having forseen this.'

Mr Banwell sat down and grasped the handles.

'Now concentrate,' said Psyche.

'And no foolin',' added Mrs Banwell.

Psyche glanced doubtfully at the lady. 'Perhaps, madam,' he said, 'we may be looked upon by the shade of Mr Lupton as disturbing influences, and it would therefore be wiser for us to leave the room.'

When the occultist returned in half-an-hour or so, Banwell was still holding the metal handles, but the wires, instead of frisking merrily around, still drooped listlessly.

'There are no results,' said Banwell, throwing down the handles, 'and what's more, there won't be any. Lupton's chucked me. I feel it in my bones.'

'Strange,' reflected Mr Psyche. 'You were doing so well, and you seemed to be working in such perfect unison. What object can he have in leaving you in the lurch like this?'

Banwell shook his head despondently. 'I don't know,' he said.

'Stop!' exclaimed Psyche. 'How much have you made out of your paintings?'

'She has it down,' replied Banwell. 'Maria, Maria,' he called out, 'what do the sales tot up to?'

'Two thousand eight hundred pounds, ten shillings,' said Mrs Banwell, entering the room with account-book in hand. 'And there's that sale of Saturday to add to it. That makes three thousand pounds, ten shillings.'

'Ah!' said Mr Psyche. 'Now I see it. Isn't that the precise sum Lupton owed you? Ten shillings over, I believe. He has settled his account with you. He's not going to do more, and in justice you can't expect it. I'm afraid you've painted your last picture, Mr Banwell.'

'What!' exclaimed Mrs Banwell. 'Have I only married a bookseller?'

'A man with £3,000 ready money, a house and furniture, and a snug little business in the City,' remarked Mr Psyche, with some severity.

'I married a painter making ten thousand a year,' said the lady bitterly. 'Banwell of Pitt Alley only makes six 'undred – and not always that. He's a shopman, too.'

'Madam,' retorted Mr Psyche, 'you are ungrateful. Mr Banwell's occupation is as honourable, if not as dazzling as a painter's, and is far more solid in the long run. You have both of you cause for congratulation. You have not only got your money back, Mr Banwell, but you have found a wife.'

'You're right there,' said the lady. 'He's found a wife who will look after him, and see he doesn't fool his money away again. Put on your hat, Banny, and we'll go down to the shop. I've run it since I sacked your man on our weddin'-day, and it's not doin' badly. If I don't make it 'um, I'll know why.'

Mrs Banwell did indeed make things hum. Sometimes as he dances to the tune she calls, Mr Banwell regrets his experiment in occultism, but his rapidly increasing wealth reconciles him, on the whole, to the situation.

On Bank Holidays it is his custom to go to the Tate Gallery, where he stands before a couple of paintings signed 'Aylmer Lupton', and marvels how he did them

Sleuth: Jules de Grandin

VII

The Poltergeist

Seabury Quinn

Though the first supernatural sleuths in fiction were undeniably British, the theme caught on in America and from the late twenties until the advent of World War II, there were a considerable number of 'Phantom Fighters' doing battle with the spirit world in the pages of books and magazines. Pre-eminent among these was a dapper little Frenchman living in America named Jules de Grandin, a man small in stature but large in ego, vanity and wit. For almost twenty years from 1927 to 1945, his investigations into supernatural manifestations were the most popular stories to appear in the now-legendary pulp magazine Weird Tales, *and with his chronicler Dr Trowbridge, a New Jersey GP, he tackled horrors of every shape and kind to deservedly earn the epithet of being 'the best-known supernatural detective in weird fiction'.*

De Grandin was the creation of Seabury Quinn *(1889-1969), a writer, attorney and for some time editor of a magazine for undertakers! Though his style was often verbose and florid, he was actually more popular with readers of* Weird Tales *than some of the legendary contributors like H.P. Lovecraft and Robert Howard, and almost every one of his ghost hunter stories topped the readers' polls. Today, these stories are undeservedly neglected, so it is a pleasure to be returning to print one of de Grandin's closest calls from 1927 in which he becomes involved with one of the most unpleasant types of ghost, a poltergeist ...*

'And so, Dr de Grandin,' our visitor concluded, 'this is really a case for your remarkable powers.'

Jules de Grandin selected a fresh cigarette from his engine-turned silver case, tapped its end thoughtfully against his well-manicured thumbnail and regarded the caller with one of his disconcertingly unwinking stares. 'Am I to understand that all other attempts to effect a cure have failed, Monsieur?' he asked at length.

'Utterly. We've tried everything in reason, and out of it,' Captain Loudon replied. 'We've had some of the best neurologists in consultation, we've employed faith-healers, spiritualistic mediums, even had her given 'absent treatment', all to no avail. All the physicians, all the cultists and quacks have failed us; now –'

'Now, I do not think I care to be numbered among those quacks, Monsieur,' the Frenchman returned coldly, expelling a double column of smoke from his nostrils. 'Had you called me into consultation with an accredited physician –'

'But that's just it,' the Captain interrupted. 'Every physician we've had has been confident he could work a cure, but they've all failed. Julia is a lovely girl – I don't say it because she's my daughter, I state it as a fact – and was to have been married this fall, and now this – this disorder has taken complete possession of her and it's wrecking her life. Robert – Lieutenant Proudfit, her fiancé – and I are almost beside ourselves, and as for my daughter, I fear her mind will give way and she'll destroy herself unless *somebody* can do *something*!'

'Ah?' the little Frenchman arched the narrow black brows which were such a vivid contrast to his blond hair and mustache. 'Why did not you say so before, Monsieur le Capitaine! It is not merely the curing of one nervous young lady that you would have me undertake, but the fruition of a romance I should bring about? *Bien*, good, very well; I accept. If you will also retain my good friend Dr Trowbridge, so that there shall be a locally licensed and respected physician in the case, my powers which you have been kind enough to call remarkable are entirely at your disposal.'

'Splendid!' Captain Loudon agreed, rising. 'Then it's all arranged. I can expect you to –'

'One moment, if you please,' de Grandin interrupted, raising his slender, womanishly small hand for silence. 'Suppose we make a *précis* of the case before we go further.' He drew a pad of note-paper and a pencil toward him as he continued:

'Your daughter, Mademoiselle Julie, how old is she?'

'Twenty-nine.'

'A most charming age,' the little Frenchman commented, scribbling a note. 'And she is your only child?'

'Yes.'

'Now, these manifestations of the *outré*, these so unusual happenings, they began to take place about six months ago?'

'Just about; I can't place the time exactly.'

'No matter. They have assumed various mystifying forms? She has refused food, she has had visions, she shouts, she sings uncontrollably, she speaks in a voice which is strange to her – at times she goes into a death-like trance and from her throat issue strange voices, voices of men, or other women, even of little children?'

'Yes.'

'And other apparently inexplicable things occur. Chairs, books, tables, even such heavy pieces of furniture as a piano, move from their accustomed places when she is near, and bits of jewelry and other small objects are hurled through the air?'

'Yes, and worse than that, I've seen pins and needles fly from her work-basket and bury themselves in her cheeks and arms,' the captain interrupted, 'and lately she's been persecuted by scars – scars from some invisible source. Great weals, like the claw-marks from some beast, have appeared on her arms and face, right while I looked on, and I've been wakened at night by her screams, and when I rush into her room I find the marks of long, thin fingers on her throat. It's maddening, sir; terrifying. I'd say it was a case of demoniacal possession, if I didn't disbelieve all that sort of supernaturalism.'

'Um,' de Grandin looked up from the pad on which he had been industriously scribbling. 'There is nothing in the world, or out of it, which is supernatural, my friend; the wisest man today can not say where the powers and possibilities of nature begin or end. We say "Thus and so is beyond the bounds of our experience," but does that therefore put it beyond the bounds of nature? I think not. Myself, I have seen things as no man can hear me relate without calling me a liar, and my good, unimaginative friend Trowbridge has witnessed such wonders as no writer of fiction would dare set down on paper, yet I do declare we have never yet seen that which I would call supernatural.

'But come, let us go, let us hasten to your house, Monsieur; I would interview Mademoiselle Julie and see for myself some of these so remarkable afflictions of hers.

'Remember,' he turned his fixed, unwinking stare on our patron as we paused for our outdoor things in the hall, 'remember, if you please, Monsieur, I am not like those quacks, or even those other physicians who have failed you. I do not say I can work a cure. I can but promise to try. Good, we shall see what we shall see. Let us go.'

Robert Beauregard Loudon was a retired navy captain, a widower with more than sufficient means to gratify his rather epicurean tastes, and possessed one of the finest houses in the fashionable new west side suburb. The furnishings spoke of something more than wealth as we surveyed them; they proclaimed that vague, but nevertheless tangible thing known as "background" which is only to be had from generations of ancestors to the manor born. Original pieces of mahogany by Sheraton and Chippendale and the Brothers Adam, family portraits from the brush of Benjamin West, silver in the best tradition of the early eighteenth century smiths, even the dignifiedly aloof, elderly coloured butler, announced that our patient's father was in every way an officer and a gentleman in the best sense of the term.

'If you will give Hezekiah your things,' Captain Loudon indicated the solemn old negro with a nod, 'I'll go up and tell my daughter you're here. I know she will be glad to –'

A clanking, banging noise, like a tin can bumping over the cobbles at the tail of some luckless terrier, interrupted his remarks, and we turned in amazement toward the wide, curving staircase at the farther end of the long central hall. The noise grew louder, almost deafening, then ceased as abruptly as it began, and a young girl rounded the curve of the staircase, coming slowly toward us.

She was more than middle height, slender and supple as a willow withe, and carried herself with the bearing of a young princess. A lovely though almost unfashionably long gown of white satin and chiffon draped its uneven hem almost to her ankles, and about her slender bare shoulders and over her arms hung a richly embroidered shawl of Chinese silk. One hand rested lightly on the mahogany rail of the balustrade, as though partly for support, partly for guidance, as she slowly descended the red-carpeted steps. This much we saw at first glance, but our second look remained riveted on her sweet, pale face.

Almost unbeautifully long it was, pale with the rich, creamy pallor which is some women's birthright and not the result of poor health, and her vivid, scarlet lips showed in contrast to her ivory cheeks like a rose fallen in the snow. Brows as delicate as those of a French doll, narrow, curving brows which needed no plucking to accentuate their patrician lines, dipped sharply together above the bridge of her small nose, and lashes which even at the distance we stood from her showed their vivid blackness veiled her eyes. At first I thought her gaze was on the steps before her, and that she made each forward movement with slow care lest she fall from weakness or nervous exhaustion, but a second's scrutiny of her face told me the truth. The girl walked with lowered lids. Whether in natural sleep or in some supernatural trance, she was descending the stairs with tightly closed eyes.

'*La pauvre petite*,' de Grandin exclaimed under his breath, his gaze fixed on her, '*Grand Dieu*, friend Trowbridge, but she is beautiful! Why did I not come here before?'

Out of the empty air, apparently some six feet above the girl's proudly poised head, a burst of mocking, maniacal laughter answered him, and from the thick-piled carpet suddenly rose again the clang-bang racket we had heard before she came into view.

'*Hélas!*' De Grandin turned a pitying glance on the girl's father, then: '*Nom de Dieu!*' he cried, ducking his head suddenly and looking over his shoulder with rounded eyes. Against the wall of the apartment, some twenty feet distant, there hung a stand of arms, one or two swords, a spear and several bolos, trophies of the captain's service in the Philippines. As though seized by an invisible hand, one of the bolos had detached itself from the wall, hurtled whistling through the air and embedded itself nearly an inch deep in the white wainscoting behind the little Frenchman, missing his cheek by the barest fraction of a centimetre as it flew whirring past.

The clanking tumult beneath the girl's feet subsided as quickly as it commenced, she took an uncertain step forward and opened her eyes. They were unusually long, purple rather than blue in colour, and held such an expression of changeless melancholy as I had never seen in one so young. It was the look of one foredoomed to inescapable death by an incurable disease.

'Why' – she began with the bewildered look of one suddenly roused from sleep – 'why – Father! What am I doing here? I was in my room, lying down, when I thought I heard Robert's voice. I tried to get up, but It held me down, and I think I fell asleep. I –'

'Daughter,' Captain Loudon spoke gently, the sobs very near the surface, for all his iron self-control, 'these gentlemen are Dr de Grandin and Dr Trowbridge. They've come to –'

'Oh,' the girl made an impatient gesture which yet seemed somewhat languid, as though even remonstrance were useless, 'more doctors! Why did you bring them, Father? You know they'll be just like all the rest. Nothing can help me – nothing seems any good!'

'*Pardonnez-moi,* Mademoiselle,' de Grandin bent forward in a formal, European bow, heels together, elbows stiffly at sides, 'but I think you will find us most different from the rest. To begin, we come to cure you and give you back to the man you love; and in the second place, I have a personal interest in this case.'

'A personal interest?' she inquired, acknowledging his bow with a negligent nod.

'*Morbleu*, but I have. Did not the – the thing which troubles you, hurl a bolo-knife at me? *Sacré nom,* no *fantôme*, no *lutin* shall throw knives at Jules de Grandin, then boast of the exploit to his ghostly fellows. *Nom d'un petit Chinois*, I think we shall show them something before we are finished!

'Now, Mademoiselle, we must ask your pardon for these questions,' he began when he had reached the drawing room. 'To you it is an old and much-told tale, but we are ignorant of your case, save for such information as your father has imparted. Tell us, if you please, when did these so strange manifestations begin?'

The girl regarded him silently a moment, her brooding, plum-coloured eyes staring almost resentfully into his agate-blue ones.

'It was about six months ago,' she began in a lifeless monotone, like a child reciting a rote-learned but distasteful lesson. 'I had come home from a dance in New York with Lieutenant Proudfit, and it must have been about 3 o'clock in the morning, for we had not left New York until midnight, and our train was delayed by a heavy sleet-storm. Lieutenant Proudfit was stopping overnight with us, for we are – we were – engaged, and I had said good-night to him and gone to my room when it seemed I heard something fluttering and tapping at my window, like a bird attracted by the light, or – I don't know what made me think so, but I got the impression, somehow – a bat beating its wings against the panes.

'I remember being startled by the noise, at first, then I was overcome with pity for the poor thing, for it was bitter cold outside and the sleet was driving down like whiplashes with the force of the east wind. I went over to the window and opened it to see what was outside. I' – she hesitated a moment, then went forward with her narrative – 'I was partly undressed by this time, and the cold wind blowing through the open window cut like a knife, but I looked out into the storm to see if I could find the bird, or whatever it was.'

'Ah?' de Grandin's little eyes were sparkling with suppressed excitement, but there was neither humour nor warmth in their flash. Rather, they were like two tiny pools of clear, adamant-hard ice reflecting a cloudless winter sky and bright, cold winter sunshine. 'Proceed, if you please,' he commanded, his voice utterly toneless. 'You did open your window to the tapping which was outside. And what did you next?'

'I looked out and said, "Come in, you poor creature!" ' the girl replied. 'Even though I thought it was a bat at the pane, my reason told me it couldn't be, for bats aren't about in the dead of winter, and if it had been one, much as I hate the things, I couldn't have slept with the thought of its being outside in my mind.'

'Ah?' de Grandin repeated, his voice raised slightly in interrogation. 'And so you did invite what was outside to come in?' Level as his tone was, there was a certain pointedness in the way he spoke the words, almost as though they were uttered in faintly shocked protest.

'Of course,' she returned. 'I know it was silly for me to speak to a bird that way, as if it could understand, but, you know, we often address animals in that way. At any rate, I might have saved myself the chilling I got, for there was nothing there. I waited several minutes till the cold wind almost set my teeth to chattering, but nothing was visible outside, and there were no further flutterings at the window.'

'Probably not,' the Frenchman commented dryly. 'What then, please?'

'Why, nothing – right away. It seemed as though the room had become permanently chilled, though, for even after I'd closed the window the air was icy cold, and I had to wrap my dressing gown about me while I made ready for bed. Then –' She stopped with an involuntary shudder.

'Yes, and then?' he prompted, regarding her narrowly while his lean white fingers tapped a devil's tattoo on his chair arm.

'Then the first strange thing happened. As I was slipping my gown off, I distinctly felt a hand grasp me about the upper arm – a long, thin, deathly cold hand!'

She looked up defiantly, as though expecting some sceptical protest, but: 'Yes,' he nodded shortly. 'And after that?'

The girl regarded him with a sort of wonder. 'You believe me – believe I actually felt something grasp me?' she asked incredulously.

'Have you not said so, Mademoiselle?' he returned a thought irritably. 'Proceed, please.'

'But every other doctor I've talked to has tried to tell me I didn't – couldn't have *actually felt* such a thing,' she persisted.

'Mademoiselle!' the little man's annoyance cut through the habitual courtesy with which he treated members of the gentler sex as a flame cuts through wax. 'We do waste time. We are discussing you and your case, not the other physicians or their methods. They have failed. We shall give them none of our valuable time. *Bien.* You were saying –'

'That I felt a long, cold hand grasp me about the arm, and a moment later, before I had a chance to cry out or even shrink away, something began scratching my skin. It was like a long, blunt fingernail – a human nail, not the claw of an animal, you understand. But it had considerable force behind it, and I could see the skin turning white in its wake. Dr de Grandin' – she leaned forward, staring with wide, frightened eyes into his face – 'the welts *formed letters*!'

'U'm?' he nodded unexcitedly. 'You do recall what they spelled?'

'They didn't spell anything. It was like the ramblings of a Ouija board when the little table seems wandering about from letter to letter without spelling any actual words. I made out a crude, printed *D*, then a smaller *r*, then an *a*, and finally a *c* and *u* – D-r-a-c-u. That was all. You see, it wasn't a word at all.'

De Grandin was sitting forward on the extreme edge of his chair, his hands grasping its arms as though he were about to leap from his seat. '*Dracu*,' he repeated softly to himself, then, still lower, '*Dieu de Dieu!* It is possible; but why?'

'Why, what is it?' the girl demanded, his tense attitude reflecting itself in her widened eyes and apprehensive expression.

He shook himself like a spaniel emerging from the water. 'It is nothing, Mademoiselle,' he assured her with a resumption of his professionally impersonal manner. 'I did think I recognized the word, but I fear I must have been mistaken. You are sure there were no other letters?'

'Positive. That was all; just those five, no more.'

'Quite yes. And after that?'

'After that all sorts of terrible things began happening to me. Father has told you how chairs and tables rise up when I come near them, and how little objects fly through the air?'

He nodded, smiling. 'But of course,' he returned, 'and I, myself, did see one little thing fly through the air. *Parbleu*, it did fly unpleasantly close to my head! And these so strange sleeps you have?'

'They come on me almost any time, mostly when I'm least expecting them. One time I was seized with one while on the train and' – her face flushed bright coral at the recollection – 'and the conductor thought I was *drunk!*'

'*Bête!*' de Grandin murmured. 'And you have not heard the voices – the noises which sometimes accompany you, Mademoiselle?'

'No, I've been told of them; but I know nothing of what occurs while I'm in one of these trances. I don't even dream; at least, I have no dreams I can remember when I wake up. I only know that I am apt to fall asleep at any time, and frequently wander about while unconscious, waking up in some totally different place. Once I walked half-way to the city while asleep, and narrowly escaped being run down by a taxicab when I came to in the middle of the street.'

'But this is villainous!' he burst out. 'This is infamous; this must not be allowed. *Mordieu*, I shall not permit it!'

Something of the girl's weary manner returned as she asked, 'How are you going to stop it? The others all said –'

'*Chut!* The others! We shall not discuss them, if you please, Mademoiselle. Me, I am not as the others; I am Jules de Grandin!

'First, my friend,' he turned to me, 'I would that you obtain a competent nurse, one whose discretion is matched only by her ability. You know one such? *Très bien.* Hasten, rush, fly to procure her at once. Bid her come to us with all celerity and be prepared to serve until relieved.

'Next' – he seized a pad and scribbled a prescription – 'I would that Monsieur le Capitaine has this filled and administers one dose dissolved in hot water at once. It is somnol, a harmless mixture of drugs, pleasant to the taste and of undoubted efficacy in this case. It will act better than chloral.'

'But I don't want to take chloral,' the girl protested. 'I have enough trouble with sleep as it is; I want something to ward off sleep, not to induce it.'

'Mademoiselle,' he replied with something like a twinkle in his keen little eyes, 'have you never heard of combating the devil with flames? Take the medicine as directed. Dr Trowbridge and I shall return soon, and we shall not rest until we have produced a cure, never doubt it.'

'This is the strangest case I ever saw,' I confided as we drove toward town. 'The girl's symptoms all point to hysteria of the most violent sort, but I'm hanged if I can account for those diabolical noises which accompanied her down the stairs, or that laugh we heard when she reached the hall, or –'

'Or the knife which nearly split the head of Jules de Grandin?' he supplied. 'No, my friend, I fear medical science can not account for those things. Me, I see part of it, but not all, *parbleu*, not near enough. Do you recall the ancient medical theory concerning icterus?'

'Jaundice?'

'But of course.'

'You mean it used to be considered a disease, rather than a symptom?'

'Precisely. One hundred, two hundred years ago the craft knew the yellow colour of the patient's skin was due to diffused bile in the system, but what caused the diffusion? Ah, that was a question left long unanswered. So it is with this poor girl's case. Me, I recognize the symptoms, and some of their cause is plain to me, but – ten thousand little red devils! – why? Why should she be the object of this persecution? One does not open a window in the wintertime to bid a non-existent bat or bird enter one's house, only to fall victim to such tricks as have plagued Mademoiselle Loudon since that winter's night. No, *morbleu*, there was a reason for it, the thing which tapped at her pane, being outside that night, friend Trowbridge, and the writing on her arm, that too, came not without cause!'

I listened in amazement to his tirade, but one of his statements struck a responsive chord in my memory. 'You spoke of "writing" on her arm, de Grandin,' I interposed. 'When she described it I thought you seemed to recognize some connection between the incomplete word and her symptoms. Is *dakboo* a complete word, or the beginning of one?'

'*Dracu*,' he corrected shortly. 'Yes, my friend, it is a word. It is Rumanian for devil, or, more properly, demon. You begin to see the connection?'

'No, I'm hanged if I do,' I retorted.

'So am I,' he replied laconically, and lapsed into moody silence from which my best attempts at conversation failed to rouse him.

Lulled into counterfeit rest by the drug de Grandin prescribed, Julia Loudon passed the night comfortably enough, and seemed brighter and happier when we called to interview her next morning.

'Mademoiselle,' de Grandin announced, after the usual medical mummery of taking temperature and pulse had been completed, 'the day is fine. I prescribe that you go for a drive this morning; indeed, I strongly urge that you accompany Dr

Trowbridge and me forthwith. He has a number of çalls to make, and I would observe what effect the fresh air has upon you. I venture to say you have had little enough of it lately.'

'I haven't,' the girl confessed. 'You see, since that time when I wandered off in my sleep, I've been afraid to go anywhere by myself, and I've even shrunk from going out with Father or Rob – Lieutenant Proudfit. I've been afraid of embarrassing them by one of my seizures. But it will be all right for me to go if you and Dr Trowbridge are along, I know,' she smiled wistfully at him.

'Of a surety,' he agreed, twisting the ends of his trim little blond mustache. 'Have no fear, dear lady; I shall see no harm comes to you. Make haste, we would be off.'

Miss Loudon turned to mount the stairs, a suggestion of freedom and returning health in the spring of her walk, and de Grandin turned a puzzled countenance to Captain Loudon and me. 'Your daughter's case is far simpler than I had supposed, Monsieur le Capitaine,' he announced. 'So much I have been accustomed to encountering what unthinking persons call the supernatural that I fear I have become what you Americans call "hipped" on the subject. Now, when first Mademoiselle detailed her experiences to me, I was led to certain conclusions which, happily, have not seemed justified by what we have since observed. Medicine is helpful in most cases of the kind, but I had feared –'

A perfect pandemonium of cacophonous dissonances, like the braying of half a dozen jazz bands suddenly gone crazy, interrupted his speech. Clattering tin cans, jangling cowbells, the wailings of tortured fiddles and discordant shrieks of wood-wind instruments all seemed mingled with shouts of wild, demoniac laughter as a bizarre figure emerged in view at the turn of the stairs and half leaped, half fell to the hall.

For an instant I failed to recognize patrician Julia Loudon in the grotesque thing before us. Her luxuriant black hair had escaped from the Grecian coronel in which she habitually wore it and hung fantastically about her breast and shoulders, half veiling, half disclosing a face from which every vestige of serenity had disappeared and on which a leer – no other word expresses it – of mingled craft and cunning and idiotic stupidity sat like a toad enthroned upon a fungus. She was barearmed and barelegged; indeed, the only garment covering her supple, white body was a Spanish shawl wound tightly about bust and torso, its fringed ends dragging over the floor behind her flying feet as she capered like a female satyr across the hall drugget to the bedlam accompaniment of infernal noises which seemed to hover over her like a swarm of poisonous flies above a wounded animal struggling through the mire of a swamp.

'*Ai, ai, ai-ee!*' she cried in a raucous voice, bending this way and that in time to the devilish racket. 'Behold my work, foolish man, behold my mastery! Fool that you are, to try to take mine from me! Today I shall make this woman a scandal and disgrace, and tonight I shall require her life. *Ai, ai, ai-ee!*'

For a fleeting instant de Grandin turned an appalled face to me, and I met his flying glance with one no less surprised, for the voice issuing from the girl's slender throat was not her own. No tone or inflection of it was reminiscent of Julia Loudon. Every shrilling syllable spoke of a different individual, a personality instinct with evil vivacity as hers seemed instinct with sweetness and melancholy.

'*Cordieu!*' de Grandin exclaimed between set teeth, springing toward the girl, then halting in horrified amazement as though congealed to ice in his tracks. From every side of the room, like flickering beams of light, tiny bits of metal flew toward the girl's swaying body, and in an instant her arms, legs, throat, even her cheeks, were encrusted with glittering pins and needles buried point-deep in her creamy skin like the torture-implements driven into the bodies of the pain-defying fakirs of India. Almost it seemed as though the girl had suddenly become a powerful electro-magnet to which every particle of movable metal in the apartment had leaped.

For an instant she stood swaying there, the cruel points embedded in her flesh, yet seemingly causing no pain, then a wild, heart-rending shriek broke from her lips, and her eyes opened wide in sudden terror and consternation. Instantly it was apparent she had regained consciousness, realized her position, her almost complete nudity and the biting, stinging points of the countless needles all at once.

'Quick, Trowbridge, my friend!' de Grandin urged, leaping forward. 'Take her, my old one. Do not permit her to fall –

those pins, they will surely impale her if she drops.'

Even as I seized the fainting girl in my arms, the Frenchman was furiously garnering the pins from her flesh, cursing volubly in mingled French and English as he worked.

'*Parbleu*,' he swore, 'it is the devil's work, of a surety. By damn, I shall have words to say to this accursed *dracu* who sticks pins in young ladies and throws knives at Jules de Grandin!'

Following him, I bore the swooning girl up the stairs, placed her on her bed and turned furiously in search of the nurse. What could the woman have been thinking of to let her patient leave her room in such a costume? 'Miss Stanton,' I called angrily. 'Where are you.'

A muffled sound, half-way between a scream and an articulate cry, and a faint, ineffectual tap-tap on the door of the closet answered me. Snatching the door of the clothes-press open, I found her lying on the floor, half smothered by fallen dresses, her mouth gagged by a Turkish towel, wrists tied behind her and ankles lashed together with knotted silk stockings.

'A-a-ah, oh!' she gasped as I relieved her of her fetters and helped her, half fainting, to her feet. 'It took me, Dr Trowbridge. I was helpless as a baby in its hands.'

De Grandin looked up from his ministrations to Julia Loudon. 'What was the "It" which took you, Mademoiselle?' he inquired, folding back the shawl from the girl's injured limbs and deftly shoving her beneath the bedclothes. 'Was it Mademoiselle Loudon?'

'No!' the nurse gasped, her hands still trembling with fright and nervousness. 'Oh, no, not Miss Loudon, sir. It was – I don't know what. Miss Loudon came upstairs a few moments ago and said you and Dr Trowbridge were taking her motoring, and she must change her clothes. She began removing her house dress, but kept taking off her garments until she was – she was –' she hesitated a moment, catching her breath in long, labouring gasps.

'*Mordieu*, yes!' de Grandin cut in testily. 'We do waste time, Mademoiselle. She did remove her clothing until she was what? Completely nude?'

'Yes,' the nurse replied with a shudder. 'I was about to ask her if she needed to change *all* her clothes, when she turned and looked at me, and her face was like the face of a devil, sir. Then something seemed to come down on me like a wet blanket. No, not like a blanket, either. It clung to me all at once, but it was transparent, sir. I could feel it, but I couldn't see it. It was like a – like a terrible, big jelly-fish, sir. It was cold and slimy and strong, strong as a hundred giants. I tried to call out, and *it* oozed into my mouth – choked me; ugh!' She shuddered at the recollection. 'Then I must have fainted, for the next thing I knew everything was dark, and I heard Dr Trowbridge calling me, so I tried to call out and kicked as hard as I could, and –'

'And *voilà* – here you are!' de Grandin interrupted. 'I marvel not you are *nerveuse*, Mademoiselle. *Cordieu*, are we not all so?

'Attend me, Trowbridge, my friend,' he commanded, 'do you remain with Mademoiselle Stanton and the patient. Me, I shall go below and procure three drinks of brandy for us – yes, *morbleu*, four I shall obtain, for one I shall drink myself immediately, right away, at once, before I return. Meantime, watch well Mademoiselle Julie, for I think she will require much watching before all is done.'

A moment later the clatter of his heels sounded on the polished boards of the hall floor as he hastened below stairs in search of stimulant.

'It is damnable, damnable, my friends!' the little Frenchman cried a few moments later as he, Captain Loudon and I conferred in the lower hall. 'This *poltergeist*, it has complete possession of the poor Mademoiselle Julie, and it has manifested itself to Mademoiselle Stanton, as well. *Pardieu*, if we but knew whence it comes, and why, we might better be able to combat it; but all, all is mystery. It comes, it wreaks havoc, and it remains. *Dieu de Dieu de Dieu de Dieu!*' He strode fiercely back and forth across the rug, twisting first one, then the other end of his diminutive moustache until I thought he would surely drag the hairs from his lip.

'If only we could –' he began again, striding across the hall and bringing up before a buhl cabinet which stood between two low windows. 'If only we could – ah! What – who is this, Monsieur le Capitaine, if you please?'

His slender, carefully manicured forefinger pointed to an exquisite little miniature which stood in a gold easel-frame on the cabinet's top.

Looking over his shoulder, I saw the picture of a young girl, black-haired, oval-faced, purple-eyed, her red lips showing against the pallor of her face almost like a wound in healthy flesh. There was a subtle something of difference – more in expression than in feature – from the original, nevertheless I recognized the likeness as a well-executed portrait of Julia Loudon, though it had been made, I imagined, several years earlier. 'Why,' I exclaimed in astonishment at his question, 'why, it's Miss Loudon, de Grandin!'

Ignoring my remark, he kept his fixed, unwinking stare upon the captain, repeating, 'This lady, Monsieur, she is who?'

'It's a picture of my niece, Julia's cousin,' Captain Loudon returned shortly; then: 'Don't you think we could occupy our time better than with trifles like that? My daughter –'

'Trifles, Monsieur!' de Grandin cut in. 'There are *no* trifles in a case such as this. All, all is of the importance. Tell me of this young lady, if you please. There is a so remarkable resemblance, yet a look in the eyes which is not the look of your daughter. I would know much of her, if you please.'

'She was my niece, Anna Wassilko,' the captain replied. 'That picture was made in St Petersburg – Petrograd – or Leningrad, as it is called now – before the World War.'

'Ah?' de Grandin stroked his moustache gently, as though making amends for the furious pulling to which he had subjected it a moment before. 'You did say "was", Monsieur. May I take it, then, that she "is" no more?' He cast a speculative glance at the portrait again, then continued: 'And her name, so different from yours, yet her appearance so like your daughter's. Will you not explain?'

Captain Loudon looked as though he would like to wring the inquisitive little Frenchman's neck, but complied with his request instead. 'My wife was a Rumanian lady,' he began, speaking with evident annoyance. 'I was stationed for duty at our legation at Bukharest in 1895, and there I met my wife, who was a Mademoiselle Seracki. I was married before returning to floating service, and my wife's twin sister, Zoë, married Leonidas Wassilko, a young officer attached to the Russian embassy, about the same time.

'Things were beginning to move a little, even in those days. One or two near-quarrels with European nations over the

Monroe Doctrine had warned even the lunkheads at Washington that we'd best be getting some sort of navy in the water, and there was no time for a protracted honeymoon after our marriage. I had to leave my bride of two months and report for duty to the flagship of the Mediterranean Squadron. Anna, my wife, stayed on at Bukharest for a time, then moved from one port to another along the European coast so as to be fairly near me when I could get infrequent furloughs. Finally I was moved to the China station, and she went to live with her sister and brother-in-law at St. Petersburg. Our baby Julia and their little girl, Anna, were born on the same day and resembled each other even more than their mothers did.

'Following the Spanish War and my transfer to home service, my wife divided her time between America and Europe, spending almost as much time in Russia as she did in Washington. Julia and Anna were educated together in a French convent and later went to the Smolny Institute in St Petersburg.

'Anna joined up as a nurse in the Russian Red Cross at the outbreak of the World War, and was in France when the Revolution broke. That probably saved her life. Both her parents were shot by the Bolshevists as reactionaries, and she came to live with us after the Armistice.

'Somehow, she didn't take very well to American ways, and when Robert – Lieutenant Proudfit – came along and began paying court to Julia, Anna seemed to take it as a sort of personal affront. Seems she had some sort of fool idea she and Julie were more than cousins, and ought to remain celibate to devote their lives to each other. To tell the truth, though, I rather fancy she was more than a little taken by Proudfit herself, and when he preferred Julia to her – well, it didn't please her any too much.'

'Ah?' de Grandin breathed, a trace of the heat-lightning flash which betokened excitement showing in his cool eyes. 'And Mademoiselle Anna, she is –'

'She – died, poor child,' Loudon responded.

'She did commit suicide?' the Frenchman's words were so low we could scarcely hear them.

'I didn't say that,' the captain returned coldly.

'*Pardonnez-moi*, Monsieur le Capitaine,' the other shot back, 'but you did not say otherwise, and the pause before you mentioned her death – surely that was something more than a tribute of momentary regret?'

'Humph! Yes, you're right. The poor youngster committed suicide by drowning herself about six months ago.'

'Six months, did you say?' the little Frenchman's face was so near his host's that I feared the spike of his waxed moustache would scratch the captain's cheek. 'Six months ago she did drown herself. In the ocean? And Mademoiselle Julie's engagement to Lieutenant Proudfit, it was announced – when?'

'It had just been announced – but look here, I say, see here –' Captain Loudon began violent protest, but de Grandin was grinning mirthlessly at him.

'I look there, Monsieur,' he replied, 'and I see there. *Parbleu*, I see far past! Six months, six months, everything, it dates from six months of yore! The death of Mademoiselle Anna, the engagement of Mademoiselle Julie, the tapping at her window, the beginning of these so strange signs and wonders – all are six months old. *Grâce à Dieu*, my friend, I begin to see the light at last. Come, Trowbridge, my friend, first for the information, then the action!'

Turning on his heel, he mounted the stairs, three at a time, beckoning me violently as he did so.

'Mademoiselle – Mademoiselle Julie!' he cried, bursting into the patient's room with hardly a perceptible pause between his knock and the nurse's summons to enter. 'You have not told me all, Mademoiselle, no, nor near all! This Mademoiselle Anna, who was she, and what relation was there between you and her? Of haste, speak quickly, it is important that I should know all!'

'Why,' Miss Loudon looked at him with startled eyes, 'she was my cousin.'

'But yes, that much I know. What I desire to learn is if there was some close bond, some secret understanding between you.'

The girl regarded him fixedly a moment, then: 'Yes, there was. Both of us were in love with Lieutenant Proudfit; but he seemed to prefer me, for some reason. When Anna saw he was proof against all her wiles – and she was an accomplished coquette – she became very morose, and talked constantly of suicide. I tried to laugh her out of the idea, but she persisted. Finally, I began to believe she was serious, and I told her "If you kill yourself, so will I, then there'll be two of us dead and nobody any the happier." '

'Ah?' de Grandin regarded her intently. 'And then?'

'She gave me one of those queer, long looks of hers, and said, "Maybe I hold you to that promise, cousin. *Jizn kopyeka* – life is but a kopeck – maybe we spend him, you and I." And that was all she said at the time. But two months later, just before Lieutenant Proudfit and I announced our engagement, she left me a note:

> Have gone to spend my kopeck. Remember your promise and do likewise.

'Next morning –'

'Yes?' de Grandin prompted.

'Next morning they took her from the bay – drowned.'

'A-a-h!' he let the single syllable out slowly through his teeth with a sort of hissing finality. 'A-a-ah, at last, Mademoiselle, I do understand.'

'You mean –'

'*Parbleu*, I mean nothing less. Tonight, she did say? *Morbleu*, tonight we shall see what we shall see!

'Stay you here, friend Trowbridge,' he ordered. 'Me, I go to procure that which is necessary for our work this night!'

He was through the door like a shot, rushing down the stairs three steps at a stride, banging the front door behind him without a word of farewell or explanation to his astounded host.

Darkness had fallen when he returned, a small black bag in his hand and an expression of unbridled excitement on his face. 'Any change in our patient?' he demanded as he entered the house. 'Any further manifestations of that accursed *poltergeist*?'

'No,' I reported, 'everything has been singularly calm this afternoon.'

'Ah, so? Then we shall have the harder fight tonight. The enemy, he does marshal his forces!'

He tiptoed to the sickroom, entered quietly, and took a seat beside the bed, detailing his experiences in the city with lively interest. Once or twice it seemed to me the patient's attention wandered as he continued his recital, but his conversation never faltered. He had seen the beautiful flowers in Fifth Avenue! The furs in the shops were of the exquisiteness! Never was there such a parade of beauty, culture and refinement as could be found in that so wonderful street!

I listened open-mouthed with wonder. Time given to extraneous matters when he was engaged in a case was time wasted according to his ideas, I knew, yet here he sat and chattered like a gossiping magpie to a girl who plainly took small interest in his talk.

Eight o'clock struck on the tall clock in the hall below, still he related humorous incidents in his life, and described the chestnut trees and the whistling blackbirds at St Cloud or the students' masked balls in the Latin Quarter. 'What ails the man?' I muttered to myself. 'He rambles on like a wound-up phonograph!'

It must have been about a quarter of nine when the change began to show itself in our patient. From polite inattention her attitude toward the Frenchman became something like open hostility. In another five minutes she seemed to have lost all remembrance of his presence, and lay with her eyes turned toward the ceiling. Then, gradually but surely, there came into her already too thin face a pinched, drawn look, the sure sign of physical and nervous exhaustion.

'Ah-ha, we do begin to commence!' de Grandin exclaimed exultantly, reaching beneath his chair and opening the little black bag he had deposited there.

From the satchel he produced an odd-looking contrivance, something like the toy rotary fans to be bought at novelty shops – the sort of fan which consists of three twisted blades, like reversed propeller wings, and which is made to whirl by the pressure of the thumb against a trigger fitted in the handle. But this fan, instead of having blades of coloured metal, was supplied with brightly nickeled arms which shone in the lamplight like a trio of new mirrors.

'Observe, Mademoiselle; behold!' de Grandin cried sharply, signing to me to turn the electric bulbs on full strength at the same time.

The girl's languid gaze lowered from the ceiling a moment and rested on the little Frenchman. Instantly he advanced the mirror-fan to within six inches of her face and began spinning it violently with quick, sharp jerks at the rotating loop. '*Regardez, si'l vous plaît,*' he ordered, spinning the whirling mirrors faster and faster.

The three bright pieces of metal seemed to merge into a single disc, but from their flying it seemed that countless tiny rays of light fell away, like water scattered from a swiftly-turning paddle-wheel. For an instant the girl regarded the bright, whirling mirrors without interest, then her eyes seemed gradually to converge toward the bridge of her nose as they sought to follow the fan's rotations, and a fixed, rapt expression began to steal over her features.

'Sleep, sleep and rest. Sleep and hear no orders from those who wish you ill. Sleep, sleep – *sleep*!' de Grandin commanded in low, earnest tones.

Slowly, peacefully, her lids lowered over her fascinated eyes, her breast rose and fell convulsively once or twice, then her gentle breathing told us she had obeyed his command and lay fast in quiet sleep.

'What –' I began, but he waved me back impatiently.

'Another time, my friend,' he promised with a quick gesture of warning. 'At present we must not talk; there is too much at stake.'

All through the night he sat beside the bed, raising his whirling mirrors and commanding sleep in tones of suppressed fury each time the girl stirred on her pillow. And each time his order was implicitly obeyed. The patient slept continuously till the first faint streaks of dawn began to show against the eastern sky.

'Now, then,' he cried, springing from his chair, reopening his black bag and bringing forth – of all things! – a hyssop of mistletoe bough. Around and around the room he dashed with a sort of skipping step, for all the world like a country woman fanning flies from the house in summertime.

'Anna Wassilko, Anna Wassilko, who has wandered beyond the bounds of the tomb,' he ordered as he waved his little brush-broom, 'I command that you return whence you came. To Death you have said, "Thou art my lord and my master," and to the Grave, "Thou art my lover and my betrothed." Your business in this world is done, Anna Wassilko; get you to the world you chose for your dwelling place when you cast your body into the sea!'

Near the window, where the dimming electric bulbs' light mingled with the beams of the waning moon and the flushing rays of the coming morning, he repeated his command three times, waving his brush forward and outward toward the ocean which surged and boomed on the beach a quarter-mile away.

Something seemed to brush by him, something invisible, but tangible enough to stir the white scrim curtains trailing lazily in the still air, and for a moment I thought I caught the faint penumbra of a shadow cast against the ivory wall. A monstrous thing it was, large as a lion, yet like nothing I had ever seen or imagined, for it seemed to resemble both a bat and fox, with long, pointed snout, claw-armed forepaws and great, spike-edged wings extending to each side from close behind the head.

'Get you gone, unfortunate one,' de Grandin cried, striking directly at the shadow with his sprigs of mistletoe. 'Poor soul who would collect the wager of a thoughtless promise, hie you back to your own place and leave the ordering of other lives to God.'

The terrible shadow rested against the pale wall another fraction of a second, then, like smoke borne away in a rising breeze, it was gone.

'Gone,' de Grandin repeated softly, closing the window and shutting off the lights. 'Call the nurse, I pray you, friend Trowbridge. Her duties will be simpler hereafter. A little medicine, a little tonic, and much rest and food will see Mademoiselle Julie as well as ever.'

Together we tiptoed into the hall, roused the sleeping nurse and turned the patient over to her care.

'And now the other time you spoke of last night has come, I suppose?' I said, rather huffily, as we drove home. 'You were close-mouthed enough about it all while it was happening. Will you explain now?'

'Most certainly,' he returned in high good humour, lighting a cigarette, breathing in a great lungful of smoke, then discharging the vapour with a sigh of gusty content. 'It was most simple – like everything else – when once I knew the answer.

'To begin: When first Captain Loudon explained his daughter's case, it seemed like one of simple hysteria to me, and one which any capable physician could cure. "Why, then," I ask me, "does Monsieur le Capitaine seek the services of Jules de Grandin? I am not a great physician." I have no answer, and at first I decline the case, as you know.

'But when we go to his house and behold Mademoiselle Julie all unconscious as she wandered about, I was of another mind; and when I hear the noises which accompanied her, I was of still a third mind. But when that evil one hurled a knife at my head, I said to me, "*Parbleu*, it is the challenge! Shall Jules de Grandin fly from such a contest."

'Now, across the Rhine from France, those *boches* have some words which are most expressive. Among them is *poltergeist*, which signifies a pelting ghost, a ghost which flings things around the house. But more often he is not a ghost at all, he is some evil entity which plagues a man, or more frequently a woman. Not for nothing, my friend, did the ancients refer to Satan as the Prince of the Powers of the Air, for there are many very evil things in the air which we can no more see than we can behold the germs of disease. Yes.' He nodded solemn affirmation.

'But when Mademoiselle Julie tells me of the mark which came on her arm, and I recognized the Rumanian word for demon, I think some more. And when she tells me of the bird or bat which fluttered at her window and yet was not there, I recognize many things in common with other cases I have observed.

'Foolish people, my friend, sometimes say, "Come in," when they think the wind has blown their door ajar. It is not well to do so. Who knows what visible terror awaits without, needing only the spoken invitation unthinkingly made to enter? For attend me, my friend, very rarely can the evil ones come in unless they are first invited, and very rarely can they be gotten out once they have been bidden to enter. So all these things fit together in my mind, and I say to me, "*Morbleu*, we have here a *poltergeist*, and nothing else. Certainly."

'But why should a *poltergeist* attach his evil self to that sweet Mademoiselle Julie? True, she are very pretty, but there are other pretty women in the world of whom the *poltergeister* do not seek shelter.

'Then when the demon tell us he hold her completely in his power and makes her to dance almost nude in her father's house and sticks pins and needles in her, I hear something else. I hear him promise to take her life.

'Why? What have she done that she must die?

'Then I see the picture of Anna Wassilko. Very like Mademoiselle Julie she was, but there was a subtle something in her face which makes me know she was not the same. And what story does Monsieur le Capitaine tell when I ask about her? Ah, now we begin to see the light! She were Rumanian by birth and partly by ancestry. Very good. She had gone to school with her cousin, Mademoiselle Julie. Again good. She had lived in the same house here, she had loved the same man, and she had committed suicide; best of all. I need now only a little reassuring as to the reason why – the result I already know.

'You know what Mademoiselle Julie told us; it all fitted in well with the theory I had formed. But there was work to be done that night.

'The demon which made Julie do all kinds of things she knew not of had promised to take her life. How to circumvent her? That was the question.

'I think. "This young woman goes off into trances, and does all manner of queer things without knowing of them," I inform me. "Would she not do much the same in a state of hypnosis?" Assuredly. Very well, then.

'I procure me a set of whirling mirrors, not because there is any magic in them but because they are the easiest thing to focus the subject's attention. Last night I use them, and hypnotize Mademoiselle Julie before the *poltergeist* has a chance to conquer her consciousness. Hypnotism, when all is said and done, is the rendering of a subject's objective mind passive while the mind of the operator is substituted for that of the subject. The *poltergeist*, which was really the *revenant* of Anna, had substituted *her* mind for Julie's on former occasions; now I get there first, and place my mind in her brain. There is no room for the other, and Mademoiselle Julie can not take suggestions or brain-hints from the ghost and destroy herself. No, Jules de Grandin is already in possession of her brain-house, and he says "No Admission" to all others who try to come in. Mademoiselle Julie slept peacefully through the night, as you did observe.'

'But what was all that monkey business with the mistletoe?' I demanded.

'*Tiens*, my friend, the monkey's business had nothing to do with that,' he assured me. 'Do you, perhaps, remember what the mistletoe stands for at *Noël*?'

'You mean a kiss?"

'What else? It is the plant held sacred to lovers in this day, but in the elder times it was the holy bush of the Druids. With it they cast many spells, and with it they cast out many evil-workers. Not by mistake is it the lover's tree today, for it is a powerful charm against evil and will assuredly lay the unhappy ghost of one who dies because of unfortunate love. *Voilà* – you do catch the connection?'

'I never heard that before –' I began, but he cut me short with a chuckle.

'Much you have never heard, Trowbridge, my friend,' he accused, 'yet all of it is true, none the less.'

'And that hideous shadow?'

He sobered instantly. 'Who can say? In life Mademoiselle Anna was beautiful, but she went forth from the world uncalled and in an evil way, my friend. Who knows what evil shape she is doomed to wear in the next life? The less we think on that subject the better for our sleep hereafter.

'Come, we are at your house once more. Let us drink one glass of brandy for luck's sake, then to sleep. *Mordieu*, me, I feel as though I had been stranger to my bed since my fifth birthday!'

Sleuth: Dr Muncing

VIII

The Sinister Shape

Gordon MacCreagh

If the verbose Jules de Grandin was far from a traditional ghost hunter, American readers could always turn to Dr Muncing, a resourceful and brave gentleman who tackled some of the most vicious phantoms to be found in the pages of macabre fiction and well-earned the high-esteem in which he was held by readers of Strange Stories. *Described somewhat prosaically as an 'Exorcist', he lived quietly in a small stuccoed house and passed almost unnoticed until called into action. Only his eyes set him apart, according to his creator, Gordon MacCreagh (1895-1958) for 'they were deep set, brooding eyes, suggestive of a knowledge of things that other sober citizens did not know.'*

This description actually matched that of MacCreagh himself, for he had spent the early years of his life travelling in the far-flung corners of the Earth and had experienced many strange adventures which he later utilised in a whole variety of stories. It is possible that there is more than a little personal experience in the 1932 story he tells here of Dr Muncing – but the experience is not one, I am sure, any reader would care to encounter!

Dr Muncing stepped out of an early morning train in the chill, salty dawn of Ocean City and shivered with an ill premonition. He did not know why he had come. He had been planning to take a vacation somewhere else; but something had impelled him to change his plans and come to Ocean City instead. It was an uncomfortable urge of something pressing. Dr Muncing shook himself and looked around him.

Solicitous hotel runners in gold-lettered caps recited the scenic and culinary merits of their respective hostelries. The doctor looked at them without the least interest, undecided.

A name caught his eye. Hotel Bathurst. The broad gold letters were just the slightest bit tarnished and the man the vaguest trifle less spruce than his rivals. But something made Dr Muncing feel that Bathurst was the hotel he wanted.

Some *thing* again. The letters were all wrong. That 'BA', combination, and the fourth letter 'H', the eighth in the alphabet. He didn't like it. He didn't particularly like the strong impulse that attracted him to it.

It was not a comfortable impulse; not just a vague hunch. It was a distinct urge that impelled him, an insistent influence against his will that drew him on. A feeling wholly unpleasant. He might have resisted it of course. But much of Dr Muncing's success in his work of battle against the more evil things of the borderland was of necessity a result of acting upon impulses. With quick decision he gave his bag to the man and followed him to the car.

Short questions during the drive elicited the information that the Bathurst was a hotel patronized mostly by the theatrical profession. None of that offered any clue to the impulse. Dr Muncing wondered darkly.

The premonition of unpleasantness received quick impetus upon his arrival at the hotel. In spite of the early hour a scurrying and a confusion was in the lobby. Bellhops hurried aimlessly, doing nothing. A few wide-eyed guests, showing evidences of having dressed hastily, whispered in groups.

Words such as 'horrible ... fearsome ... the most frightful sound I ever heard in my life ...' passed in shuddering agreement.

A large, very blonde lady behind the desk wrung her plump white hands distractedly and moaned:

'That it should happen in my house! My God, why must it happen to me?'

A car roared up to the door and a burly man with a brusque and officious manner entered.

'Where is it?' he asked importantly.

A dozen voices told him eagerly:

'Fourth floor. Room forty-eight.'

Four and eight again. Dr Muncing was always quick in decision. He stepped up to the man and handed him his card on which was inscribed, 'Dr Muncing, Exorcist.'

The man glanced at it. The title, doctor, caught his eye. The last word was unfamiliar in his business of extracting the solid facts out of material mysteries; but this was no time to bother. He grunted satisfaction.

'Good. Better come along, Doc. I couldn't connect with our own man this early; had to leave a call for him. All right, boy; shoot her up.'

On the fourth floor frightened faces peered from doorways. A woman huddled in a chair at the floor desk, rocking with her head buried in her arms while her body shook in great hysterical sobs. The elevator boy pointed dumbly in the direction of room forty-eight.

The plainclothes man strode briskly down the corridor. Over his shoulder he said:

'Phone call said the whole floor was awakened by a frightful scream and the floor clerk rushed to the room and found a guy laid out all twisted on the bed. Something about a tall thin feller and the window too. Sounded foolish; but we'll get the woman in as soon as we've had a look around.'

While scared faces stared at him in horrid fascination he pushed open the door with professional callousness and entered, Dr Muncing on his heels.

The window shade kept the room unpleasantly gloomy; but there was plenty enough light to see an emaciated figure in pajamas on the bed, twisted, as the floor clerk said, in a hideous contortion.

The detective grunted.

'Huh. Don't need a physician to tell me that this one is out. But look at him anyhow, Doc.'

While Dr Muncing made quick tests for any possible lingering life, the other with trained eyes took in all details of the room. He shot the window shade up with a whir and let in the early daylight. The window sash was open. The man leaned out and made critical note of the outside distances. He came back to the bed and looked at the body.

'What's the verdict, Doc?'

Dr Muncing's face was darkly serious.

'Quite dead of course. There's not an external mark on him, but every bone in his body seems to be broken; smashed small from the inside.

The detective scowled and his eyes swept the room rapidly once more.

'Huh – that's a funny one. Not a mark on him; nothing upset; no furniture broken; no signs of a fight; nothing. A body tied in a knot like it had been done with a derrick, and an open window. But, what the heck, there's nothing human could get out there. Let's call that woman in.'

Dr Muncing nodded; but mechanically. He stood with head high, his strong black brows drawn together in a frown, nostrils wide and twitching, as though sniffing. He was feeling, sensing, trying desperately to catch some vague aura or impression that remained in the room. The impression was uncomfortable; more than that, evil and menacing.

He went to the window, as the detective had done, and looked out. The wall was sheer. No projections, no ledges or roofs. He measured with his eye the distances to adjoining windows. He drew his head in again, nodding darkly with thin lips sucked in a tight line.

Outside the door was the detective's voice, not unkind but determined.

'Come along, my girl. Nothing's going to hurt you. I don't want to make it hard; but, we've got to have your description. Hey, Doc; cover it up, will you? This dame's got the horrors.'

He pushed the floor clerk before him.

'Now about this man you say you saw. Tell me exactly where and how he stood.'

The woman came in, twining convulsed fingers round a moist handkerchief and biting her lip to control hysteria. She cast a shuddering glance towards the bed; and, finding to her relief that the twisted form upon it was decently covered, she controlled herself sufficiently to stammer her tale.

'I – I was reading at the desk there – I wasn't asleep. Suddenly I heard the scream. It was – God have mercy, it was the most horrible noise I've ever dreamed in a nightmare. I ran to the door and knocked. There was no answer. I – the knob turned to my hand and I looked in, and –'

Shudders choked her words and she covered her face with her hands. Dr Muncing quickly put his arm about her shoulders and spoke soothingly.

'Don't tell us about the man on the bed. Don't think of that. Just tell us about the other one.'

The woman sensed protection in the muscular arm, and understanding in the voice. She got a grip on her nerves.

'He was – it wasn't quite daylight yet; the room was dim. All I could see was a very tall man – not his face. Only his shape – my God, his frightful shape. It was that that frightened me more than – than that other. I don't know why; but it was somehow horrible. Just the shape. Dark and thin and frightfully tall. He – it seemed to reach the window in one stride and it pulled aside the shade and stepped out. Just like that. All elbows and knees and then it was gone. Then I – I screamed and other people came from their rooms.'

'Let's get this straight,' snapped the detective. 'Other people came. Did they come at once? They'd be witnesses that nobody came out of this room. That's important, because no human person could go out of that window. It would take an eight-foot man with a ten-foot reach to touch the next window sill. I tell you nothing human could get out of that window.'

Dr Muncing nodded.

'You are right, officer. Nothing human. Still –' He pointed with his eyes at the shrouded huddle on the bed.

The detective frowned. His voice was dubious.

'I've got to look into rope-ladder possibilities; though I'd say that's out from the start. A rope against three floors of lower windows would make quite a racket. Still, that tied-up knot isn't normal. Something must have killed him.'

Dr Muncing nodded agreement again. Very softly and full of dark meaning, he said:

'You are very right again, officer. Some *thing* quite surely killed him.'

The detective looked at him, his eyes dilating.

'What d'you mean? What weird stuff are you driving at, Doc?'

Dr Muncing shook his head.

'I don't know, officer. I don't know – yet. There are more horrible things in heaven and earth than are dreamed of in your police records. You go ahead on your own methods. I'd like to verify from your coroner's autopsy my opinion that there was nothing organically wrong with this man. Still, I'll bet that he has been sick for some days and I'll bet that his doctor has never found the trouble in all his medical books. I must go and see that man if I can possibly get his address from the office.'

The detective scowled reflectively and lit a cigarette to conceal an uneasiness that came over him.

'You're a cheerful one, Doc, to have on a murder case. You give me the willies with your unholy talk. If this guy has had a doctor, like you say, I guess I'll come along with you and talk to him. I want to know what kind of sickness ties a man up into that kind of a knot.'

The physician who had been attending the sick man, a Dr Perkins, turned out to be an alert-eyed little man with the inquiring manner and quick movements of a bird. He was momentarily shocked to hear of his patient's horrible and sudden death. Then he shrugged.

'I suppose one should call it a tragedy; but it was, after all, only a hastening of what seemed to be inevitable. Whatever was the matter with him was more than my poor skill could fathom.'

'So I thought,' said Dr Muncing. 'You found nothing organically wrong?'

'Nothing. Nothing at all. It was the most perplexing case of all my experience as a general practitioner. There was nothing wrong with the man; I'll stake my reputation on that. He was just wasting away and he responded to no treatment. Something was sapping his vitality.'

Dr Muncing assented soberly.

'Quite right, Doctor. Without any manner of doubt, some *thing*.'

The detective exploded.

'There you go again, hinting at deviltries of some kind. Come across, Doc. What have you got up your sleeve? I'm sure one of those know-it-all sleuths of the story magazines; I'm not above taking a hint from anybody. Let me in on your dope.'

Dr Muncing held up his hand. His compelling eyes held the detective.

'One minute, sergeant. The doctor here has verified just what I guessed. Take the phone and verify one more guess, will you, while I ask the doctor a few more questions; and then I'll tell you all I know. Call up the hotel and ask if there aren't some more sick people.'

The detective stepped into the hall where the telephone was and the mumbling of his voice into the mouthpiece came to the two men while Dr Muncing asked questions. Suddenly the voice came loud in a startled exclamation.

'By Cripes!' and then, 'The hell you say!'

The man came back to stare at Dr Muncing with dilated eyes. Thickly he said:

'You're a wizard, Doc. And there's hellishness afoot somewhere. There's two other sick ones; and neither do their doctors know what they've got. And there's a maid on the top floor out of her mind and moaning about a horrible tall dark thing.'

Dr Muncing sprang to his feet. Flinging a quick thanks to Dr Perkins, he caught the detective by the arm and hurried him to the street. There he hailed a taxi and pushed the detective in. The latter obeyed without resistance; he was following a knowledge greater than his own. In the taxi Dr Muncing rapidly explained to the bewildered detective the outlines of what he guessed and the rudiments of the darker mysteries of life. He found no difficulty in reducing many years of occult study in many countries down to a few lucid details. Muncing's work was so unusual and so few people knew anything about it, that he was constantly called upon to explain his science.

'We have no time to go into history or abstruse arguments,' said Dr Muncing. 'You accept the findings of expert criminologists as probable truth. You will take the word of another detective on things that you may not be familiar with yourself. Well, I am a ghost detective.

'No, don't interrupt. Let me tell you what I know; and later, perhaps – if we get out of this alive – we can argue.

'I don't have to tell you that what you call ghosts do exist. Most people – though they like to pooh-pooh such things – have an inherent feeling that they might meet a ghost some time in a dark place. You probably have your own superstitions.

'Well, they are not superstitions. They are hereditary memories. Our forefathers knew a great deal about spirit life that we have drowned in modern materialism. Oriental people still know a great deal.

'What most people do not know is that there exist many distinct forms of spirit life and that they function each according to their attributes. Some forms are well disposed to human life; some are harmless; some are malignant.

'We have to deal here with a malignant form. From its action I judge it to be an elemental. Elementals are primal earth forces – formless, eyeless, faceless. You will understand them perhaps by applying the great truth of evolution to all things. Elementals are spirit forms that have just not evolved at all. They exist, where shall I say? For want of a better word; they exist along with various other spirit forms on the other side of the veil that divides spirit from man.

'Sometimes it becomes possible for a spirit form to break through the veil and to manifest itself on the human plane. Never mind how they break through. They are attracted in various ways. In order to break through they must first be attracted by humans, consciously or unconsciously. The vibration theory may account for some. When they do break through we, in popular language, see a ghost.

'All elementals, possibly on account of their inferiority, hate humans who have progressed further in the scale of evolution. Having broken through into the human plane, an elemental must continue to draw sustenance from humans in order to continue to manifest. It can establish contact with some human who is sick, weak, whose power of resistance is at a low ebb. Thereafter it continues to draw vitality from its victim just as the vampire draws its sustenance in blood – till there is no vitality left.

'That in itself is bad enough. But the human victim, robbed of all vitality, does not quietly die, as do vampire victims. For the elemental, finding its victim useless, vents all its hate upon him by rending the last life from him with a vicious force, and then casts the twisted shell of what once was a man aside and turns to find another victim in a favourable condition of low resistance.'

The detective had listened with wide eyes, knuckles showing white where his hands gripped his knee. These things sounded fantastically impossible; but Dr Muncing's cold enunciation of them forced a reluctant belief in their gruesome possibility. And there was the evidence of the broken, twisted body and the telephone addenda from the hotel. All of them, things normally inexplicable.

The detective drew a long, tremulous breath and then fired what he thought was a poser.

'If this thing is a spook – which I don't admit yet – what brought it here? I thought that spooks hung around in old houses; monasteries and such like places where there'd been murders.'

Dr Muncing was able to laugh happily.

'There you are. Your own established superstitions. Why do you believe that? Because your forefathers knew it; because it is history; because people still know it. But make no mistake. While some forms of spirit life are attracted to their associations in old houses, others – elementals – are attracted directly to humans; they can fasten on to them wherever they may live.'

The doctor had a desperately logical answer to every doubt. The detective propounded another – not a doubt this time; a question looking for information.

'And this spook thing, can it hurt other people too; people who aren't sick? Us?'

Dr Muncing nodded seriously.

'Under the right conditions, yes. Conditions in the Bathurst are right. If it has established contact with three victims its power may be immense.'

'What do you figure brought it to the Bathurst?'

'I don't know,' replied the doctor. 'Maybe the number combinations of its name opened the way. There are deeps in numerology that no man has fathomed. Maybe its victim did or thought or possessed some luckless thing, to attract it. Maybe just the fact that there were three prospects whose physical vibrations provided the right sort of non-resistance was sufficient.

'These are things that I do not know. I can do no more than guess in the dark. I do not know how this malignant entity was able to exert some queer force that impelled me, personally, to come here. But from that I deduce that I have had contact with this elemental evil before. It has reason to hate me more than all other humans; and it has drawn me to this place because it feels it has contacted with some new power, that will enable it to destroy me. I don't know yet what this power may be or just how the thing has been able to exert it from a distance. But I feel positive that the whole plan of campaign is aimed at me.'

The doctor stated his case with cold conviction. No exaggeration, no assumption of knowledge that he did not possess, no heroics. Here was something at last that the detective could understand. A force for evil directed deliberately against an individual who stood for law and order. It was a condition that he himself had faced many a time. And the doctor faced the condition calmly, without hint of hesitation just as any officer of the law might.

There was inspiration in that attitude. The detective braced himself. It had been the dark unknown that had seemed so horrible. Now he felt that he knew quite a good deal about the ways of spooks. He shrugged.

'Well, it sounds like a lot of hooey to me, Doc. But you got your nerve all right. And I'm assigned to clear up this murder. So I'll throw in with you. Let me just phone headquarters to send a man to look up marks around the window and fingerprints; and then we'll take a look at this maid that's gone queer on the top floor.'

Upon arrival at the hotel they found a physician already in attendance upon the maid. She had been moved to a bed in a vacant room, and there she lay in a state of collapse, moaning incoherent things and rolling staring eyes that saw nothing.

The physician was quite at a loss.

'There's not a thing the matter with the girl,' he told them. 'No hurt of any kind. But there seems to be some awful fright. All she does is mutter something about a horrible shape.'

Dr Muncing nodded.

'Do what you can. We'll be back.'

He drew the detective away.

'There'll be attics above this top floor; trap-door entrances. That's where we must look. And listen – get this very straight because you'll need to know just what you are up against. This is no empty shadow that groans and rattles chains. It has drawn human vitality sufficient to materialize in exaggerated resemblance to the human form from which it has taken that vitality. By the process of multiplication of energy known to all spirit forms it has built up that energy to a force sufficient to tear you and me apart. Few spirit forms can face bright light. Therefore this thing will be lurking through the day in dark places; attics.'

The detective heaved up his shoulders in a great shrug.

'If I believed the half of what you told me, Doc, I'd be taking cover faster than from a crook gang with machine guns. But I'm with you; so you know just about what I think.'

At the end of that long hallway, rungs let into the wall led to a square trap above. Dr Muncing, with a grim little smile, waited. The detective was quick to catch on to his motive. He grinned at him.

'You haven't got me scared yet, buddy,' he grunted; and he slowly climbed the ladder. With a thrust of his burly shoulders he flung the trap door back and disappeared into the gloomy hole.

Dr Muncing deliberately waited below. He heard the man's heavy footsteps move in a small circle above. Still he waited. It was being alone in the dark that tried a man's unbelief in ghosts. Suddenly the detective's voice came.

'Doc. Hey, Doc.'

Within the second it came again; urgent, anxious.

'Hey, Doc. Come on up!'

In a flash Dr Muncing was up the ladder and beside the man. It was he who was grinning now, though rather thinly and without mirth.

The detective drew a shaky breath. His face was sheepish and had by this time lost all of its gruff assurance.

'By golly I – I guess I'm a fool. For a minute there I was getting rattled. But – there's something up here, Doc?'

Dr Muncing laughed shortly.

'So? You felt it, did you?'

'Felt what?' The detective was boldly positive again. 'If I'd felt anything I'd have taken a crack at it. What d'you think I felt?'

Dr Muncing was grimly uncompromising.

'Fear,' he said. 'Just the first swift stab of it – and you haven't seen the thing yet. I told you fear was one of its attributes. You'll have to hold your nerve with an iron grip because this thing knows how to wrench out the very roots of fear.'

The detective's voice came very soberly.

'By golly, Doc, you've almost got me believing you. There was something getting my goat. But – I'm with you.'

'Good man,' said Dr Muncing. 'Let's take a look around.'

The attic space in which they stood was a long, wide barrack of a place. Dim light filtered through a cobwebby louvre opening. Ghostly grey BX electric cable wandered snakily over the open ceiling beams. The peaked roof shingles were lost in the gloom above. Only a track of three planks made walking space down the middle of the empty area. A false step on either side and one's foot would plunge through the ceiling of the room below.

At the far end another dim ventilation louvre showed that the attic extended on both sides. Apparently it was all like that, a dusty, musty, emptiness of king posts and cross beams that covered the whole building, which was constructed with wings and a centre, like a letter E.

'Helluva place to go spook hunting,' grumbled the detective with an attempt at jocularity to keep up his spirit.

Dr Muncing said nothing, but advanced slowly, the detective as close to his side as the narrow plank track would allow. In the gloomier central portion barely lit from the dim ends the doctor was very cautious. A faint metallic clink in his pocket told that he had handled something. If over-wrought imaginations were not building figments out of nothing, soft echoes and vague scuffling noises indicated that something was moving somewhere.

'We've got to be sure,' said the doctor, 'that it is up here and that it is It.'

They advanced together cautiously. Arrived at the end, the detective fastened a spasmodic grip on the doctor's arm.

'There! By God, I'll swear I saw something duck round the far corner.'

'Come on,' said the doctor shortly.

Both men felt a tingling of their skin as they started forward. The detective pressed on. Having seen something, all his training as a man-hunter came to the fore. He reached that corner ahead of the doctor. With a sudden shout he snatched his pistol and fired into the further darkness.

Nothing happened. Then in a few seconds – almost as though it were a foul odour given off by some beast of the skunk family – a hot wave of hate swept back and eddied round them. It was a sensation almost solid. They could feel the furious malice of the thing. A chill ran along the detective's spine.

'That was foolish,' said Dr Muncing quietly. 'You can't shoot a ghost. But I knew you had your gun; otherwise I would never have brought you up here.'

'God of Heaven!' breathed the detective. 'I take it all back, Doc. I don't know what I saw, but it was a long and a fearful shape of something. And what use is a gun then, if you can't shoot a thing like that?'

Dr Muncing nodded. He spoke with ominous seriousness.

'The sinister shape that frightened the women to hysteria. You're beginning to believe, yes? But listen now again. You've got to know this. It is a law of the universe that to every natural ill Nature has provided an antidote. We don't know all the antidotes; but science is continually finding more of them.

'There are repellants as well as attractions for all spirit forms. The old timers practised a mumbo-jumbo and called it magic. Rubbish. There is no such thing as magic. They knew some of the rules, that's all.

'The repellant for an elemental is – cold iron. I don't know why. But it has been known for all the ages. The amulets of all oriental people – who knew a lot more than we do – are made of cold iron. Your lucky horse shoe is cold iron. The material of which your gun is made is a thousand times better safeguard here than all your bullets. Better still is natural iron; the antidote to the primal earth spirit as Nature primally made it. Best of all, because of its purest natural form, is meteorite iron. An elemental can approach cold iron only in circumstances of extraordinary power. Now come ahead.'

Quickly they traversed that passage and came to what would correspond to the lower arm of the E. A blind passage. If the thing were here at all they had it cornered.

'It can't go through that ventilation louvre,' whispered Dr Muncing. 'I mean, it could squeeze through the slats, but it can't face daylight. Come on.'

It was a foolish, in fact a quite stupid, advance to make, as Dr Muncing perfectly well recognized afterwards. That louvre was particularly cobwebby and dim. The corner was dark. The elemental malignance had been drawing power from no less than three sick persons. And lastly – a law which the doctor well knew – anything cornered instantly builds up a psychological increase of power.

With perfectly insane recklessness, however, he advanced along the narrow plank track, over the open ceiling beams, the detective, sublime in his ignorance, with him.

Like an offensive odour again heavy hate assailed them. Tangible, almost stifling. The gloom in the far corner became gloomier. Long, black shadows of beams threw patterns. If the thing were there it was indistinguishable amongst the other shadows.

Under ordinary circumstances Dr Muncing would have taken warning right there. The sheer overwhelming force of the hate projection was evidence of the power that the thing had been able to gather to itself. But in some amazing manner he seemed to have lost all caution. Not only caution but simple common sense was lacking. The detective, bold in his ignorance, followed the lead of the expert. But he felt the menace of the thing.

'By God,' he muttered hoarsely. 'I'll swear it's getting darker.'

And it was. A blackness in the corner thickened and seemed to bulge out at them. Malignance, almost triumphal, swirled about them. Then fear in a sudden rush clutched at their senses. Like an animate intelligence tearing to break down their resistance.

At that at last Dr Muncing felt that he had come too far; that he had pitted himself against a condition of power far greater than he had realized. He knew that he had come just where the thing wanted him.

A desperate thought of retreat came to him. But it was a long passage back over the narrow and insecure planks. Then fear in an overwhelming surge tore his grip of himself to shreds of frazzled, screaming nerves. A choked cry of hideous panic came from the detective. And with it the horror broke upon them.

The shadow towered up before them. A palpable, monstrous, deformed thing. An inhuman noise issued from it; a ululation of hell's triumph. The unleashed malignance of all the ages enveloped them. And the *thing* launched itself at them.

Both men agreed afterwards that at that moment they saw their own spirits apart from themselves, torn from them and whirled in a strong wind.

The detective's shout was a strangled groan. With desperate effort he hurled himself aside – any side, anywhere.

His heavy body struck violently against the doctor.

Together the two bodies came down. There was a smashing sound. Wood splintered. Plaster cracked. The bright light of God's good day broke blindingly upon them. A short, swift descent, and a thud. They had smashed through the lath and plaster ceiling into the room below.

Above them, through the jagged hole, sounded a noise like beasts snarling in rage. Angular concentrates of darkness moved furiously in the gloom, as though long arms struggled to reach them; the more furious because they could not face the bright light. Like a stench again, consuming hate settled down upon them. Then slowly the malignance ebbed from the opening.

Both men were badly shaken. Death had been terrifyingly close to them. They were bruised and the breath had been knocked out of them. But their shock was mental much more than physical. The terror of that primal evil in the thick dark still shook them.

The room through the ceiling of which they had mercifully broken happened to be untenanted. Dr Muncing pulled himself together with a strong effort. He dragged himself to the plaster-littered bed and sat with his head in his hands.

With the sudden fall and the plunge into bright daylight, common sense had come back to him. The thread of some queer influence had snapped. His mind grappled with the phenomenon of his so nearly fatal stupidity.

'How could I do it?' he kept asking. 'I should have known – I did know, that it had a tremendous store of power. I knew that conditions were just right for it. What lunacy made me walk right into its trap? How did it influence me to come here in the first place? An elemental in itself is of too low an order of intelligence to influence the human mind. That rule is absolute. What new and deadly trick is this?'

The detective was concerned with a more practical aspect of the case. His heavy, ruddy face was white and great drops of perspiration clung to his forehead.

'Blessed saints!' he kept muttering. 'Holy Mother! I don't know what I've seen nor what black section of hell has broken out and come to this house. But God help us, what's to do? What can mortal man do against a thing like that? Fifty cops couldn't fight that thing. Save us, is it safe anyway to sit under that hole where it can look at us?'

Dr Muncing shook himself out of his uneasy consideration upon the new menace of mental influence. The detective was right. Practical considerations were paramount. Precautions had to be taken.

'It can't come at us in the light,' he assured the detective. 'All the police in the world wouldn't be any good. They *might* be able to chase it out of here. But it would be loose somewhere else in the world and would find another victim. We can't destroy it. It is a spirit form and so cannot be killed.'

'Holy Mother!' The awfulness of that thought shook the detective. 'Is it a piece of everlasting hell itself? What can we do?'

'The only thing we can do is to starve it. By a merciful dispensation of Providence the thing has its limitations. It has made its contacts and has materialized. In order to continue to manifest on this material plane it *must* continue to draw energy from its victims. It must eat.

'We must cut off its supply. We must protect its two remaining victims from further drain upon their vitality – by cold iron on their persons; and their rooms must be kept brilliantly lit throughout the night. We must bar all exits to the attic with cold iron; the louvre openings; everything. That won't be difficult. Stove lids, gas piping, anything will do.

'Fortunately the thing cannot easily break through the natural resistance of people who are not sick, whose vitality is strong. In fact it seems that there are only certain people whose vital vibrations are right for it; with whom it can establish contact. Every day – or rather night – that it cannot renew its supply of human vitality it grows weaker. Till shortly it will not have power enough to materialize at all. It will be forced back to spirit form, to the limbo from which it came.

'That is the only way we can deal with it. We *must* so deal with it. Otherwise it will remain a curse at large in the world.'

With a material job in hand the detective was full of energy. Full, too, of an almost religious obsession as to the need of driving this unholy thing back to the nether pit.

'I'll fix that end of it, Doc,' he declared with a crusador's spirit. 'Leave it to me. I'll have those trap-doors and things fixed up in no time. No need to tell the hotel folks what it's all about. I'll just say the police are in charge.'

'By no means tell anybody,' said the doctor. 'Fear engenders vibrations favourable to occult forces. I shall go and see these two sick people and try to make them understand what we want to do without scaring them.'

At the hotel desk the doctor inquired for particulars about the two sick people who were so mysteriously sick. The large blond lady gave garrulous details.

There was Mr Beckett in room sixty-two who had the snappiest monologue act in vaudeville. A fine, generous gentleman he was too; and it was a shame and a disgrace that the doctors who took his good money couldn't even tell him what was wrong with him.

And there was Mr Lubine in nineteen who used to play the two-a-day; but there was not much call for his specialty these days, and he was reduced to a come-on booth at the beach. A hypnotist he was and one of the best in –

'What? What's that?'

Dr Muncing's sudden shout startled the lady back to her tremulous condition of the early morning. Her nerves were in no condition to bear another shock.

'A hypnotist, you say? God of everlasting wonders! What cunning guile is this?'

He hurried from the desk muttering, leaving the lady to gaze tearfully after him. A hypnotist? So that was how it was done? The malignant thing, absorbing with the man's vitality a portion of his attributes, had been able to project a hypnotic suggestion to its enemy. Dr Muncing was sure now that this was the same elemental evil that he had combatted before. On that occasion owing to the stupidity of others, the elemental had won; the doctor had failed to starve it out. Now it knew the danger of the doctor's profound knowledge, just as a criminal knows and fears the danger of a clever detective.

Dr Muncing smiled a tight and very crooked smile. So that

was how the thing had been able to influence his mind and had lured him here where it had no less than three coincidental sources of power. That was how it had fooled him into advancing into its lair in the face of conditions that all his knowledge told him were in its favour.

Dr Muncing whistled and wiped his brow. What an insidious and deadly danger that was! His lips set in a hard line. He would not be caught with that trick again. And he must immediately warn the detective against that sly menace.

Together they made the rounds of the top-floor halls. The various trap-doors had been guarded with immense quantities of iron. Hardware of all kinds had been nailed, screwed, or attached by cords, as conditions permitted, to every possible outlet. From outside, festoons of gas pipe hung over the ventilation louvre.

'And we've shoved nails and stove bolts into the mouse holes,' said the detective with an official pride in his thoroughness.

Dr Muncing told him that an elemental was no such attenuated thing that it could ooze through a mouse hole. It was a material body capable of doing material harm. They went to the patients' rooms and immunized those.

Inventing a story about a prowling gang of burglars, Dr Muncing instructed them about keeping doors and windows closed and lights burning bright. Over the brass hardware of the doors he hung packets of meteoric iron.

'To-morrow,' he said to the detective, 'we shall know whether we have missed anything. If the patients look better it will be proof that we are being successful. If they are worse –'

'Don't worry that I've overlooked anything,' the detective interrupted. 'If the devil spawn is anything bigger than an ant we've got him bottled in the attic.'

In spite of which boast, a furious knocking woke the doctor with the first streaks of dawn, and a white-faced boy brought a story that a watchman had seen a long, dark figure skulking up a staircase.

Muncing immediately investigated in company with the detective and discovered that the ironware about one of the trap-doors had been removed and stacked neatly in a corner.

'What the hell!' swore the detective. 'I thought you said it couldn't touch iron.'

But Dr Muncing with a very serious expression continued his inquiries. They elicited the information that a hotel employee on one of the upper floors had moved them. He appeared to be hazy in his recollection of just why he had done so. He supposed that probably they must have looked unnecessary, as well as untidy.

The furious detective would have struck the bewildered employee. But Dr Muncing held his hand.

'Remember,' he told him meaningly. 'It hypnotized us to follow it right into its den.'

The detective's hand dropped. Amazement and awe were in his expression.

'Holy Saints! If it can do that against our precautions – Do you think it got at the sick ones again?'

'Come on,' snapped the doctor.

A hurried call at number sixty-two disclosed that everything was intact and that Mr Beckett had slept well and looked refreshed.

But the report from number nineteen was not so reassuring.

Mr Lubine lay in his bed, completely exhausted. And his window that had been so carefully protected was wide open.

Tactful, painstaking inquiry disclosed that he had been unable to sleep, it had been hot. So he had opened the window for fresh air and had turned out the glaring lights.

Dr Muncing drew the detective out of the room. His manner was very troubled.

'There are times,' he murmured, 'when I almost believe in a personal devil. What a diabolic jest upon life! Hypnotising the hypnotist with his own medicine!'

'God of Mercy,' groaned the detective. 'What can we ever do against that damnable trick?'

'Nothing,' said Dr Muncing with flat conviction. 'Nothing at all. I had hoped to starve this thing out. But as long as that man lives it will always be able to influence somebody to leave a loop-hole somewhere. His hypnotic art is his own death sentence. We can only hope that he does not live too long.'

The detective stared at him with big eyes as he assimilated the helplessness of that thought.

Three days of watching and futile precautions passed. Always somebody somewhere was insidiously impelled to remove some carefully built barrier of cold iron. The doomed hypnotist grew horribly weaker. And then, one day just before the dawn that frightful, soul-searing scream rang through the hotel once more.

The detective and Dr Muncing almost collided with each other at the door of number nineteen. Together they tore it open and dashed in. But only to verify what they already knew.

The body of the wretched hypnotist lay distorted in a gruesome contortion.

The detective, in spite of his anticipation of the tragedy, was stunned by the hideous inevitability of it. But Dr Muncing was full of grim energy. His strong nostrils quivered with the prospect of encounter and a tight smile pinched his lips.

'S-ss-so,' he hissed very softly. 'The thing has been foolish enough to kill its source of supply. It has perhaps learned enough to circumvent our barriers. 'But' – he nodded very purposefully – 'perhaps now we can trap it.'

The detective stared at him.

'What do you mean, trap it? You're not going to try and catch that thing? And you can't kill it, you told me.'

Grimly Dr Muncing expounded the law.

'Every spirit form can be exorcised – if you know how. Every ghost, as you would put it, can disappear. A spirit form may disintegrate itself voluntarily. Or – if one has the knowledge and the necessary courage – conditions may be made so unpleasant for it that it disintegrates itself back to the fourth dimension. If we can catch our elemental and force it to de-materialize, it is right back where it came from – beyond the veil once more. A completely new set of conditions must be found in order to let it break through again.'

'How?' was all that the detective said through set teeth.

Dr Muncing was deadly deliberate.

'Have you got plenty of plain guts? I mean, nerve enough to meet this thing in a locked room? But I know you have. You'll see it through with me? Live or die?'

The detective's eyes were held by the doctor's compelling stare. Slowly he nodded. Dr Muncing held out his hand.

'Good man. Listen then. This thing as a low grade of intelligence. To-night it will try to get into the other sick man's room. Well, we'll leave the road open – and you, my nervy friend, and I, we shall be waiting for it!'

Like steam slowly escaping the breath came heavily through the detective's nose. But his eyes remained fixed on Dr Muncing's. His jaw muscles swelled over gritted teeth. He nodded.

'Good man,' said Dr Muncing tersely again. 'Go ahead and arrange about having the patient moved into another room, and hang all the iron in the house around it. I've got some preparations to make yet. I've been getting ready for this for the last three days. I've got a long session now with a carpenter and an electrician. Probably a blacksmith, too. See you at ten o'clock to-night.'

For the detective it was an awful day of foreboding and gloomy conjecture. A day that dragged its minutes into interminable hours. Fearsome though the thought was of facing the elemental thing, he welcomed each new hour that led on to the evening as being one hour the less to wait in suspense.

Not a minute before ten p.m. did Dr Muncing show up. He was tense.

'Come on,' he said shortly. 'They turn off the main lights here at ten. We want to be in position right away.'

The sick man's room was stuffy with recent occupancy and want of air. Dr Muncing's first act was to throw the window up to its fullest extent. The detective breathed like a nervous horse, but said nothing. Laconically, Dr Muncing outlined his plans.

'I've been having a surprise built here for the thing. That will give us an advantage – and let me tell you, we'll need it. We must just sit tight in the dark till it comes. Chairs in the corner farthest from window and bed. Not a peep, not a sound to warn it. And then, if it comes, it'll be it or us.'

The detective never knew whether minutes or hours or days passed. Time was an interminable ache of apprehension. Comfortable human noises in the hotel ceased. Unfamiliar noises shuffled and whispered down passages. Probably humans too – or mice. But the detective quivered at each one. Faint clicks came from without the window. Insects or summer bats. The detective groped for Dr Muncing's arm in the dark.

The doctor leaned softly over to whisper reassurance.

'Don't bother about noises. It will be as silent as a ghost when it comes; and then whatever happens will happen fast. Hold your nerve for that minute; and then, whatever happens, don't let the iron amulet out of your hands.'

Black eternity passed again. Suddenly both men drew a sharp breath at the same time. There had been no sound; but a roundish object the size of a grapefruit was dimly outlined above the window-sill. For minutes it stayed as motionless as a lurking animal. A formless, indistinguishable shape; a blur in the outer darkness.

At last it moved. It rose above the sill. An extraordinarily long angle of a raggy elbow heaved up from below. A gaunt shoulder followed; and then another fantastic elbow. There the thing hung in grotesque silhouette. The grapefruit thing was obviously its deformed head. It turned as though listening.

The detective experienced the same cold fear that he had at his first meeting with the thing in the attic; and again, almost as an animal odour, the sense of hate wafted into the room.

His grip closed hard on Dr Muncing's arm. Its rocklike steadiness reassured him.

Slowly, with infinite caution the shadow drew itself over the sill; all long raggedy arms and abnormally attenuated legs. Now it stood wholly within the room; a shadow against the outer dimness, deformed, grotesque, immense

Then things happened fast. Dr Muncing stretched out a cautious arm and pressed a button. With a rasp and a heavy metallic clang a sliding shutter slammed down into its groove, cutting off even the dim square of outside night. The room was in black darkness.

A snarling squealy noise sounded by the bed. A choked 'My God' from the detective. Then a click; a familiar sputter; and a blaze of light from a powerful theatre arc lamp.

Crouching in sudden afright the sinister shape loomed enormous in all its exaggerated deformity; menacing in spite of its startled surprise. But it was to the face of the thing that the eyes of both men were attracted. A faceless face. A smudge. A smear of mouldy, doughy substance. Shapeless, shrunken, incredibly evil. Yet there were eyes; dead slatey grey with darker diagonal slits of irises; and a frothy gash of a mouth. A formless face of fear and of unbelievable fury.

A sound of rage issued from the mouth and the Thing hurled itself at the window through which it had come. In the same movement, like an animal arresting its leap in mid-air, it shrank from the iron sheet that had clanged into place. With inhuman speed, snarling as it twisted, it changed its leap into a plunge across the room and lunged an abnormally attenuated arm at the arc lamp.

There was a crash, a tinkle of smashed carbon rods, and the room was blotted into black darness once more.

Out of the dark came a roaring noise, an incoherent howl of triumph. The detective felt himself whirled off his feet into the air by an irresistible force. He commended his soul to God.

Then, mercifully, there was a sputtering noise and a spurt of blue flame. Another arc blazed bright. A sputter, once more. Another. Again another. The room was flooded with light that hurt the eyes.

The detective found himself on the floor. Vaguely he was conscious of Dr Muncing shielding his eyes from the glare and advancing with incredible courage against a shapeless blackness that condensed in a corner, holding in his hands a queer, five-sided emblem of iron.

From it and from the blinding lights the black shadow shrank. Farther into the corner and yet farther. The lights seemed to penetrate it, to eat it up. Its solid blackness paled. It thinned out. The baseboard was visible through it; the pattern of the wall paper. Presently there was no shadow. Nothing. Only a stifling odour of baffled hate.

Dr Muncing advanced resolutely into the corner. He pressed his pentagon of iron into the farthest nook. There he left it and he came to lift the detective to his feet. Great beads of perspiration stood on his forehead. His strong hands were trembling. He hid his own agitation under a cover of brusqueness.

'What in thunder did you do with the iron amulet I told you not to let out of your hand? Dropped it to reach for your gun, huh? You poor fool, you've been nearer to horrible death than you'll ever be able to understand.'

The detective was not resentful at this.

'Is – is it gone?' was all he wanted to know.

Very slowly and very soberly Dr Muncing nodded.

'By the grace of God, yes. And by the grace of God again, the conditions that allow a thing like that to break through into the human world come, very fortunately, seldom. This elemental evil is exorcised. Or, as you will tell the tale to your unbelieving fellows, this ghost is laid.'

IX

Panic In Wild Harbor

Gordon Hillman

Of all the American supernatural sleuths, my favourite is the remarkable Cranshawe, whose cases appeared in the decade leading up to World War II and were then reprinted in the nineteen sixties. Although there is a little of both John Silence and Carnacki in Cranshawe, there is a stylishness about his demeanour and a variety in the locations to which he is drawn (he even crosses the Atlantic on one occasion to solve the mystery of a screaming skull that has baffled all the local ghost hunters!) which sets him apart from the rest.

Sadly, we know little about Gordon Malherbe Hillman *(1909-1960), the creator of the resourceful Cranshawe, beyond the fact that he was a regular and evidently knowledgeable contributor to the popular American magazine* Ghost Stories, *which provided lovers of the supernatural with a monthly feast of stories and essays in both fact and fiction. It has been suggested that Hillman may at one time have been a seaman as a number of his stories deal with maritime subjects. Be that as it may, the following story, 'Panic in Wild Harbor' which was first published in* Ghost Stories *in September 1939, is as memorable a tale of the sea and its mysteries as one will find anywhere …*

In all my friend Cranshawe's portfolio of psychic experiences, there is none more ghastly or unearthly than the weird affair at Wild Harbor. Cranshawe, being a trained psychic investigator and perhaps one of the best-known in America, catalogues it simply as 'phenomena in a New England coast town.' But Cranshawe is always conservative.

It all began when a telegram was laid on our table.

Cranshawe read it, signalled to his Japanese valet and tossed the wire over to me. It read:

Engage you immediately to probe ghastly mystery. Come at once.

It was signed by the town officials of Wild Harbor.

'I know the place,' said I, but Cranshawe had already called to the valet.

'Pack the bags and get two seats on the Boston train,' he snapped.

'This may be a most remarkable case,' he turned to me. 'I've heard something, I believe, about this place. A bell rings at uncanny intervals.'

'Rot,' said I. 'You can't expect to find ghosts in a summer resort nowadays. Wild Harbor's full of artists and barelegged girls in the season. The only thing that's ghastly about the town is the smell of fish.'

Cranshawe was already sorting out his equipment; his note-books, his camera, the telescope he always took with him, and a dozen other odds and ends.

'You're always so sceptical,' he said. 'That's why I'm taking you with me. If what I fear is true, horror stalks in that town, and a good, sane, sensible scoffer is exactly what I need as a witness. Come along.'

I must confess that, as we began our adventure, I shivered a little at the memory of my other experiences with Cranshawe. But the sight of Wild Harbor reassured me. It was such a sleepy little fishing town, and more sleepy now than it would be later, for the summer season had not yet begun. Ordinary, box-like New England houses were everywhere. The inhabitants were peaceably going about their business, while a quarter of the town's police force was down at the station, picking his teeth and watching the train come in.

'Well, here we are,' said I, 'and not a ghost in sight.'

A short man in a faded blue suit came running up to meet us, and if ever a man was agitated, he was. His very eyes held a hint of dark terror, and his voice shook when he spoke.

'Mr Cranshawe?' he said 'Thank God you've come. These things can't go on – they mustn't! It's too ghastly –'

'I have brought a friend to help me,' said Cranshawe, and the three of us climbed into one of the town taxicabs and went rattling over the cobblestone streets.

'The whole town's terrified,' the little man was saying, 'and if the tourists get wind of it, our summer season's ruined. We count on you, Mr Cranshawe; we count on you!'

It was quite idiotic. Here was the little man babbling away as though we were living in the Dark Ages; yet through the cab window I could see the fish nets drying, and the red front of a five-and-ten-cent store, and could hear the newsboys crying the Boston papers.

I couldn't catch much more of the conversation, for the little man was leaning toward Cranshawe and whispering in his ear. But I could tell from the way his hand shook that he was frightened out of his wits.

We stopped in front of a big white house, with a green lawn in the rear sloping gently to the harbour. The house stood by itself, away from all others, and at the far corner of its ground rose the red chimney of a paint factory.

'You'll come in?' said Cranshawe to the little man.

'*Me*?' he shuddered. 'I can't. I don't dare. That bell and the face and … Goodbye!' With that he slammed the door in our faces.

The cab was gone in a cloud of dust, and Cranshawe and I stood in front of the white picket fence looking up at the old house.

'What's he afraid of?' I asked testily, for I was tired from the long train ride.

'Horrors,' said Cranshawe. 'Horrors that he does not understand. One of them's the bell above you.'

I looked up and, there, just below the flat window's-walk that adorns the top of all sea captains' houses, hung a bell – an old, worn ship's bell, gone green in places from rust and damp. No rope led to it.

'Every Friday at midnight, it tolls ten times,' said Cranshawe. Then he led the way to the front door of the house, opened it, and we stepped inside.

A very ordinary house it was, too. Old haircloth chairs and sofas, a ship's lantern in the hall, rugs and bric-a-brac picked up from the four corners of the earth, lithographs of sailing vessels on the wall. In short, the house of a sea captain.

Then I thought of something.

'How can the bell ring?' I asked. 'It has no rope.'

'It tolls,' insisted Cranshawe calmly. 'It tolls ten times.'

'But why ten?'

Cranshawe lifted one of the lithographs from the wall.

'Ten men,' he said, 'went down on the schooner, *Golden Wind*, at twelve o'clock on a Friday night two years ago. What's that?'

It was a long, drawn-out hello, and as we stepped outside on the porch, a stout, red-faced seafaring man was waving to us from beyond the fence.

'Mr Cranshawe!' he called. 'It's Cap'n Starbuck.'

'Come in!' Cranshawe called back, but the Captain shrugged his shoulders.

'Not I!' he said. 'Will you come out here, sir?'

Cranshawe and I walked over to the gate. I could not help marvelling how men could entertain such supernatural fears when the sun shone down and all the day was fair. Now, I marvel how they could have lived at all, side by side with that house of evil.

'I haven't been in that house,' said the Captain shakily, 'since what happened a year ago today. Nothing on earth would ever get me in there again. Clear out, sir! Clear out quick! I warn you!'

'Now my advice to you, Cap'n,' said Cranshawe, quite seriously, 'is to clear out yourself. Go far away, go to California, and straighten out your nerves. And go at once ...' he paused, looking still more serious. 'At once – before it's too late.'

The Captain's hands shook.

'I been ready to go,' he muttered, 'and now I got my affairs in shape, I will. But I'm bound to sail to the banks tomorrow in the *Hallowe'en*. The moment I get back, I'll start for California, and thank you kindly, sir.'

He turned quickly and shambled off down the road. Cranshawe raised his voice in a last warning. 'Don't go near the sea, Captain! Don't go near the sea!'

Stark fear glinted in the old seaman's eyes, but he shouted angrily: 'By God! Alive or dead, I'm not afraid of *him*!'

When we went back into the house, the swift twilight was already falling.

'What the devil did he mean!' I said.

Cranshawe calmly lit his pipe. But his eyes were not calm; they darted about as if he were expecting something weird –

something uncanny and horrible.

'Two years ago,' he droned, 'the *Golden Wind* was racing the *Hallowe'en* up the coast, racing to be in first with the catch of fish. Cap'n Starbuck drove his ship headlong into a fog; a fisherman's horn sounded dead ahead. Cap'n Starbuck was at the wheel. He took a chance and kept to his course. There was a crash, and that's all he knows – except that the *Golden Wind* went down with nine men and its Portuguese skipper.'

'Ten men in all,' said I, shuddering. 'And the bell tolls ten!'

Cranshawe knocked out his pipe.

'Precisely,' he said. 'Cap'n Starbuck came back here to this house. A year ago he was found unconscious, with his hand upon the knob of this very front door. He has never stirred a foot onto his own land or into his own house since. Now, if the summer colony gets wind of this, they'll stop coming to Wild Harbor, so the city fathers called on me. Let's have a sandwich.'

The sandwich and the cup of coffee which Cranshawe had provided made me see again how foolish the whole business was. An old sea dog falls unconscious in his house, the wind makes a bell toll – and there you have a pretty tale of terror. Besides, I reasoned, all seafaring folk are superstitious.

By half-past ten, I was yawning my head off. By eleven, I said to Cranshawe, 'I'm not going to wait for your old bell. I'm going to bed.'

'Righto,' Cranshawe said, with a yawn. 'The front room's made up.'

The lights were on in the hall; they were on in the cheery little bedroom, and, after a last look out at the harbour, I undressed and slipped placidly between the covers. Then I switched the lights off and waited for that phantom bell.

I watched the hands on my radium-faced watch racing toward midnight. They came together on the hour, and I strained my ears.

The bell did not toll on the hour, nor at the quarter nor at the half, so I shrugged my shoulders and turned over to sleep.

At last, I chuckled, Cranshawe had come on a wild goose chase!

It must have been a foghorn that wakened me – for its eerie wail was still ringing in my ears when I sat bolt upright in bed.

The horn sounded suddenly again, on a keen, high note of terror, and I stepped to the window from which the sound seemed to come.

As far as I could see stretched a white sheet of fog, and through it twinkled the red and green riding lights of a schooner. The horn had stopped; there was no sound; but out of the fog loomed the broken bow of a ship, heading into shore. That ship was ghastly white, and she seemed to move in her own circle of light, a dull, greenish, corpse-coloured glow. In she came and in, till it seemed she must touch the sea wall. Her foremast was a tangled wreck, her bulwarks broken down and slimy with weed.

The fog clung close about her; yet that ghastly green glow illumined the long, rutted, weed-hung decks, the splintered wheel-house, the ribbon of sail stringing from the broken mast. By the mast, and seemingly supported by a spar, a tall shadow was twisted.

A sudden shift in the light revealed it plainly as that greenish flicker played about the bows. Sailors call that light 'corpse-fire,' and in a flash I knew why. The tall shadow was not a shadow at all – it was a sailor, his arms outflung as if to clench some unknown thing, and his face was not the face of any living man!

As I shuddered and gripped the window curtains, I saw plainer still – the splinter of the spar had pierced clean through that silent shadow!

For a moment I fancied I knew, recognized, remembered the man who bore that ooze-green face, the man cut clean through by that splintered spar. Then horror upon horror loomed from the wreathing fog.

A ship's lantern made a spark of white upon the lawn – a loathsome, deadly white; but outside of that one spark, the lantern threw no light at all. There was no glow around it; the fog was no brighter there, and stare though I might, I could see nothing behind or beside that lantern. Waist-high it was, as though a man were carrying it. It even swung with the motion of a man's arm, but there was no man there.

Straight it came, as if bearing down upon me. Then, with a start, I realized it was rising to the height of a man's shoulder, then above his head – a shuddering, eerie dead-white spark in a sea of fog, a silent signal of horror.

Behind it lay the silent ship, the figure still inert upon the transfixing spar – and terror held me fast. Move my legs I could not; my head seemed riveted to one position on my shoulders. But even so, my fear-crazed brain registered the approach of something sinister.

Something, I knew, was creeping out of that fog, creeping down upon me like the hunter of a wild animal. And I was the animal, caught in a mesh of cold fear, my legs paralyzed, my arms like water, my eyes staring straight into the white welter.

In a panic I stretched a clammy hand out to the revolver under my pillow. A jerk and it was mine, though I could scarcely hold it.

Then the lantern glowed level with my eyes, glowed with its dead light that illumined nothing. It moved as if a man were carrying it across the veranda roof, but no man was there. And all the time I had the feeling of some Terror coming from the fog …

The lantern's light was so bright it hurt my eyes; yet it lit nothing in the night outside nor in the room. I raised my revolver and then I saw –

First a hand, misshapen, twisted like a claw; and though that hand held no lantern, held nothing at all, the light was still there. The hand moved blindly toward the window pane. It had no thumb, and the nails were like long talons.

As I stared, a scream – a hideous, racking scream – came through the fog. It came from that sepulchral ship, from that ghastly shape impaled upon the splintered spar. It was the scream of a man in utmost agony – of a man on the point of death – and the claw crept close to the catch on the window.

My icy finger slid on the trigger and my revolver, slid slowly as death, and I could see the hammer rise as that 'corpse light' shone full upon me and I was face to face with the Horror of all Horrors.

There was a Thing behind the lantern – huge, transparent, so that I could see the death ship through it – a Thing in the semblance of a man.

Long earrings such as Portuguese seamen wear glittered dully, the hair above them was matted with salt and seaweed, and – it is nearly beyond me to tell it, even now – that Thing had no face!

More because my finger twitched than because I willed it, the revolver went off with a deafening roar. The window crashed. My wrist was caught as if by claws, the revolver clattered to the floor, and I could see nothing – nothing that can be mentioned even now – save two long earrings.

I must have screamed. I must have struggled, for my arm was slashed as if by sharp claws – and suddenly I was at the door, with the soft patter of footfalls behind me! Not the footfalls of a living man – rather those of an animal, and I wrenched at the knob and stumbled down the stairs, scream upon scream tearing from my throat.

Above my cries, drowning them out, arose the deafening tolling of a bell. Slow strokes and sure – like the toll of a dead man's doom. *One – two – three –*

I caught feebly at the stairhead, and screamed again, while those footfalls pattered soft behind me, closer – closer –

'*Four – five – six*,' the bell was still tolling.

A cold shiver seized me. *Eight – nine – ten –*

Though the clamour still went on, I could not cry out again.

The bell tolled thirteen, and stopped dead!

Then I lost track of everything.

I awakened in the warm sunshine of the library, with Cranshawe bending over me, a whisky glass in his hand.

'The bell!' I whispered, for my voice seemed gone. 'The bell tolled thirteen!'

'Thirteen!' said Cranshawe, and his face went even paler. 'I didn't count. I heard you calling and rushed out. Lucky I caught you as you fell.'

'I didn't fall,' I said weakly. 'There was some Thing –'

But Cranshawe was not even listening.

'Thirteen?' he mused. '*Thirteen*! And there's a fishing schooner just come up the bay with her flag at half-mast. Old man, I'm afraid we're in for more terrors.'

'There aren't any more,' I whispered. 'there can't be.' And, still shivering all over, I told him the horrors of that awful night.

He was just helping me to rise, when a shout came from the outer door, and the little man we had met at the station came in, creeping fearfully, as if in abject terror.

'Mr Cranshawe!' he cried. 'Oh, my God, it's horrible! The *Hallowe'en* was sunk last night and every man aboard save one.'

Cranshawe looked stunned. 'I told Starbuck to stay away from the sea,' he said, as if to himself.

'The *Hallowe'en*,' said the little man, peering about him in fear, 'sailed on the evening tide. The *Mary B.* picked up one man. He says – he says that off the Graves Shoal, they ran into a fog, and out of it loomed a ship – all white – and the white ship ran them down! Its foremast was a wreck – What say, sir?'

'Nothing,' I shook my head. 'Go on.'

'And as they struck, Cap'n Starbuck was up for'ard, and one of the white ship's spars pierced him through and through. All that the man the *Mary B.* picked up can remember is the Cap'n screaming, and one more thing –'

'What's that?' asked Cranshawe.

'He says that the white ship – the one that struck them – was the *Golden Wind* – the ship that Cap'n Starbuck sent to the bottom two long years ago last night!'

The little man was ashen pale; his hands were quivering, and he flinched as Cranshawe suddenly spoke.

'How many were lost aboard the *Hallowe'en*?'

I could have told him, even before the little man spoke.

'Thirteen!'

Cranshawe snapped his notebook shut.

'We'd better help my friend out of here,' he said. 'He's had – a bad fall!'

The little man lifted me on one side, and Cranshawe on the other. I was hardly able to walk.

'What are them?' said the little man, and drew back swiftly.

I looked down. My pyjama sleeve was crushed back, and on my forearm there were four red marks, like the gashes left by four sharp talons. My wrist was so stiff I could not move it.

'I tripped in the night,' I said weakly. 'The fog was so thick I couldn't see –'

The little man took hold of my arm again, but he was shaking all over.

'There wasn't any fog in Wild Harbor last night,' he said.

Cranshawe snapped at him.

'Don't mind about that,' he said. 'Take him across the street and get him a cup of coffee. I'll bring down his clothes. I'm going upstairs, anyway, to have a look around.'

I was propped up in an easy chair in a pretty little cottage across the street. Out on the porch, the housewife and the little man were still rattling on about the horrible wreck of the *Hallowe'en*, when Cranshawe came in and shut the door on them.

'Old man,' he said solemnly, 'I found everything as you said. The window is smashed, there are pools of sea water on the floor, the whole place smells of dank weed and ocean bottoms – and I found your revolver with one chamber empty. Only it's not a revolver any more. Some terrific force has twisted it into scrap iron.'

I shuddered.

Just then a boy came shouting down the street. I could not help hearing what he cried from door to door:

'There's a wreck come ashore at the Graves with a dead man on it.'

'Was it the *Hallowe'en?*' I could hear a woman ask, but the boy's voice blurred so I could not hear it any more.

The little man came hastily into the room, his face a mask of utter horror, and I asked weakly, 'Is it the *Hallowe'en?*'

'It isn't the *Hallowe'en!*' cried the little man in near hysteria. 'It's the *Golden Wind*, up from the sea bottom after two years – and aboard her, hung on a spar is ...'

I waved him to silence. I knew who hung on that spar. I remembered at last that dead face on the dank deck of the dead ship. And I wanted to know no more.

'Mr Morse,' said Cranshawe, 'that ends the tolling of the bell and the apparitions of the face – that is not a face – in the fog. Nothing more will disturb you or your summer visitors. The dead man's vengeance is complete.'

I rose weakly. The talon marks were still scarlet on my arm, and I put on my coat gingerly.

'But what's the explanation of this whole terrible business?' quavered the little man as we walked out into the sunshine.

'You must make your own,' Cranshawe told him. 'One man's guess is as good as another's.'

Sleuth: Miles Pennoyer

X

The Case of the Bronze Door

Margery Lawrence

Curiously, fictional supernatural sleuths have been in rather short supply in recent times, though this situation may well be reversed after the success of Ghostbusters. *Still, though, there have been a trio of writers who have kept the tradition alive and they contribute my last three selections. The first of these is* Margery Lawrence *(1895-1969), a prolific novelist of adventure and romance stories, who created Miles Pennoyer as a direct result of her conversion to spiritualism and deep interest in the supernatural.*

Pennoyer lives at the most suitable address of number 7, Queer Street, and is assisted by Jerome Latimer, a young man with the 'psychic sensitiveness' necessary to help his mentor in his magical work. In introducing a collection of the Pennoyer stories in 1945, Margery Lawrence described him as a 'psychic doctor who deals in the ills that beset the soul rather than the body of man' and admitted that his exploits had also been partly inspired by those of John Silence and Dr Taverner. Pennoyer is, though, very much his own man, and in the story here proves himself most worthy of being compared with those two distinguished predecessors.

It was a magnificent thing, and I exclaimed with wonder and admiration when I first saw it, one night when I went to dine with my old friend Miles Pennoyer at his roomy flat overlooking the Thames.

He had turned the top floor of an old riverside house in Blackfriars – the famous 'No 7 Queer Street', of which I spoke in my foreword – into an enviable bachelor flat. Certainly it was lonely and out of the way according to most people's tastes – below him were offices, bleak and empty every night, and but for Friedl, his old Bavarian housekeeper, and Hans his wolf-hound, he lived there entirely alone; but he preferred it – indeed, declared it necessary. High-perched there above the river, with the tall house below him silent and deserted, he could breathe freely, he said. It was either that or going to live in the country, since for his work he was forced to avoid, as far as possible, living in too close contact with the crowd. So this delightful top-floor eyrie was perfect for his requirements.

It was a lovely spring evening, and the wide windows behind the window-seat stood open. I flumped down upon the brown velvet cushions and leaned luxuriously back. The sunlight lay along the old polished boards of the floor, warming the faded colours of a gorgeous Persian silk rug that lay before the fireplace into life and vitality. Below, a whistle hooted faintly in midstream, and the masts of the shipping rose heavenwards like a serried row of pointing fingers; there was a light, warm breeze, and across the river, beyond the tumbled roofs, the sky curved sweetly, faintly blue and flecked with tiny tufts of cloud like feathers.

Pennoyer poured me out a whisky and soda, and I stared contentedly round the room – and saw the screen.

It stood at one end of the long, low-roofed room, fastened flat against the wall. It fitted curiously well into the background of mingled old and new that was Miles Pennoyer's setting; dark brown velvet hangings, deep leather chairs well worn and cushioned, rows of books running round three sides of the room to a height of some four feet from the ground – and all about, oddments of ancient art of any and every kind. A Russian ikon of silver gilt set with gleaming rough-cut jewels, a Venetian mirror over the mantelpiece, a Byzantine Madonna, glowing in sombre colours from a cracked wooden panel. A slipware tyg, two Ming kylins, blue as the heart of turquoise, a Turkish scimitar with a carved and enamelled hilt, the rust of old blood still upon it – and now, set flat against the end wall, the screen!

I jumped up at once and went over to examine it more closely.

'That's a magnificent piece of work, that screen. Where did you pick it up, you lucky devil?' I said.

Pennoyer smiled and splashed iced water plentifully into his glass. He drank no alcohol, as became a man interested in his particular sort of work – for Miles Pennoyer, though most people called him Doctor, was not a doctor in the strictest sense of the word. Not a doctor, that is, of the body. His doctoring lay in a direction much more difficult and intangible. A woman once called him a 'doctor of souls', and perhaps this description may pass as well as any other, though to me it savours rather irritatingly of conventional religion – which, since I am a rabid anti-clerical, always rubs me up the wrong way! But to resume ...

I flattened my nose against the screen in envy and admiration. It was not, I discovered, actually a screen at all, but a door of bronze weathered with age to a green-brown sheen exquisitely rich. A great double door, seven foot high by about six wide, fastening in the middle with a giant wheel-shaped sort of lock, and with huge hinges shaped like Mah-jongg pieces on each side. It was covered with a magnificent design in incised and chiselled work, and I guessed its date as somewhere about the Sung dynasty; its dignity and elegance, combined as only the Chinese know how to combine them, was as satisfying as a perfect meal, as the kiss of a woman who understands kissing, as a book one reads and reads again and loves afresh at every reading. I sighed, and turning my back on the thing, came to the fire where Pennoyer waited for me, his deep-set eyes intent on my face.

'Where did you get it?' I asked discontentedly. 'You've got some priceless stuff, I know, but that's simply magnificent!'

He nodded.

'It was given me,' he said. 'Quite recently. By – a patient, since I suppose I've got to call those I try to help "patients" for want of a better word.'

He drank a deep draught of iced water and set his glass down as I sat up, instantly alert.

'You've got a story about the thing, Pen!' I accused him.

He laughed and nodded.

'Yes! And since I think it's one worth putting on record, I may as well admit that one of the reasons for which I asked you round to-night was in order to tell you the story.'

I settled back luxuriously.

'Good thing you didn't tell me so before dinner,' I said, lighting one of the good cigars Pennoyer keeps for his guests – as he drinks no alcohol, so he neither smokes nor eats meat, since to do any of these impairs the delicacy of the psychic vibrations on which so much of his success as a 'doctor' depends. 'I would have gulped it down so fast that I would never have done justice to Friedl's cooking! Go on now – I'm all attention.'

*

It happened (said Pennoyer) about three or four months ago. I was dining at the Club one night – the Travellers I mean, where I'm regarded as one of the few members who doesn't quite conform to standard and is therefore vaguely suspect! (His lean dark face creased into amused wrinkles.) They tolerate me because my Uncle Benbow is a peer of the realm, and therefore the argument is that if I *am* superficially queer, at heart I must be sound! I go there sometimes, as you know, because after dealing all day with strange twists and tangles of the human soul, it soothes me to sit awhile and relax – bask, if you like – in the atmosphere of a place where practically everybody, including the staff servants, is beautifully and restfully – even monotonously! – normal.

Well, I was sitting eating my usual 'mess of rabbit-food', as dear old Uncle Benbow calls it – being a vegetarian and a non-drinker-or-smoker is another nail in my coffin with the diehards! – when old General Satterthwaite tottered up, puffing and blowing. He slumped into a chair beside me, and at the moment I was rather annoyed, I must admit, because I wanted to be left alone. I wanted – mentally – to snooze, as I was frightfully tired.

But the General's a friend of Uncle Benbow's, and one has to be polite – and after a preliminary of grunts and snorts, the old boy suddenly came out with something rather interesting.

'You go in for this – spiritualistic business, don't you?'

The utter scorn and contempt he put into the word "spiritualistic" was delightful! I stared at him, but made no answer – frankly, I couldn't imagine what he was getting at.

He snorted again, louder than before.

'Don't believe in it – all damn rot! But all the same ...' He snorted once more, and I began to laugh.

'I *could* start an interesting argument as to what you mean by that overworked word "spiritualistic", I said. 'I don't suppose it's what *I* mean. But if you don't believe in it, why introduce the subject?'

The old boy blinked and coughed evasively.

'Don't believe in it myself,' he grumbled, 's'far as I'm concerned, I mean! All mumbo-jumbo – fakes and trickery and so on. But all the same …' He ruminated a moment and then brought out, with a queer mixture of contempt and urgency, the reason for his unusual visit to my lonely corner table. 'All the same … I wish you'd go and see my nephew, John Satterthwaite? Lives in Westminster – making a name for himself at the Bar – married a Trehoweth. Good old Cornish family – nice girl. God-child of mine, 'smatter of fact. Couple of kids too, boy and girl – marriage turned out well – not like some of the damned modern youngsters' marriages. Here to-day and gone to-morrow …'

He puffed into his white moustache, and I stared at him.

'If everything in John Satterthwaite's garden is as good as you say, what's worrying you about him?' I said.

He grunted, staring at me obliquely from his squinty little eyes, set in the heavy folds of ruddy flesh above the white moustache.

'Er – well, there you are! Marriage OK – but there's *something* upsetting it, all the same. *She* told me about it. She's worried – came to see me the other day. Funny story.' He puffed and snorted again. 'Wish you'd look him up. You might remember him. John Satterthwaite. He was at school with you – years your junior, but he hasn't forgotten you. Had a sort of hero-worship of you, what?'

Then I remembered! A lean, dreamy little youngster who had attached himself to me with a devotion almost embarrassing when we were both at Marlborough. An odd kid – I'd forgotten all about him. But as the old General talked I 'saw' him suddenly as clearly as I see you now, in a clear mental picture. The same youngster, but older, a man grown for all he had retained his wide blue gaze and sensitive mouth … and the eyes that looked into mine were suffering eyes. Eyes that begged, that implored help …

I rose from the table and held out my hand to the General.

'I *would* like to see John again, tremendously,' I said. 'And if you'll let me have his address I'll write him asking if I may come down and look him up some time soon.'

'Right,' grunted the old man. 'But mind – don't let him think you want to see him because of anything. *He* doesn't know there's anything wrong – at least, that's what I gather from his wife. Just let him know you ran into me and we got talking about him, and all that, and that you wrote off your own bat, see?'

I saw – and wrote to John Satterthwaite by that night's post, suggesting a meeting, to which he returned a delighted letter inviting me to dinner. And two nights later I descended from a taxi before a tall house in Smith Street, Westminster.

Old General Satterthwaite's description of his nephew's abode as a 'flat' was not quite accurate. Actually the young couple and their children occupied the whole house, with the exception of the ground floor, this being used as a bachelor flat by the owner of the house, an elderly barrister who was a friend of John's.

The hall was the usual narrow, rather gloomy affair, smelling vaguely of furniture polish and mackintoshes, and furnished with an umbrella-stand, a coat-rack and a black wooden settle upon which nobody ever sat – but a 'pram' at the far end, and a child's scooter beside it, brought a flavour of humanity into the rather bleak austerity of the place. I hung up my hat and coat and followed the maid upstairs to a small landing on the first floor – where there were two doors, one directly facing the stairs and one at the side – and as I set foot on the landing the door at the side flew open and John Satterthwaite pounced out on me, seizing my hands and shaking them with an almost feverish eagerness.

'*Pen*! Man, I'm delighted to see you. I've often wondered what on earth had become of you … come in, come in!'

He ushered me through the open door into a snug little book-lined study facing the back of the house – evidently John's own particular sanctum, if a rack of pipes, deep leather chairs, a paper-littered desk and various briefs tied with the traditional red tape did not lie. There was a blazing fire on the hearth, and a small table was drawn up near the fire with various drinks upon it. John was on the verge of pouring me out a stiff whisky and soda when I stopped him.

'Don't drink, old chap!' I laughed. 'Can't, with the sort of work I do!'

'I'm sorry,' said John, and his slightly crestfallen expression was precisely the snubbed little boy I remembered at Marlborough. 'I didn't know ...'

'How should you know?' I said, warming my hands at the leaping flames. 'It's merely part of my job. I don't drink because I've got to keep my psychic vibrations steady; a golf-pro who wants to keep in form doesn't drink either because he has to keep his eye steady.'

John eyed me respectfully.

'I'd heard – vaguely – the sort of work you'd taken up,' he said. 'You always used to be interested in queer sorts of things, even at Marlborough, I know – though of course I didn't know you very well then. I was only a miserable little junior, and you were awfully decent to take any notice of me at all! As far as that goes, it's frightfully decent of you to take the trouble to look me up, with all your work and your name and everything.'

I began to laugh.

'For two pins you'd call me "sir",' I said. 'Forget it, John! After all, though I may be grey and your wig's still got its pristine blackness, there isn't more than ten years or so between us all told.'

He grinned in return – and within five minutes thawed out so completely that we were yarning away, prefacing every sentence with 'd'you remember?' just as two old friends always do, and enjoying ourselves thoroughly.

A step sounded outside, and I turned as John extended a welcoming hand to the small, slim figure in black advancing into the ruddy circle of firelight. As I took her hand in mine I stared at her quite frankly, curious and interested. As you know, in the treatment of psychic ills, a man's cure depends – so often, so terribly often! – upon the woman he has married.

I saw a pretty young girl of about twenty-five or so, with reddish-brown curly hair and a short freckled nose, bright grey-blue eyes with a charmingly candid, eager expression in them as she searched my face with interest at least equal to mine. I shook her hand, made the usual pleasantly conventional greeting and turned again to the fire. I was relieved – and yet at the same time faintly disappointed. She was kind and sweet and loyal; obviously devoted to John and longing to do something to help him … it was a great advantage, that last, of course, since I have had to do battle sometimes for a man's soul with a woman who is either instinctively antagonistic to me and my methods, or else frightened to death (which is almost as bad!) or worst of all, who deep within herself does not *want* her husband to recover! D'you remember the Green Monster case, eh? That was pretty grim? And yet – I was faintly disappointed.

Looking at John's lean-drawn, intelligent face, remembering his passion for books and art, the discussions, amazingly deep and thoughtful for such a little chap, that we used to have together, I seemed to sense that, sweet as she was, this pleasant, sincere little woman he had married was somehow – inadequate! Good and sweet and kind – yet somehow not the kind of outstandingly fine-fibred creature I had pictured as John Satterthwaite's mate. If you get my meaning, I felt that in a crisis she'd do all she knew, pull her damndest – but that she simply would not have the strength for her help to be *worth* a damn! D'you get me?

Well, to go on. We went upstairs to dinner, which was served in a pleasant room on the floor above John's study – a room that, from its scattered toys, work-basket, women's magazines and light, fresh decoration, was as plainly Mrs Satterthwaite's sanctum as the study was John's.

The food was excellent. Clear soup, fish, cutlets with vegetables – for once really well-cooked – and fresh fruit, as John did not care for sweets; and my hostess chattered cheerfully about the children – who, I gathered, with their nurse, occupied the top floor of the house – about John's recent successful "win" in an important case, about the theatre and the latest thing in hats, and John contributed his share of the talk …

It was when the pink-cheeked little maid whispered to her mistress, 'Where'll you take coffee, 'm?' that for the first time I sensed a faint strain in the atmosphere that had been pleasantly friendly and normal during dinner. Margaret Satterthwaite glanced at her husband oddly as she replied, with a curious diffidence that at once made me prick up my mental ears:

'Er ... in Mr Satterthwaite's study, I think, Mary.'

But even as she spoke I saw John stiffen with suppressed irritation.

He spoke at once, and sharply.

'Why on earth in the study, Meg? This is the third time lately that you've suggested that – and you know we always have it in the drawing-room!'

'I know, darling,' she murmured uncomfortably. 'But it's a big room ... a bit draughty ... the study's so cosy, and Dr Pennoyer ...'

He cut across her stammered excuses sharply by speaking to the maid, standing looking doubtfully from one to the other.

'Put it in the drawing-room as usual, Mary!' Then to Margaret again with that curious edge to his voice. 'Cold – rubbish! There's been a fire as big as the one in the study all day.'

He was palpably annoyed, and I was sorry for the little thing, sitting looking piteous, her big eyes roving miserably from her husband to me and back again – so I stepped swiftly into the breach.

'If it's as cosy as this room and the study it must be delightful,' I said. 'I've never seen more charming quarters – nor eaten a better dinner. I must congratulate you on your housewifely qualities, Mrs Satterthwaite, if it isn't out of date to say such a thing!'

The compliment brought a smile, but it vanished as we passed out of the dining-room, went down the stairs to the landing where John had greeted me, and entered the door that faced the top of the stairs that led up from the hall.

The moment I entered the room I realized that the first floor, which was now two rooms – John's study, facing the back, and a large room, the drawing-room, facing the front – had originally been one very big room. L-shaped, with the lower 'bar' running across the front of the house, and the upright bar running from front to back. At some time, some owner, who found the large room unwieldly and needed an extra room, had built a wall or partition across the junction of the two bars of the 'L', and this created two separate rooms. But still the front half – the present drawing-room – though shorn to half its original size, was a large and handsome room, with a deep fireplace at one side, walls tinted faintly green, and an attractively-worked plaster ceiling the colour of clotted cream; the old parquet floor was waxed and polished till it shone like a sheet of brown amber, and the windows were draped, from pelmet to floor-level, with breadths of a charming green and gold French damask.

There were several cosy chairs grouped about, covered in the same damask, and a long sofa-divan, placed at right angles to the fire, was piled with green and gold cushions. Beside it was a low table where the coffee equipment was already set out, and there was a 'baby' grand piano – for both John and his wife were musical. A white sheepskin rug lay before the fire; there was a walnut bookcase and a writing-table to match; two shell-shaped arched niches, one either side of the fireplace, were filled with more books, and several bowls of ruddy shag-headed chrysanthemums stood about. Altogether a delightful room. Essentially and charmingly English – without a foreign note, one would have said.

Therefore you can imagine what a start I got when, after warming my hands at the fire – for the room was coldish despite John's retort to Margaret at dinner – I turned to face down the room and encountered, fixed flat against the wall that had been built to divide the original room into two – *that.*

Pennoyer nodded towards the Bronze Door.

'It took up more than half the entire stretch of wall – the door by which we had entered from the landing was just beside it, and looked completely dwarfed by this splendid winged double-shield of dusky-gleaming metal. It was magnificent – and as utterly incongruous as a macaw in a dovecot! What had brought it there? I wondered – and wondering, noted two things. One, that John had lingered behind us as we entered the room, and was standing beside the Door, running his fingers lovingly along the darkly-shining surface of the metal – and the other, that Margaret's hands, as she poured out the coffee into the three waiting cups, were shaking unaccountably. But the impression was a fleeting one, and broken at once as John came up to the fire, and Margaret, the cups filled, handed them round. Still, the impression had been made, and was to recur to me again – that the germ, as it were, of the trouble lay behind the Bronze Door.

'Behind' a door that was set flush, flat like a picture against a flat wall? Yes, you may well laugh! But that *was* the phrase that came to my mind. And as you know, I've been trained not to disregard phrases, however apparently trivial, that come into the mind. They are indicative – descriptive, perhaps, is a better word – of impressions; and though words may not be important, impressions most certainly are.

I nodded towards the Door, and spoke precisely the words you spoke when you first saw it.

'Where *did* you get that?'

I sensed rather than saw Margaret grow curiously tense as I spoke, and John's instant flash of half-defensive suspicion was odd – and instructive. He eyed me half-truculently, half-defiantly.

'Where did I get it? I found it in a one-eyed antique shop in Peking, if you want to know.' He drained his coffee cup with elaborate unconcern. 'About a year ago, Meg had been very ill and was ordered abroad, and I'd come into a nice little legacy, so we packed the children down to the country, to Meg's mother, and went off for six months. Went all over the place, and incidentally stopped at Peking. I was prowling down a dirty little street, and I saw it.' His eyes lingered on it hungrily, lovingly. 'It was standing at the back of the shop, half-hidden with carpets and stuffs and so on hung over it. That gorgeous thing! D'you wonder, I felt I couldn't leave it there to be used as a sort of super-washing line?'

'I can't think what possessed you to want it!' It was Margaret speaking, a faint tremor of resentment in her pretty voice. 'You've never been particularly keen on antiques before.'

John's reply was instant, defensive.

'How often have I tried to explain that I don't know? I just *did* want it. And I still do. I wouldn't be without it for the world.'

His eyes dwelt on the Door almost adoringly, and I saw her lips tremble.

'And I hate it!' she muttered.

John compressed his lips.

'Don't let's start that again, for God's sake!' he growled. 'Haven't we argued enough about it?' He forced a laugh that was patently unreal. 'Let's leave it at that, darling, shall we?

That I like it and you don't. But for goodness' sake don't let's squabble before poor old Pennoyer, or he'll wish he'd never come!'

She looked up at me. I saw the glazed look of tears in her eyes, and again a rush of compassion swept over me for a valiant little childish soul up against something she instinctively feared, but could not understand. Again I rushed into the breach.

'That's all right, John,' I said, laughing. 'If you're going to stand on ceremony with me I shan't come again. Don't bother about me – I'm one of those comfortable people you can regard as a chair or a table.'

Meg thanked me with a rather watery smile and with some murmured excuse about seeing the children, left the room, obviously still on the verge of tears.

John, watching her go, turned impulsively to me.

'Miles, I'm a brute! You must think me an awful cad.' His miserable, repentant eyes searched my face. 'I ought not to snarl at her, poor darling – but I don't seem able to help myself somehow.'

I felt this was where care was needed.

'I dare say you're overtired for some reason,' I said cautiously. 'Been doing too much? It always makes one edgy and then one takes it out on one's nearest and dearest.'

He sighed, then laughed rather forcedly, and sank down upon the divan beside the fire. I was sitting in a deep chair on the opposite side, and between us the vivid firelight lay like a pool of molten gold. At the far end of the room the Bronze Door faced us, austerely beautiful, gleaming sullenly where the dancing light caught it. Hinges clamped solidly against the wall, and where the two leaves met locks, those magnificent wedge-shaped locks of old China, were tight-closed, fastening the two halves together like two close-sealed lips … yet why was it that as I looked at it, I had that curious feeling that if Something happened – *what*, I did not know – the Door might open? And that if it opened it would not open upon a blank wall, but upon – something else? But John was speaking, and for a moment I had to banish impressions and listen to what he was saying. He was obviously shy, uncomfortable – not so much reluctant to talk as unable to put what he wanted to say into adequate words.

'It's … it's about that screen … that Door, I mean.' He indicated the shimmering bronze panel, immobile, rigid against the wall. 'She's right – in a way – it's creating a sort of split between us, the first we've ever had. I love the Door – it's funny. I've never had that feeling about anything before, and I'm not a collector. But it simply fascinates me … and Margaret loathes it …'

'She wasn't with you when you bought it then?' I said.

John shook his head.

'We'd been travelling about for two or three months, and were in Peking for a fortnight. Margaret's got an uncle in the Consulate there, and we were taking China in our stride, as it were. The day I found the Door Meg wasn't with me – she had a headache or something, so I left her to rest in our hotel and wandered about for an hour or two. I bought her some jade beads I thought she'd like, and I was poking about to find some amber as well and I saw – this!'

He raised his head and looked down the long room at the Bronze Door, and I swear the look that came across his eyes was the look that one sees only in the eyes of a lover who sees his mistress approaching him. Hungry, adoring …

'So you bought it?' I spoke as colourlessly as I could – I was deliberately schooling myself to neutrality; obliterating myself so that he could expand, let himself go.

He turned astonished eyes on me.

'But of course! How could I let it go? I couldn't. Don't you see?'

I didn't see – yet. But his assumption that of course I understood what he meant without his going into details of explanation was useful, and I said nothing, only nodded silently as he went on.

'I couldn't take it home to the hotel, of course, but I gave 'em a cheque there and then and told 'em to pack it safely for transport to England. Then I went back to the hotel. Margaret was better – she was delighted with the beads and interested in what I told her of the Door …'

'So it happened that she didn't see it at all until you came home?' I asked.

John nodded.

'Not until we came home – that's only two months ago.' His voice was rueful. 'I knew it would arrive before us and I'd written home to my head clerk – he's an invaluable chap – to tell him to have it unpacked and put up along the wall there. And the moment Meg walked in and looked at it – what do you think happened?'

I shook my head, and the finish of his sentence startled me somewhat.

'She fainted! Right here in my arms.' His anxious eyes probed mine. 'Gave a sort of gulping cry and collapsed without a word – and when she came to she burst into tears and begged me to get rid of the thing! Can you beat it?'

'I can't – at present,' I said cautiously. 'Hasn't she ever told you why she dislikes it?'

He shook his head.

'No. I don't think she knows. She just hates it, that's all. And I ...' His eyes roved down the room again and once more the look of yearning love came into them. 'I could no more get rid of it than I could cut out one of her darling blue eyes – and yet it looks like coming between us in the end! Things are getting more and more difficult.'

He sighed, and getting up, stood warming his hands at the fire, his back for the minute to the room, as he went on, speaking half to himself, half to me.

'You must think me a complete fool, to waste your time on this your first visit to us talking about what must sound a very common-or-garden row between a couple who can't agree about a mere piece of old bronze-work!' His tone was unhappy, morose. 'But honestly – I can't help feeling there's something more in the situation than just that. *Why* does Margaret loathe the thing so – and why do I love it? I can't ...'

His voice trailed away – but for the last few words I confess I had not been listening. I had been watching the Door, and suddenly I had a feeling, a feeling so strong, that *Something* stood pressed close, listening, to the further side of the Door! Something strong, almost dynamic, evil yet not wholly evil – something imperious that called imperially, imperatively! Something that sent out to the man beside me a wave of force so strong that it seemed to me he must needs hear and obey ... something that struck me in a note of danger, hovering, imminent, that woke every psychic nerve in my body into instant alertness!

I sat up, startled – and then the room door opened. Margaret entered, and as though a tap had been sharply turned off, the 'current', whatever it was, stopped. Whatever it was that had been flowing towards John from the Bronze Door was broken, deflected – and I was for the moment thankful. I felt a trifle shaken. Her entrance prevented further private talk, for which I was again rather thankful, as I had gathered plenty of impressions to work on for one night at least.

The rest of the evening passed in pleasant trivial chat, and at about eleven-thirty I took my leave and a taxi back to my eyrie here.

I deliberately avoided any form of concentrated thought as I undressed and got into bed. Settling down, I crossed my feet at the ankle and linked my hands together to ensure the 'locking' of the psychic current within my body, sent out a mental SOS for advice, and within a few minutes drifted into a sound sleep. I dreamt most curious dreams! Dreams in which John Satterthwaite – but an older and a different John – and two women played the chief parts; dreams coloured with blood and fire and old tears; dreams lit with gold and glory unspeakable; dreams too tangled and wandering to remember clearly on waking. But in the morning when I awoke I found written on the blank pad of writing-paper I always keep beside my bed, these words! 'Question the woman Margaret.'

As usual, They had responded, and I had my instructions.

I wrote a note to Margaret thanking her for a charming evening, and asking her to ring me up – I did not ring up myself for fear of striking a time when John was at home. I wanted to ask her to come and see me alone, and for obvious reasons I did not want John to think I wanted to talk him over with his wife.

She responded eagerly, and we arranged a meeting for tea at the Ritz – one of the quietest and most discreet meeting-grounds I know.

I was punctual to our time, but she was already waiting for me, her eyes fixed with an anxious hopefulness on the big entrance, and my heart warmed to the little thing as she eagerly grasped my hand.

In her smart black suit and expensive furs, with a chic velvet hat framing her soft brown curls and round face, she looked oddly like a small child trying to be sophisticated as she faced me over the shining glass and silver of the tea-table, but her blue eyes met mine bravely.

'I – I hoped you'd ring me up,' she said. 'I've been so unhappy. I can't even begin to tell you … I wanted *so* much to talk to you!'

I nodded.

'And I to you, Mrs Satterthwaite!'

'I hate deceiving John,' she said ruefully, 'but I *couldn't* tell him I was going to see you! You see, he doesn't want me to talk to you – for fear I get you on my side over that beastly Door!' Her laugh was forlorn. 'As though, if I couldn't persuade him to get rid of it …'

'If *you* can't, it isn't likely that I can,' I agreed. 'But can't you tell me something of the inner reason of your dislike of the thing? There must be some – *real* reason, I mean? A reason beyond mere dislike of its looks.'

She shook her head.

'It isn't its looks. I think it's gorgeously handsome – though personally I like more simple, rather more cosy things to live with. Yet I think I've got sufficient taste to appreciate the beauty of old things.' She frowned. 'That's what I can't understand, myself. I can *see* how magnificent this is! I can appreciate what a cinch it was for John to find it, and buy it at the price he paid – oh, awfully little compared with what it's worth? And yet …' Her face paled apprehensively. 'I go grey with fear every time I see the thing! Did John tell you what happened when I first saw it?'

I nodded, watching the expressive face.

'I suppose you can't tell me just what rushed through your mind at that moment – no matter how trivial?' I suggested. 'It might – help me.'

She shook her head.

'No! Nothing – that is, nothing beyond a sudden quite extraordinary and unreasonable shock of terror. A feeling as though something that I'd forgotten for ages – forgotten so that I never knew I'd known it, if you get what I mean? — had risen up before me, and I'd fainted with sheer horror, realizing that it was still there! Not gone or forgotten at all. Still there, more terrible and powerful than ever … and it's getting stronger, you know, and John weaker, every day. He's not half the man he was. He's thin and irritable and nervy, like a man who takes drugs, and I've got an awful feeling that unless we can *break* this – whatever it is – he'll somehow go under, though *how*, I don't know … do you understand?'

I nodded. She was telling me more than she knew in these stumbling sentences.

'Go on,' I said.

She hesitated, eyeing me apprehensively, and I hastened to reassure her.

'I won't laugh, whatever you say. Go on.'

She stared at me, and now the grey-blue eyes were darkly violet with fear.

'Do you know, I used to love sitting there after dinner in that room, but now I hate it so much that, as you saw last night, I do all I can to avoid going there at all. And if you ask me just what I feel … well, I've always got the feeling that – *there isn't any wall behind the Door at all!*'

I stared at her. This was interesting! *Very* interesting. So she felt it too …

'Do you get any impression of *what* is behind the Door?' I asked.

Again she shook her head. No. No. She felt merely that there was no wall there. As though if the locks were forced apart – which they couldn't be now, John said, they had rusted so long that they had grown welded together, and to force them would break them – but *if* they were, that the Door would open, not upon the blank wall of an English house, but upon a world of its own! A world that she could not, dared not visualize … but a world that did not terrify John, at least, as the mere idea of it terrified her!

I leapt to the alert at once.

'Then he has the same – impression too?'

'Oh, yes! But he doesn't know I know. He – he talks about it in his sleep – he – he *longs* for it, and that's the dreadful part! He's not fighting against the influence at all, that's what is so terrifying, and that's why we can't hope for the least co-operation from him, do you see? You saw how angry I got when I differed from him about the Door – and when he's asleep, or dozing before the fire, he calls and cries for it to open, open and let him through! He talks about a House that's on the other side, and sometimes about a Garden too … and when he gets that far' – her eyes dilated – 'he starts talking in some language I don't understand! And once – he fell asleep in the drawing-room after dinner. I was coming in very softly so as not to wake him, he'd had a tiring day' – she drew a sharp scared breath – 'and he was talking that language *again*! And – I *know* it sounds crazy, but just at the moment that I paused at the threshold to listen, I got the impression that *somebody was answering him*!' Her eyes, wide with fear, stared into mine. 'Somebody was talking to him – and *in the same language*!'

'That's *most* interesting,' I said. 'Have you any idea what the language was?'

Her eyes were darker than ever, her voice was a mere whisper as she made answer.

'I thought – I don't know – but it *sounded* to me like Chinese. I know something about China – my uncle spent years there and he taught me a little Chinese – enough, at least, to know what it sounds like. But that's the terrifying part, don't you see? John doesn't speak any Chinese!'

Well, she'd given me more than a useful lead – and confirmed my own impression that the germ of the whole trouble lay in the Bronze Door. But what *was* the trouble? One day when I knew John was in Court and the coast was clear, I went down to the house and prowled round the damn thing, examined it, deciphered the various phrases woven into the engraved decoration – for I've a working knowledge of most Eastern languages, as you know, and rather more than that of Chinese – but there was nothing, as far as outward appearances go at any rate, to give me any clue. Nor did I get any 'feeling' that time, as I had the first night … evidently the Entity that lurked behind the Door was clever and wary enough to be able to 'cut' at will any psychic vibrations that extended beyond the Door. And until I could find out who – or what – that Entity might be, that was plainly reaching out after John Satterthwaite to trap and hold him, I was stumped! I tried the Min Yiu process (you remember it, with the five leaves of acanthus and the thrice-knotted thread) and the Yimghaz test, both generally pretty useful, but never got a thing. I'd have tried the Ritual of Hloh, only I hadn't the proper materials, and it might have taken months to find them, and unless I was gravely wrong in my conclusions, John's case admitted of no delay. Besides, the door might have defeated even the Ritual of Hloh! Whatever – or whoever – was working on John Satterthwaite through that inanimate slab of bronze was well versed in magic, that was plain. So at last, baffled, I sent out a message once more to Them for advice, and got it as before, scrawled on the pad beside my bed.

'To lure a lion within reach of the hunter, bait the trap with the meat that the lion desireth.'

I knew now what to do, and it only remained to await my chance. If John had been a willing partner, it would all have been easy – but I knew that that was past praying for. He was already ranged, subconsciously at all events, on the side of the Enemy, and all I could do would be to await my chance and take him unawares. So I took to frequenting the house in Smith Street pretty often, and saw, to my concern, that despite obvious and valiant efforts on both their parts to maintain at least an outward semblance of happy normality, the strain between the young couple was becoming more tense, more fine-drawn every day. In a thousand ways it showed itself – the shadows under Margaret's eyes were growing darker, the harassed lines on John's face etching themselves deeper and deeper, his appetite flagging, his temper becoming more and more edgy. At last one day at dinner he flared up into a furious temper over some triviality, and she burst into tears and ran out of the room. Instantly repentant, he rushed after her, but returned after a few minutes looking dashed and ashamed of himself. I looked at him reflectively as he sat down, flushed and frowning – again looking absurdly like the small boy I used to know – and determined to force the issue.

'Look here, John,' I said, 'you aren't being fair to Margaret.'

He looked at me with haggard, unhappy eyes.

'Don't I know it? I hate myself – but it's getting worse and worse. She's getting on my nerves – and yet I adore her! She's so sweet and gentle and all I want in a woman ...'

'Then why treat her this way?' I asked, reasonably enough.

He shook his head hopelessly.

'Blest if I know! It's almost as though something was getting at me! Egging me on to be difficult and moody, pointing out all the time in dozens of little ways how irritating she is, what stupid little mannerisms she has, how she can't spell properly, scatters bath-powder all over the bathroom and always puts the oil into the salad-dressing first instead of the vinegar ... oh, a thousand little idiotic things that either didn't matter at first or that I loved her for! But now it's as if there was a kink in my mind that found everything I found lovable and childish and dear in her – even if it wasn't clever – now simply stupid and exasperating ...'

He paused. But now I had got him talking I wasn't going to let him stop.

'Even ...' I paused for a moment, for this point wasn't specially easy to mention. 'Look here, forgive me if I'm over-frank. But has this new impulse, whatever it is, separated you for the moment from your wife? Physically, I mean?'

He nodded shamefacedly and played with the stem of his wine-glass.

'Er – yes. For some time past, as a matter of fact. I ... I just feel I've got to be alone. It's extraordinary, but I simply *must* be alone these days. And of course ...' He stumbled and flushed scarlet but went doggedly on. 'It's – er – difficult for Margaret to understand why. We've only been married a few years, we're still young ... and dammit, it's difficult for *me* to understand why too! Till now I've thought it the happiest and loveliest thing in the world to go to sleep with her dear curly little head on the pillow beside me, and her hand in mine. But now ...' He made a hopeless gesture. 'Now all I know is that I've simply got to be alone.' He rose with a helpless shrug and moved towards the door. 'I'm beginning to believe there's something in what she says – that the Door hates her and wants to squeeze her out of my life, fantastic as it sounds! It's certainly since I had the thing that this miserable business has started.'

'Then why,' I suggested as I followed him down the stairs, 'why don't you take the bull by the horns and *make* yourself get rid of it?'

He shook his head gloomily.

'Too late now.'

We were walking up the long drawing-room towards the fire now. Reaching the divan, John flung himself morosely upon it and lay, his dark head against a pile of coloured cushions, his eyes, set in hollows that were surely now too deep and shadowed for the eyes of a healthy young man of barely thirty, fixed on the Bronze Door.

He stared sombrely at it as he spoke again, half under his breath.

'Too late! I *can't* let it go.'

I said nothing. There was nothing to say – but I knew that at last opportunity was coming my way, as it always does if one waits long enough.

I sat and watched him in silence as he lay brooding, eyes fixed on the great glimmering sheet of carven bronze … Mary brought in coffee, and with the coffee came a tiny note addressed to me from Margaret. A pathetic little note excusing herself from coming down again on that useful feminine plea, a headache. Sorry as I was for the poor child, obviously crying her eyes out on her lonely bed upstairs, I sighed with relief as I threw the note into the fire – nothing could have suited me better than to have her out of the way to-night. John was here – alone. Bait for the trap …

Now I knew what to do as clearly as though it was written up before me! Now, unless something went very seriously wrong, Whatever or Whoever waited behind the screen of the Bronze Door could be lured into the open, faced, and – I hoped – defeated. If not … well, it looked as though a promising marriage would go the way of many other marriages, to sad and sorry wrack; and what was worse, a promising young man would be caught half-way between this world and the next – trapped, helpless, never in this life, possibly not for many lives, to regain his freedom. And for this, even more than for the mere saving of poor simple little Margaret's happiness, I was prepared to do battle with all the strength and knowledge at my disposal …

We drank our coffee – and since I knew that an extra drink or two on the top of the wine he had drunk at dinner would make John more malleable to my will, I suggested that my teetotal principles might be waived for once in favour of some remarkably fine brandy that I knew he possessed. I managed to pour my share unseen into a flower-vase, but John, absent and unhappy, since without asking he had guessed the contents of Margaret's note, consumed two good-sized glassfuls, and under the combined influence of the spirit, the warm fire, his own depression, and the waves of silent force that I was deliberately sending towards him to will him to sleep, within less than ten minutes I saw it was with difficulty that he was keeping awake. His eyelids flickered, he yawned and sat up with a jerk and a smiled apology.

'For goodness' sake – I'm a perfectly frightful host, Pen! Feel so damn sleepy – don't you think perhaps I'd better send you home and go to bed?'

But that was the last thing I wanted! I wanted him to sleep in the room beside the Bronze Door – only I didn't want to tell him so! I wanted him completely lax, quiescent. Sending out all the mental force at my command I smiled at him and reached towards his cigar-box.

'Not a bit, old man! Having broken my rules over drinks I want to break 'em over smoking – I used to be a great cigar-smoker, and those look good. Lie back and have ten minutes' snooze while I smoke, and when you wake there's something I'd like to discuss with you.'

It worked! Within five minutes that cigar was burning merrily – a tragic waste, as it was a beautiful Corona – burning merrily within the grate, and John was lying sleeping on the divan, his body lax, his lean handsome young face smooth, at peace in the golden glow of the firelight. The trap was baited. Now for the catch …

It seemed untold hours that I sat there motionless within the deep chair. The house was deathly still, only the distant hoot of a passing taxi broke the silence of the night outside, and the occasional crackle and flare as the flames caught a fresh log amongst the pile that filled the huge old-fashioned grate. Now and then I glanced at the clock, but it seemed to march slower and ever more slowly as the hands worked on towards midnight. But waiting never worries me – as you know, one has to do so much of it in my job – and I knew that if I waited long enough my trap would be sprung. Never before – I had discovered that! – never before had John gone to sleep in the shadow of the Door; never before had he been so completely at its mercy. And it was not likely that this chance would be missed ...

I knew I would succeed when at last I sensed a tiny ripple, a mere thread of vibration, as it were, coming stealing through the room towards the sleeping man – a 'feeler' sent out from the other side of the Door to test the atmosphere. Deliberately I had made myself, after willing John to sleep, as neutral, as non-existent as possible, so as to leave open the way to the trap – and within a few moments that first vibration was followed by others and still others until the entire room was quivering and throbbing as though I was in the centre of some infernal power-house. Have you ever felt the amazing power of suction of an earthly engine when it is going full speed ahead? The almost irresistible pull and drive of it? Well, though obviously nobody except those with trained psychic sense could have felt or heard any such thing, I tell you that that was the feeling I got in that room – and I realized that whatever force was working from beyond that Door, was working to 'Draw' John towards it. To suck him into its vortex, sweep him away ... but *where?*

The sleeper stirred and flung out an arm towards the Door – and suddenly he began to speak. Confused mumbling mostly, and I strained my ears, but could not gather more than a few fragments ... yet, enough to know that Margaret had been right. He was talking Chinese! John, who had visited China only once for a week or so, on that one and only occasion when he had bought the Bronze Door! I realized at once, of course, that it was not the John of to-day who was speaking, but an older John. A John I didn't know ... and moreover, he was speaking in Chinese that I could not understand at all easily, although I find little difficulty in conversing in modern Chinese. But John was talking the exquisite Chinese of olden days, the all but forgotten Mandarin language only spoken by a few, and those of great and ancient nobility.

The sinister Force gathered and whirred about him until I almost heard the hum, like a colossal dynamo, of its vibrations ... but on sending John to sleep I had built a mental Barrier about him that I knew it could not penetrate. Round and round I felt it go, nosing and poking like something almost human, then flinging itself afresh, as though angry and baffled, at the Barrier. But the Masters did not train me for nothing, and the Barrier held! So at last the Force, gathering itself together, withdrew frustrated, as a tide withdraws, back towards the Door ... and I knew that now the Sender of the Force must admit defeat, or come forth in person to do battle with me!

I sat tense, waiting – then, even as I stared, without a sound the Door opened. Without a sound its ancient locks fell apart, it swung back, silent and smooth as though gliding on new-oiled hinges – and I saw that, as I had felt the first time I saw it, behind the Door *there was no wall at all*!

Through the wide square opening I looked direct into a Chinese room. A room belonging not to the China of to-day, but to Old China – that marvellous civilization that is now only a memory. The floor was covered with fine-woven matting, a great vase of ox-blood porcelain stood in a corner on a black-wood stand, a magnificent embroidered curtain where the five-clawed Dragon sprawled in glittering metallic green upon a background of the royal Yellow hung on one side, and in the background a carved redwood sliding-screen, as fine as lace, was pushed half aside to show a garden where the sun shone on drooping silvery-leaved willows behind an old stone well. Grey pigeons with green and purple throats pecked and cooed beside a great clump of rose-white peonies, a fringe of yellow laburnum blossom hung swaying from the eaves above, and the scent of odorous woods, of flowers and spice and sunshine stole about me. Sunshine and willow trees and peonies ... and I sat in an English room with a wood fire, and outside was an English winter's night ...

But I had no time to analyse. For into the Chinese room, from the garden outside, there walked a Woman! Straight towards the open Door she came – and I knew that, as I had hoped, the Sender of the Force had come in person!

She stood there in the Doorway, motionless as a statue, both hands tucked into the long sleeves of her tunic of plum-coloured silk brocade embroidered with a flight of green and silver butterflies and buttoned high to the neck with ball-shaped silver buttons. Her narrow trousers were of heavy dark blue satin ringed with more embroidery, and her sleek black hair was built high, shining like a helmet of polished ebony, and pierced with gold and enamel pins from which hung scarlet tassels of floss silk. She stood with her tiny bound feet, encased in red embroidered shoes not bigger than those of a child of three, pressed close together; and I knew suddenly, as I watched her, that we in the West know nothing, after all, of Beauty. Of the beauty, fantastic, exotic, amazing, that died when the Old World died ...

She stood there for a moment, as though to allow me full chance of seeing her – though whether those immobile dark eyes under the casque of shining ink-black hair saw me I don't know. That woman could have gone to her death without moving a muscle of her countenance – they taught their aristocratic women self-control in the old days. And this was more than an aristocrat. She was Royal! And as she stepped delicately, like a picture from its frame, out of the Doorway and came swaying down the room towards me, I knew again that when Beauty died, so Royalty died too! For no woman of to-day, no matter what her heritage or birth or lineage, could match the utter grace of that woman's movements, balanced on her bound feet barely three inches long ...

I rose silently from my chair and faced her as she advanced. She halted about three feet away from the divan upon which lay John Satterthwaite, still sunk in a deep sleep. But now I know he was not only John Satterthwaite. I remembered his name – for with this woman came a rush of memory of many things. Chen Hwang – of course! Even now, as he lay there in the firelight, I seemed to see the Chinese aspect impose itself upon the English. The lean dark face – surely those hidden eyes were almond, that curly dark hair black and sleek, those cheek-bones high and long? I stared at her as she looked down at him; at her perfect oval face, the colour of old ivory; her eyebrows, finedrawn lines of black over long, slanting eyes heavy-lidded and dark as night; her painted mouth like a ripe red plum, tiny, close-shut, immobile – and as I looked my heart sank. For I remembered a pleasant, simple little English face set in a halo of brown curls, and I knew that against this face, still, remote, strong with the relentless strength of untold ages, poor Margaret had not only little chance, but no chance at all.

For a long moment we faced each other. Then the woman raised her head and looked at me, and I drew a long breath and passed one hand across my eyes. Strong? That first glance shook me! It was she who spoke first – if you can call it speaking. I heard, of course, not with the outer ear, but with the inner.

'Why do you try to keep him from me?'

The voice was thin, remote, still – expressionless as the ivory face, like a lovely mask. I knew the voice – now. As I knew the woman – and what I had to do. I answered quietly but firmly.

'Because, Princess, he has work to do here.'

Her eyelids flickered ever so faintly, like the movement of a moth's wings.

'I – want him. For untold ages I have searched for him. And never found him, for our ways were set apart because of sin.'

'I know,' I said.

She nodded, her fathomless eyes upon the sleeping man.

'When he bought the Door – the Door through which he used to come to me in the olden days – I knew it! So I came back to him – through the Door. And I claim him, for he is mine.'

'I know,' I said again. 'You are trying to get him back. But that, Princess, you must not do.'

There was a faint pause as she looked at me – and almost I could have sworn a flicker like the faintest shadow of a smile crossed that mask-like face.

'*Must* not? That is not a word I know!'

'That is not a word you ever knew,' I said steadily. 'But it is a word you must learn; Princess, before you can claim Chen Hwang as your own indeed. Have you forgotten the old days, and Min Tau, whom he married?'

'I do not forget.' The words were faint, but distant as pebbles dropped one by one into a bottomless well. 'That little fool! He had married her before he met me – and she was in our way ...'

'I remember,' I said. For as she spoke I saw, forming before my mental sight like a quick running newsreel, a swiftly-unfolding memory of what their lives had been, hers and John's, in that long-dead day for which they were now paying such grim toll! And needs must that I spoke the truth to her whatever it cost, for only she could truly save him.

'I remember – too well, Tang H'sien! Because she stood between you, you killed her! You gave your servants orders to strangle her – and blind with passion for you, he let you do it, though he knew he could have saved her! Now she is once more upon his hands that he may work out his duty to her – the duty he shelved for love of you in those old ancient days.'

She smiled faintly, a smile oddly compounded of defiance, cynicism and utter love, as she gazed down at the sleeping man.

'It is true, Master whom once I knew! As always, you know too much!'

I nodded.

'It is my business to know – to see further than most men.'

She looked still down at the man below her. Then she stretched out a slender ivory hand, tipped with the long golden nail-shields that marked her regal birth, to touch his head – and with an odd little shiver drew her hand back before it had reached him.

'There is a Barrier,' she said.

I nodded.

'I have placed one about him, to protect him from the Force you sent out to draw him back to you. *You* know, Princess!'

'I know,' she said. 'As in the old days, you are too strong for me in many ways – yet in others I am too strong for you! And I know that not even this Barrier that you have set about him can keep us entirely apart ... if I refuse to let him go.'

My heart sank. It was true. I could keep John safe in a measure – but *only* in a measure. Only she could give him back his full freedom, freedom to complete his work on earth and so earn his release, his honourable discharge. Only she could reclose the Door so strangely opened! But – would she? Tang H'sien in the old days had not been notable for generosity – and that small mouth was set firm as a steel trap beneath its crimson paint! Well – she must choose, and for both their sakes, with all my heart I hoped she chose aright.

She stretched forth her hand again and held it over the forehead of the sleeping man. The firelight caught and sparkled on her golden nail-shields as she did so, and in his sleep he frowned faintly and drew a sobbing breath as he murmured a name – her own. Her face was dark with trouble as she withdrew her hand and slipped it once more within her ample sleeves.

'He dreams of me,' she said below her breath. 'And you – you ask me to let him go! To *Her* ...'

'Debts must be paid,' I said. 'It is the Law.'

She bowed her head.

'It is the Law. But what if I defy the Law, as I did last time – and keep him with me? Already he is half mine, and walks the earth in a dream unseeing, half-dazed! Already he is lost to Her! He sees her only as a tiresome shadow at his side, a shadow he tries to brush away as one brushes a veil of mist that obscures reality ...'

'I know what you are trying to do,' I said. 'What you have half-done already, indeed. And I know that not even I, with all the knowledge The Great Ones have taught me, can force you to give back what you have already stolen from her – and from him. But I can prevent your stealing more! I can fasten the Barrier about him so that you cannot draw him over to you completely, as you were trying to do.'

Her black eyes narrowed dangerously.

'You came – for me – just a few days too soon!'

I smiled.

'They sent me just in time! Yet not in time to save him completely. For unless you give back what you have drawn from him, and let him rise from this tranced sleep a whole man once more, he will live out his life a man walking in a dream. Neither yours nor hers – nor even his own. Wandering, a poor bewildered shadow between two worlds, wholly alive in neither ... O Tang H'sien, I beg of you, stand back and let him go!'

Her lips twisted faintly.

'Three thousand years,' she murmured. 'Three thousand years and more since I lost him, and I had so nearly won him to me again! A short time longer, and so much of him would have been over Here with me, that his earthly body would have faded and died, lacking the inner life that sustained it – and he would have been mine altogether! Even now, the shadow of him that moves beside me in a half-waking dream, is dearer to me than my own soul ... and you ask me to let him go!'

I paused and gathered myself together. For the vibrations that flowed between us now were so strong, so warring, so rebellious, that now and again even my trained balance shook and quivered on its pedestal, and I seemed to see her, as it were, through water, now strong and clear, now broken, fading and quivering like light on a running stream – and the beauty, the utter womanliness of her, despite the ruthlessness, the cruelty that shot that womanliness through and through as one colour weaves through and over another in a piece of shot silk, tugged at my heartstrings sorely. For despite all the evil I remembered of her in the old days, I remembered good also, and nobility and gracious strength – and mightily I longed to see her take the chance I knew now that They, who make no mistakes, had given into my hands to offer her! The chance to make reparation, for her own accord, for that ancient sin ...

The firelight glimmered and sank low, and now there was only a ruddy pool upon the soft white of the sheepskin rug on which I stood. Yet as I looked again she shone out more clearly, standing there in her gorgeous robes, her lovely head inclined to listen, her still hands folded inside her sleeves, her lily-feet pressed close together as a lady of Old China should stand, her eyes fixed on the sleeping face of the man who lay prone between us – I knew that on a hair's breadth swung my chance of success, complete or only partial!

For it was true what I had told her. I could if I chose – and it might be that I would have to choose – fasten the Barrier about John for life, so that she could not draw him completely out of the physical world over to her. But I could not give back what she had already won to herself, and I shrank, appalled at the thought of the handsome, brilliant young barrister I knew doomed to a life spent, as I had said, drifting between the two worlds. A dreamer living eternally in a dream ...

'Tang H'sien!' I spoke urgently across the flickering pool of light. 'If you cling to him – if despite all I can do or say, despite any Barrier I can raise, you persist in clinging to your spiritual possession of Chen Hwang who lies here – what will you gain? You will not only have refused to pay your share of your debt to Min Tau whom you slew, but you will have hindered him from paying his – and all the weary business will be to do again in yet another life, as you well know! *All debts must be paid in full, if not in one life then in another!* Have you forgotten all I taught you, Tang H'sien?'

She shook her head, and a faint half-mocking smile parted those berry-red lips for a second.

'No, Master. I have not forgotten!'

I flung out my arms.

'Then let the memory of those lessons bring forth fruit! O

Tang H'sien, of the Royal House of Chung, be generous to this woman, who matters in the long tale of your lives with Chen Hwang but so very little! She counts for nothing, indeed, except a lesson to be learned, a duty to be done – a duty shirked that day three thousand years ago, a duty still to be done despite that shirking. Face your duty, Princess – since when have the women of the House of Chung lacked courage?'

For the first time a shade of indecision seemed to pass like a shadow across that still face, immobile as though carved from a piece of solid ivory. The reply came faintly, almost in the form of a question.

'Lacked courage …'

The firelight was fading, and beyond the figure that glittered in the shadows before me it seemed that the Chinese room that still shone out between the wide-flung wings of the Bronze Door loomed fainter, less distinct. The power was waning – I must hurry! I flung my whole soul into one final plea.

'Remember Han Loo, who thrust a knife between her breasts rather than endure disgrace! Tsang Li Shen, who drowned herself to save her father's good name. Wen Chi, who sold herself for a slave to a foreign land to buy her brother's ransom. Are you less valiant, Tang H'sien, than those other women of your ancient House?'

Now for the first time the narrow, heavy-lidded eyes met mine fully – sombre, fathomless as black glass! The delicate head reared proudly on the narrow shoulders hidden beneath the stiff plum-coloured brocade, and one long hand was lifted – in farewell?

'I am not less strong than they! If I give Him back … if I do this thing …'

'If you do,' I said steadily, 'your debt and his to this little soul whom once you slew is paid! Leave Him – go to your own place, Tang H'sien, and there abide patiently the day of meeting! Let him live out his life with this woman, let him discharge his debt. Then – then when he crosses the threshold he will come straight to you, and, all debts discharged, all sins wiped out, They will open the Gates for you both so that you may enter in …'

*

'And is that the end?' I asked as Pennoyer, pausing, poured himself out a fresh glass of soda-water.

He nodded.

'That's the end. At least, all that matters. All I remember then is a sudden flaming sensation all about me, like the touch of a giant torch passing swiftly through the room! I remember the sound of John's voice crying out something unintelligible in a voice of desolation, of agony and loss unspeakable, and as I blinked and staggered back, half-blinded and breathless, I saw that the Door was shut. Shut – and now, now I knew that there was nothing but a blank wall behind it! Tang H'sien had been true to her race and her word. She had gone – to her own place.'

He paused, staring thoughtfully into the fire.

'She was a great woman. A rare woman. A woman who can love a man is comparatively easy to find – but a woman who can love and deliberately turn her back upon love and the lover for that lover's sake, is a rare woman. But she was always rare, was Tang H'sien.'

'You knew her, didn't you?' I said. 'At least, you seemed to. And she called you Master?'

Pennoyer smiled oddly, and nodded.

'Yes, I knew her – and she me.' He rose and crossed the room to where the Bronze Door stood against the wall, a tall shield of dusky metal, its reflections of russet and dull-green, purple and copper and darkest gold ashine on its fretted surface in the firelight. He passed his fingers over it reflectively.

'John woke himself up with that last woeful cry as the Door slammed shut ... but, of course, he had no idea of what he cried out. Nor of why he cried. Said he'd had a nightmare, but oddly enough thought he felt better for it – clearer in the head. Drank another brandy, and then was all agog to rush away and beg Margaret's pardon for his bad behaviour at dinner. I noticed that as he left the room to go upstairs he passed the Bronze Door without even looking at it. Tang H'sien never did things by halves ... and a few days afterwards John made me a present of the Door. Said he couldn't think why he'd ever taken a fancy to it – after all, it was a cumbersome damn thing and out of place in an English house, and Meg hated it. So – here it stands as a souvenir, and Meg and her husband are as happy as they can be. The deeper side of John's nature is asleep again, and he thinks his wife all he has ever dreamt of in a woman. But – I hope I shall be there when he and Tang H'sien, their debts discharged, come to each other's arms on the Other Side at last – at the time when all things shall be made clear!'

Sleuth: Neils Orsen

XI

The Case of the Red-Headed Women

Dennis Wheatley

Recent reports of hauntings have shown that ghosts no longer confine themselves to old castles and isolated mansions – they are just as likely to be found in the heart of a town or city, even in a modern apartment block as this next story demonstrates. The author, Dennis Wheatley *(1897-1977), lived in the heart of London himself, and although we met from time to time to discuss supernatural matters, he never indicated that his flat was haunted. In fact, the only spirits in the place were convivial ones, for Dennis was a great wine expert and a most generous host!*

Like a number of the other supernatural sleuths in this book, Neils Orsen the hero of 'The Case of the Red-Headed Women' was based on a real person whom Dennis came to know well. He explains, 'The man's name was Henry Dewhirst, and any charm both of appearance and character which I may have succeeded in giving Neils Orsen is derived from my memories of his wise and greatly gifted original.' Dennis said that Dewhirst was not only a great occultist, but also a prophet who could see into the future, and actually predicted the enormous success which Wheatley later enjoyed as a novelist. Among the cases which Neils Orsen investigated were both genuine and fake hauntings, but perhaps the most interesting of all (and certainly it was Dennis Wheatley's favourite) is the one which follows which is based on actual events. Dennis explains, 'The background to the story is based on fact to the extent that there was at one time a flat in South Kensington that remained tenantless for several years because a succession of suicides occurred there and no one could be induced to take it even at an absurdly low rental. Moreover, it was said that all the suicides had taken their lives in the same way, namely, by throwing themselves out of the window.' With that intriguing statement, I'll leave you in Neil Orsen's company ...

Neils Orsen waited, his long, tapering fingers beating a tattoo upon the mantelpiece, his large, curiously pale blue eyes thoughtful. There was no reason for his waiting, he had made no appointment, yet the moment the door opened and he saw the tall American lawyer from the Chambers below he knew that his instinct had not failed him – his friend was very worried.

'What's the trouble, Hemmingway?' he asked at once. 'Mix yourself a drink, then sit down and tell me all about it.'

The dark-haired solicitor gave the little man a shrewd smile as he helped himself to a whisky-and-soda. 'I suppose by now I should be used to this trick of yours of always knowing what's in my mind the moment I come into the room – or perhaps before – but it still seems queer. And of course you're right – I am worried – very worried.' He leant forward suddenly, 'Orsen, this is not an ordinary case – but I think it's right down your street.'

'Well?' his host smiled.

'The situation is this,' Hemmingway began. 'A young friend of mine has just got married. He has taken an apparently charming little flat and the lease was handled by my firm, but unfortunately I was away when the deal was drafted.'

'Unfortunately?' Orsen queried.

'Yes. It just happens that I know the history of the place and I wouldn't willingly have drafted a lease of it for my worst enemy. Of course outwardly it's an amazing bargain. Owing to the fact that it has been empty for so long the rental has been reduced out of all proportion to the value of the property.'

'Why?' Orsen interrupted encouragingly.

'Well, there have been three suicides and the other tenants have always left after a week or so, complaining of an unpleasantly cold atmosphere and all telling the same curious story that on certain nights the bathroom window used to open of its own accord.'

'Was there anything unusual about these suicides?'

'On the face of it, no,' Hemmingway continued slowly, drawing at his cigarette. 'The first was a French woman of about thirty; the second, which occurred some three months later, a man of sixty; and the third an older woman – who, incidentally, was the last occupant – she died just a year ago.

Of course it may only be coincidence, but it seems very odd that all three should have chosen the bathroom window out of which to throw themselves.'

'Yes, most peculiar,' Orsen agreed, 'but there may be a perfectly reasonable explanation. As you know, four-fifths of the so-called psychic phenomena that I have to investigate turn out to be hoaxes, even though sometimes they are of a very violent and unpleasant nature. However, this may be one of the odd fifth, a genuine Saati manifestation; but what would you like me to do?'

'Just this. The flat is being re-decorated while the young couple are on their honeymoon and they will be returning in about a month's time. I've got a set of keys, so I thought that if you could go down there and see it maybe you'd know if anything really is wrong. I, personally, am quite convinced that there is something uncanny going on, and knowing your peculiar power to sense psychic manifestations I came to you. Anyway, the police would just laugh at me.'

Neils Orsen turned his head. 'Pāst! Pāst!' he called. As if from nowhere a beautiful Siamese cat leapt down on to his shoulder. 'Pāst, old man, we've been asked to go ghost-hunting again. What do you think?'

The cat purred lazily and blinked its large, pale blue eyes at Hemmingway.

Orsen held out his hand. 'Very well. Let me have the keys and I'll see what I can do. Come back in a few days' time and I'll give you the results.'

'Thanks awfully; that's a great load off my mind,' Hemmingway said, finishing his drink. 'The flat is in Collingburn Court, South Kensington; No. 35, and it's on the fifth floor.'

A week later the two men met for dinner. Not until coffee had been served would Orsen satisfy Hemmingway's curiosity.

'In a way you were right,' he began. 'That place has a most unpleasant atmosphere. I have been several times and even spent the night there in the bathroom, but I found no evidence of anything supernatural. The bad atmosphere is easily explained. Many people who like myself are of Nordic extraction are what you call *fey*, and as the seventh child of a seventh child I am so ultra-sensitive that I can pick up the unhappy vibrations of humans who have been miserable at some time or another, in at least one out of every six rooms I go into. Pāst didn't like it either. As you know, I always take him with me on cases like this because of his hyper-sensitiveness to evil manifestations.

'Being stymied in that direction I went to the police and made inquiries about the suicides. The first was a very beautiful French woman, Victorine Daubert, who lived alone with her maid. The maid was away when her suicide occurred. The second, curiously enough, was an inmate of the same block; a shipowner named Arnold Robertson. His flat was just above but he took over Madam Daubert's on her death owing to its greater accommodation. The last, Mrs Matheson, killed herself after a tenancy of only one week.

'Three points that did strike me as curious emerged from my inquiry; they are: one, that none of these people apparently had any motive for taking their lives; two, that all three suicides occurred between midnight and one in the morning; and three, the curious coincidence that both the women had very fine heads of red hair. But if there is an evil entity in that flat it does not respond to any of the usual tests for haunting; so there it is. I'm afraid there is nothing more I can do – for the present, anyway.'

'I see.' A worried frown creased Hemmingway's forehead. 'But what do you mean, "for the present"?'

'Just this. I checked up the dates upon which the tragedies took place – not the ordinary calendar dates but by the lunar months – and found that both the women committed suicide on the second day after the new moon. Of course this may mean nothing, because Mr Robertson threw himself out of the window on the fifteenth day, so there is no question of a series. But all the same, I think it would be worth my while to pay another visit two days after the next new moon. That is in about a fortnight's time and if there is any genuine Saati manifestation it should certainly take place that night. If not – well then, my dear Hemmingway, your young friends will have nothing to worry about. Oh, by the way, when do they return?'

'In about three weeks, I think.'

'Well, then, I suggest that we should both go down there a fortnight from today. What do you say?'

'That's grand by me. What time shall I meet you?' Hemmingway asked.

'It is no use our going there before midnight, so how about having a late dinner first? I will make all my arrangements that morning.'

'What do you mean, "arrangements"?'

'Oh, I shall place my special cameras in focus with the fatal window and connect up the flashlights with invisible wires. If the window is thrown open the flashlights will go off and should any psychic phenomenon appear the plates will be quite certain to register it upon their delicate surface.'

At eleven-thirty upon the pre-arranged evening Hemmingway and Orsen arrived at the block of flats.

As Orsen got out of the car he glanced up and gripping his companion by the arm whispered urgently: 'Look at those lights! Look! The bathroom is in darkness, but someone is in the bedroom.'

Hemmingway cursed. 'Burglars, I suppose.'

'We'll see,' Orsen replied grimly. Silently they climbed the stairs, then taking out his key he inserted it in the lock, but before he could turn it the door opened.

'Peter!' Hemmingway gasped. 'What on earth are you doing here? I thought –'

'I know. We weren't due back till next week and I was livid at having my honeymoon cut short but I was re-called on urgent business by my firm. As the flat was all ready we decided to come straight here from the station when the train got in to-night.'

The young man's tone was abrupt and he was obviously very tired, which perhaps accounted for the lack of surprise and pleasure he had shown upon seeing his friend.

It was an awkward situation. The last thing they wished to do was to ruin his first night in his new home by telling him of the true reason for their visit; so, having introduced Orsen, Hemmingway said quickly:

'I just thought I'd come round and see if everything was all right and as we were having dinner together I brought Orsen with me.'

Peter Wembley hesitated a moment; then his good manners overcame his reluctance to receiving visitors at such an hour after a long day of tiring travel. 'Well, it's grand to see you – come in, do. Pauline is getting ready for bed, but I was just going to have a night-cap, so you must join me.'

Hemmingway and Orsen filed past him, feeling acutely embarrassed. Their young host was obviously not very pleased to see them. Only by appearing boorish and insensitive could they keep him up for long and it was still a good twenty minutes before midnight.

'What will you have?' Peter went over to the sideboard. 'Whisky-and-soda – brandy or –'

'Whisky for me, old man,' Hemmingway said with a brightness he did not feel.

'And for you, sir?' Peter glanced at Orsen.

'May I have a glass of water? I find that it suits me best.'

The two guests sat down, but Peter stood in front of the fire rocking gently on his heels. He evidently had no intention of allowing them to prolong their visit into a midnight session.

Hemmingway glanced uneasily at Orsen, but the little man was saying with a guileless smile: 'I hear you've just returned from your honeymoon – do tell me, where did you go?'

'Italy – the South – little place called Amalfi – perhaps you know it?'

'Yes, I drove over to it once from Naples – an enchanting spot.'

Peter nodded, but he made no further contribution to the conversation.

'Of course you had good weather?' Orsen went on a little lamely.

'Um ... too cold for bathing, but the blue skies were a pleasant change.'

For lack of something to say Orsen pulled out his cigarette-case. 'Will you have one of these? They are Turks, I have them specially imported for me.'

'No thanks.' Peter shook his head.

Hemmingway felt it was time that he entered the uneven contest. They'd only been there for just over ten minutes and somehow Peter had to be kept talking until well after midnight. 'By the way, old man,' he began jovially, 'I suppose you'll be doing some hunting now you're back.'

'Rather,' the young man showed more interest now that his

favourite subject had been broached. 'I hope to get down to Leicestershire next week-end.'

'Have you still got that grand little mare you had last season?'

'Yes. She's stabled with some friends of mine; you must try her out one day.'

'Pauline's keen, too, isn't she?'

The mention of Peter's wife was unfortunate; he glanced pointedly towards the bedroom door. 'Yes. She'll be so sorry to have missed you, but I expect she's in bed by this time.'

The situation was becoming desperate. Suddenly the clock began to strike. The tiny chimes seemed to resound through the still room. Hemmingway looked up sharply, but Orsen shook his head, 'Fast,' his lips mouthed the word silently.

'I say, Peter,' Hemmingway leant forward quickly to attract his host's wandering attention, 'I had the most amusing case the other day. A young man came to me almost biting his nails with rage.'

'Really.' Peter tried to show some interest.

'Yes, it seems that his old man had done the dirty on him – left all his money to his mistress.'

'But surely he must have known what kind of man his father was and expected something like that to happen?' Orsen interrupted helpfully.

'No, no, that's the funny part, the old boy fooled him into thinking that he led a respectable and even puritanical life – pretended to disapprove heartily of modern young things – and his only ostensible form of fun was stamp collecting.'

'What was the girl like?'

'As tough as they make 'em. An innocent little thing you'd say, till she started to talk – you know the type, great big blue eyes and a mass of fluffy yellow hair. I think she was a chorus girl until old Standish picked her up,' Hemmingway trailed off lamely.

'Sickening for the boy.' Peter smothered a yawn.

Orsen began to tap his long tapering fingers on the table beside him. How much longer would they have to endure this wretched pretence of a casual visit; it was well past twelve now but nothing might happen for half an hour or more.

Hemmingway nerved himself to cross the room and refill his glass under Peter's openly disapproving stare. His thoughts were chaotic. Even while they sat there some terrible thing might be mounting unseen from the bottomless pit to claim another victim beyond the sitting-room walls.

'I believe stamp collecting is a very interesting pastime – have you ever gone in for it? A friend of mine . .' Orsen began trying desperately to keep things going.

'No, I haven't.' Peter's voice was sharp and almost rude, and shrugging irritably he began to pace the room.

The two intruders sat on – miserably racking their brains for another subject. But Orsen found it impossible to concentrate. What was the girl doing; she should be in bed by now; she would be quite safe there – but was she in bed? Or had she still to go into the bathroom to wash? He listened intently. Only the ticking of the clock on the mantelpiece disturbed the eerie silence. They seemed to have been sitting there for hours.

Even Peter was affected by the strange tension that crept into the atmosphere. He slumped into a chair and stared at the floor, apparently no longer caring whether his guests went or not. Hemmingway smoked incessantly. The uncanny stillness enveloped them all like a mantle of fog. Only the clock ticked on the mantelpiece in mechanical defiance.

Orsen stirred uneasily; his sixth sense warned him that the moment of crisis was fast approaching. Suddenly he leapt to his feet and dashed towards the further door.

Peter came to earth with a jerk. 'Hi – where are you going? That's my wife's room!' he shouted angrily.

A piercing scream made them gasp as Orsen and Peter met and struggled in the doorway. Hemminway grabbed Peter by the shoulder and hauled him back. Orsen dashed through the bedroom and was the first to reach the bathroom. It was in darkness; the window was flung wide open and a girl lay stretched on the floor beneath it. Peter, having flung Hemmingway off, leapt to the light switch but Orsen stopped him while Hemmingway picked the girl up and carried her into the bedroom.

While Peter was getting some brandy Orsen set about retrieving the cameras he had placed in the bathroom that morning. One that he had set at an angle on top of the linen-cupboard was safe; but the other, which he had fixed up on a bracket just outside the window, was gone.

When he went in to Pauline's room she was recovering. Her large grey eyes were open and terrified and her bright auburn hair glittered under the sharp bedside light.

'What happened, darling? What happened?' Peter cried, his face pale and distraught.

She passed a hand over her forehead. 'I – I can't remember anything except that when I – before I got into bed I had the most appalling thirst. I went in to the bathroom to fetch a glass of water. It seemed frightfully hot in there so I opened the window, then' – she hesitated and shuddered – 'a cold wind of incredible force seemed to sweep me up from behind and for a second I thought it was going to throw me bodily out of the window. A brilliant light flashed in my face – I remember screaming – then, I suppose, I fainted.'

Directly he could catch Hemmingway's eye, Orsen said gently: 'Well, I think we had better be going. You'll be all right now, I promise you. We'll find our own way out – don't you bother, Mr Wembley.'

As he had visited the flats in the daytime Orsen knew that the one below had a balcony and fortunately the flat was temporarily unoccupied. Having dug out the porter of the block with his pass keys, they found Orsen's camera which by great good luck was not smashed to pieces, but had got lodged in the branches of a small bay tree.

Immediately they got back to Orsen's chambers in the Temple they set about developing the plates.

'Here's the first!' the frail little man announced excitedly. 'This is the one from the camera that was on the linen-cupboard.'

Hemmingway peered over his shoulder, but it was disappointing. It showed an outflung arm with fingers crooked clutching wildly at the empty air and a shadow just behind it that might have been almost anything.

'No, no good; but the second should be ready now, we'll see if that is any better,' Orsen said, hopefully. He turned after a moment. 'Yes – just look at this!'

Hemmingway stared at the plate. He saw Pauline Wembley's face, ghastly and terrified, her eyes black and fixed, her body foreshortened as though she was being hurled through the air; but over her shoulder there was another face, only imperfectly materialized, as through it could be seen the open door of the linen-cupboard.

'That's what I wanted,' Orsen breathed, and bent down to stroke Pāst, his Siamese cat, who was gently rubbing himself against his legs. Abruptly he straightened up. 'You must get your young friends out of that flat some time tomorrow on one pretext or another – anything will do – then we can go down there and deal with this horrible business thoroughly.'

'All right; I think I can manage that. Have you found an explanation?'

'Yes – I believe so.' Orsen suddenly seemed very tired and Hemmingway knew that the crisis of each of his investigations always told heavily on his frail physique, as he was not surprised when the little man added: 'But I'm too tired and done up to talk now. Call for me here tomorrow at whatever time is convenient and I'll tell you my conclusions.'

The next morning on their way down to South Kensington, Orsen explained. 'Evil entities of this kind,' he began, 'must have something to fasten on in order to aid their materialization and make them physically dangerous. I guessed, the moment I saw Pauline Wembley's lovely red hair. All red-headed people give out a definite and curious emanation. In civilized countries this is rendered unnoticeable by extreme cleanliness – but it still remains apparent to astral sensitives. Now, as you know, apart from the suicides, three other women lived in the flat – uneasily, I grant you, but they came to no harm, as also the two men; but both the women who were supposed to have committed suicide – and Pauline Wembley who was attacked – had this peculiarity.'

'That's all very well, but how do you account for Robertson – his hair was black?' Hemmingway asked a trifle impatiently.

'If my theory is correct I shall be able to account for that when we arrive.'

On entering the flat they went straight into the bathroom. 'Look at the door of this linen-cupboard,' Orsen said. 'It is firmly shut and I am prepared to swear that it was shut last night when we rushed in here; yet in the photograph it is standing wide open. I'm convinced that this cupboard holds the key to the mystery,' and opening the door he began to remove the shelves.

'I rather think this cupboard has a false back,' he murmured a moment later. 'Yes, I was right. Look!'

Hemmingway peered inside as Orsen pulled forwards a hinged sheet of three-ply that formed a second door. Behind it a small dark stairway led up towards the flat above.

'This is the way the Thing comes,' Orsen continued softly, 'and in this case we have to deal not with an Ab-human, but with an earth-bound. Now that we've found the root of the evil we can exorcise it. I will perform a ritual purification and the poor soul will be released from the chains that still bind it to the physical. Its time is up or the Great Ones who adjust the balances in the lives of us all would never have sent me here. Afterwards, your young friends will have nothing more to fear.'

'But –' Hemmingway broke in – 'I still don't see how everything ties up. I understand what you said about only the emanations from red hair giving the Thing power to materialize physically and that being the reason why the other women were not attacked, but that does not explain the death of old Robertson.'

Orsen smiled. 'My friend, haven't you realized that the first woman, Victorine Daubert, didn't commit suicide at all? This stairway between the two flats is the key to the whole business. She was Robertson's mistress. He was jealous perhaps – in any case, he came down these stairs one night, caught her in the bathroom and murdered her by throwing her out of the window. Then, her personality preying on his mind, he took over the flat himself, lived there in misery for three months and eventually committed suicide by the same means as those by which he had killed her.

'Two such occurrences are quite sufficient to explain his haunting the scenes of these terrible moments at certain phases of the moon. He has become a blind, seeking force which no longer recognizes persons in this life and is compelled to repeat his murderous act whenever he has an opportunity.

'Each time he suffers all the agony of remorse he felt after the murder of Victorine Daubert until he can find a new victim; yet only the emanations of red hair give him the power to do so, then the wheel of his terrible penance starts to turn again.'

'It sounds extremely plausible, but how can you be certain?'

Hemmingway asked with all a legal man's reluctance to admit anything but cold hard facts.

'Compare these two photographs,' Orsen held them out. 'The first which I got from Scotland Yard is of Robertson after he committed suicide. The second is the one of Pauline being thrown towards the window last night. Behind her you will see the outlines of a face which is quite sufficiently materialized to be recognized as Robertson's.'

'By Jove, you're right! But what prevented her from being hurled to her death?'

'The flashlight of my camera going off as the window opened and operated the leads I had fixed. The Power of Darkness can always be driven back by the Powers of Light.'

XII

Apparition In The Sun

Joseph Payne Brennan

The last of our supernatural sleuths is also the one who has been doing most of late to keep the tradition alive. Already several of Lucius Leffing's cases have appeared in such prestigious American publications as Alfred Hitchcock's Mystery Magazine, *and two collections of stories have been published to considerable critical and public acclaim. He is the creation of the distinguished American poet and novelist,* Joseph Payne Brennan *(1918-   ) whose tales of mystery and horror are widely judged to be among the best currently being written.*

Lucius Leffing is a pyschic investigator and private detective who operates in the lovely American state of Connecticut, where Brennan himself was born. He is also unique among the ranks of occult investigators, as Frank Bleknap Long, the leading fantasy fiction writer and a long-time admirer of the stories has written: 'Leffing does not shout at the reader, his clients, or anyone else. But in his scholarly reserve and quietness there is a sagacity of a high order, a brilliance that blazes and sears and shatters the horrific as if it were a vessel of glass with the deadly precision of a rapier-thrust.' Need I add any more, except that 'Apparition in the Sun' may just be the most unusual ghost story you will ever read. For who ever heard of spirits actually materialising by day ...

One rainy evening in July, when I had no particular plans for either entertainment or work, I received a welcome call from my friend, Lucius Leffing, the psychic investigator.

'I can't say it will be an exciting case,' he told me over the wire, 'but it has its odd aspects. I intend to look into it tomorrow. If you would care to come along, you might drop over tonight and learn the few facts I possess concerning the affair.'

I accepted immediately. Leffing lived less than a mile away and besides I enjoyed walking in the rain. After putting on a waterproof coat and hat, I stepped forth into a refreshing summer shower.

Very shortly I arrived at the door of seven Autumn Street. Leffing shook hands cordially and ushered me into his quaint Victorian living room. The antique dark mahogany furniture was softly illuminated by gas lights which glowed along the walls. I might have stepped back into the 'nineties. I eased into Leffing's eminently comfortable Morris chair; presently he reappeared bearing two cut-glass tumblers filled with cold sarsaparilla.

'It's a queer business,' he said, settling into another chair across the room. 'A Mrs Woolmore of Prospect Street has requested my services. She is the owner of a brownstone house dating back a century or more. You might call it a mansion. The house is distinguished by a sort of abbreviated tower, or turret, which rises above the general level. The tower contains an excellent small chamber, which Mrs Woolmore has been using as a guest room. She is quite wealthy and entertains guests frequently.'

He sipped his sarsaparilla and resumed. 'Well, to put it bluntly, this tower room appears to be haunted. One guest complained of it openly and at least two others have quitted it on some pretext.'

'Sounds intriguing,' I commented. 'Do you propose to spend a night in the tower room?'

Leffing shook his head. 'By no means. The – intrusion – seems to occur during the afternoon when the sun is streaming in the tower room window.'

I felt that Leffing was pulling my leg and said so, but he denied it.

'Those are the circumstances, Brennan. At this point I cannot explain them. But tomorrow we shall run up there and see for ourselves.'

For another hour or so we talked about books and then I left. I was back early the next afternoon.

As we waited for a taxi, Leffing commented on the bright sunlight which filled his rooms. 'A good day. Perhaps our tower-room visitant will put in an appearance!'

The taxi climbed the hill to Prospect Street and within minutes we were rolling up a long private driveway bordered by huge old oak and elm trees which must have known the rain and winds of two hundred years. At the end of the drive loomed a massive brownstone, in good repair and yet melancholy with the aura of a vanished age.

I felt carried back in time and I know that Leffing did also. He gazed about with relish, a faint smile on his angular face.

But our mood of reverie was abruptly shattered by the appearance of Mrs Woolmore, who had been expecting us and opened the door.

A large-boned, rather masculine woman with a booming voice, she greeted my friend enthusiastically.

'So *good* to see you!' she told Leffing. 'I *do* hope you can rid the place of that nasty thing – whatever it is!'

Leffing bowed. 'We shall do our best, Mrs Woolmore.'

He introduced me and Mrs Woolmore led us to the drawing room.

Leffing refused drinks, pointing out that narcotics tend to dull one's psychic responses, and Mrs Woolmore launched into her tale of the tower room.

A recent guest, a young girl named Selma, had come down looking white one afternoon. At first she said she was ill, but when someone went to telephone for a doctor, she admitted that she had seen 'something' in the tower room, which had been assigned to her on her arrival the night before. She had gone up, she said, to write post cards, when she had been terribly frightened by a nameless shape which appeared just inside the window, in the direct afternoon sunlight. She said that it had some human aspects but seemed to her to be more animal than otherwise. She had used the expressions 'filthy deformed monkey,' and 'monstrous elongated toad, standing on its hind feet.' It was, she related, in constant motion; in fact, it almost appeared to be 'dancing'. She said she knew it was an apparition of some kind, because she could see the sunlight streaming through it, but she was just terrified as though it has been solid, perhaps more so.

Two other guests assigned to the tower chamber had requested different rooms. One gave the height as an excuse. The other pointed out that there was no fire escape.

Mrs Woolmore was emphatic. 'Really! We can't tolerate this in Oakhill House, Mr Leffing! When something annoys my guests, it has to go! You will put an end to it?'

Leffing arose. 'I shall attempt to, Mrs Woolmore. Where psychic manifestations are concerned, one does not make promises!'

Mrs Woolmore's expression indicated impatience. I had no doubt she secretly believed a good whack with the business end of a broom ought to rout any ordinary phantom.

But she conducted us up thickly-carpeted stairs to the tower room without further comment and pushed open a door.

'Here it is.' She strode across the chamber and turned. 'And not a ghost in sight!'

It was a small, high-ceiling room, sumptuously furnished as a boudoir. A tiny alcove held a writing desk and chair. There was one large window, through which the afternoon sun was just beginning to shine.

Leffing looked about in what appeared to be a cursory manner, but I sensed that he took in every detail.

'Thank you, Mrs Woolmore. With your permission, we shall spend an hour or two in this room. I think it best that we not be disturbed.'

Mrs Woolmore nodded vigorously. 'Stay as long as you like. And I'll see that you're not disturbed – at least not by any of us!' With that she was gone.

Leffing smiled. 'A matriarch of the old school, Brennan!'

Walking to the window, he pulled aside the flounced curtains and began examining the inside edges of the window frame. He seemed absorbed, although I could see nothing to comment on. The window was lightly screened and appeared ordinary in every respect, except that it was very slightly curved.

Presently Leffing turned from the window and sat down in the room's one armchair. 'We'll wait for the sun to strike in more fully. Meanwhile, I think we had better keep conversation at a minimum.'

I seated myself on a fragile-looking, satin-covered boudoir chair which turned out to be surprisingly comfortable, and waited.

If our vigil had been at night, I might have felt expectant; as it was I merely felt a bit foolish. It was impossible for me to imagine a phantom materializing in such an airy, innocent room with the afternoon sun beginning to enter.

Leffing sat motionless and alert, as if he were being entertained by the most engaging stage play ever performed.

I marvelled at his patience and keen attention, but as the sun began to beat in, I became drowsy. More than once I felt my head falling forward and I snapped to with alacrity and a quick eye to see whether Leffing had noticed.

If he had, he gave no sign of it.

An hour passed and I was just about to suggest that perhaps we had better call it quits, when I saw Leffing staring toward the window with a questioning look which immediately turned my gaze in that direction.

At first I saw nothing except the flood of sun pouring through the opened curtains. But even as I stared, something began to coalesce within that rectangle of sunlight.

A grey writhing monstrosity gradually took form. It appeared to be in continuous motion – leaping, twisting, squirming. It bore some resemblance to a malformed human being, but it had limbs where no limbs should be and its flattened fish-like head seemed to rise directly out of its trunk. Its limbs – legs or arms, it was impossible to say which – were hairy and thin as a spider's. It was a nightmare shape – the kind of aborted figure which is ordinarily seen only by doctors in a delivery room before it gasps out its few seconds or minutes of life.

Motionless, it would have remained a fearful enough sight – but its frenzied and incessant movement filled me with a sense of loathing. I did not feel that I could remain in the room with it for a full minute.

Leffing leaned forward in his chair, eyes narrowed, every sense keyed to its highest pitch. I had an idea he felt the same intensity of revulsion as I, but his face remained a mask.

And still the grey, foul spidery thing danced and twisted there in the sunlight, its filmy bulging eyes blank and motionless.

Suddenly Leffing stood up, numbly skirted the weaving monstrosity, strode to the window and twitched the curtains together.

Almost at once the hideous shape began to fade. It seemed

to shrink into itself, to shrivel, and abruptly it was gone.

When Leffing opened the curtains again, there was nothing visible in the patch of sun except a few motes of floating dust.

He nodded, as if to himself. 'As I thought, it comes for the sun.'

He stood lost in thought for a moment, then looked round at me. 'I think there would be no purpose in remaining longer. We will go down to Mrs Woolmore.'

We located Mrs Woolmore in the drawing room. She laid aside her magazine. 'Any luck?'

Leffing inclined his head. 'We saw the – materialization. But as yet its origin and the compulsion which draws it back are not fully clear to me. I shall need more time before I have a full explanation. In the interim I suggest that the tower room remain unoccupied.'

It was evident to me that Mrs Woolmore was disappointed that Leffing had not immediately cleared up the mystery, but she made the best of it, agreed to cooperate further in any way that she could and bid us both a cordial good-day.

On the way back to Autumn Street in the taxi, Leffing seemed lost in thought, but he did ask me one question.

'Did you experience any sense of evil when the form was there in the room?'

I almost answered in the affirmative but checked myself and finally admitted that while I had experienced an overwhelming feeling of *loathing*, I had not actually felt any sense of evil.

Leffing appeared to be satisfied with my answer and lapsed into preoccupied silence.

After he had promised to let me know if and when he had made further progress in the case, I left him at seven Autumn Street and walked home.

Nearly two weeks passed before I heard from him again. At length, one evening in August, he telephoned. He had solved the mystery of the materialization at Oakhill House, he said, and would I care to come round and hear the explanation?

I was on the street within minutes and soon found myself snugly ensconced in Leffing's gas-lit parlour.

'Further questioning of Mrs Woolmore,' he began without preamble, 'brought out the fact that until recent months the tower room had been used only for storage purposes. It was converted to a ladies' guest room late last December. That, I felt, explained why the manifestation had been reported only recently.'

He paused, putting his fingertips together. 'You may recall, Brennan, that I examined the window frame of the room rather carefully. What I noticed were a number of evenly-spaced circular marks along the edges of the frame. They had been painted over, but were still visible. They puzzled me only momentarily. I quickly concluded that at one time the tower room window had been heavily barred. The bars had been sawed out even with the frames, leaving faint outlines visible.

'Mrs Woolmore had not even noticed them and could give no explanation of their origin.

'I next delved into the past history of the house. Mrs Woolmore has owned it about four years. Previous to that it had been the property of a Hiram Calleston, a wealthy banker, who had lived there with his sister. Mr Calleston had owned the house for nearly thirty years. I could find nothing in the Calleston history to explain the materialization in the tower room. I did learn that the Callestons, like Mrs Woolmore in the beginning of her own occupancy, had used the tower room primarily for storage purposes.

'You will see, then, that the tower room had been virtually unoccupied for over thirty years. Was it possible, I asked myself, that the monster shape had been appearing all those years unseen, that it actually predated the Callestons?

'I did further research of property records. Before the Callestons, Oakhill House had been owned by the Farringtons, a powerful family who controlled one of New Haven's flourishing early carriage-manufacturing establishments.'

He frowned. 'The Farringtons, I found, were socially prominent and much admired. No stigma of scandal, no mystery and no strange rumours attached to them. It looked as if I had run into the proverbial stone wall.

'But I refused to call it quits. While turning over some old Farrington family papers in the local historical society files, I chanced upon a handwritten pay book. This little book listed the names, addresses and wage records of the Farrington family servants, domestics, gardeners, etc. I copied down the names and addresses and subsequently tried to trace these former Farrington employees.

'It seemed hopeless. The majority had died years ago; a few had simply vanished, leaving no records or addresses. Incredibly enough, however, the very last name on the list brought success! I shall not give the gentleman's name; he was listed in the Farrington pay book as "hothouse worker"; he is now approaching the century mark and is living quietly with a married niece in a suburban town.

'I hired a car and was driven out to meet him. I found him crippled with arthritis, partially blind and somewhat deaf, but still alert mentally. At first he was reluctant to talk, although he admitted readily enough that he had once worked for the Farringtons. At length, after we had chatted for some time, he told me that he knew the secret of the tower room.

'He said that the last Farrington had died over twenty years ago and he could see no harm in revealing the secret. During the days of their greatest success, he disclosed, one of the Farringtons had given birth to an abnormal infant – a "monster." It was so hideously deformed, the doctors expected it to succumb within hours. Blind, twisted and horrible as it was however, it lived. The household servants, most of long tenure, were sworn to secrecy. Outsiders were told that the creature was stillborn. Perhaps because they felt it might be cruelly used, or possibly because they believed the risk of publicity was greater, the Farringtons at no time committed it to an institution. It was locked in the tower room and its wants were filled.

'As it grew, it began to climb about the room and once was caught halfway out the window. Bars were immediately set into the window frame, probably by Farrington employees.

'The creature survived in the tower room for over forty years. Afternoons when the sky was clear, sun struck into the tower-room window for about an hour. According to my informant, the monster, blind though it was, hungered for the sun. When sunlight entered the tower room, the thing would sense it. Scrabbling to the window, it would dance and leap there in the light until the sun began to fade. As it grew older, it lay for the most part motionless in one corner of the room, but it never failed to crawl into the sunlight and caper about.

'The old man said that the servant that fed it reported that even on the last day of its life it had leaped and cavorted near the window when the sun entered.'

Leffing shook his head. 'A strange and pathetic story, Brennan. Hideous as it was, one feels compassion for the poor creature.'

I nodded. 'But why does it come back? How and why does it continue to materialize there, after all these years?'

Leffing was silent for a moment, as if carefully choosing his words. 'In my opinion, you might almost say the thing does not understand that it ever died. It still comes back because its particular kind of awareness did not fully comprehend that it had ever left. It was born and lived in total darkness. Death was, perhaps, to its strange consciousness, only a deeper darkness. Some pathetic residue of it, some shred of its non-physical being, remains in the room. When the sun enters, the compulsion of forty years impels it once again to dance in the light. It is this mindless, unreasoning compulsion which gives the poor remnant power enough to project its former physical image. It is that which we saw.'

I must admit I was not fully satisfied with Leffing's explanation, but I could suggest no other.

I inquired if he had told the full story to Mrs Woolmore.

'I have,' he said, 'and have furthermore advised her to shut up the room. The monster shape may, of course, suddenly cease to materialize – yet it may go on appearing for many more years. I cannot foretell.'

'Is there no way to – banish it?'

Leffing shrugged. 'Exorcism would be useless. The thing is not evil; I doubt if it even has an awareness of evil, as we know it. It is virtually mindless. Exorcism would be of no avail. No, the monster is not possessed.'

He stood up, rather wearily, I thought. 'Well, Brennan, even though Mrs Woolmore's problem remains, another case is solved. The solution of a case calls for a small celebration. Would you join me in an ounce or two of brandy?'

I joined him, and never in my life did brandy taste any better.